NOT SO GOODE

GOODE GIRLS

Jasinda Wilder

NOT SO GOODE

ONE

Charlie

APANICKED CALL FROM MY SISTER IN THE MIDDLE OF THE night.

I'd ended the call, thought about my course of action for a hot minute, and then I'd thrown a bunch of things together, knowing in the back of my mind that I might not be back in Boston for a while. If ever.

And then here I was, on the highway to New York state, at seven-forty in the morning.

Call it serendipity.

I was on my second large cup of gas station coffee, and I'd already eaten two bear claws. Between the caffeine and the sugar, I was pretty buzzed. I didn't normally indulge in junk food like this, but I wasn't normally woken up at three in the morning by a hysterical sister begging me to come rescue her...from what I wasn't entirely sure.

I called Lexie again once I was on the freeway, headed to Sarah Lawrence College where she was a student—I'd managed to talk her into going back to bed and getting some sleep, but still hadn't gotten any kind of concrete details from her about why she was so upset.

So, to recap, at 3 a.m. my middle sister, Lexie called me, sobbing hysterically and begging me to come rescue her. This was unusual in many respects, as Lexie simply did not cry, ever, no matter what. She never ever asked for help, no matter what, and she would not accept help from anyone, about anything, ever. She was vehemently, obstinately, comically independent, and had been since she was a little girl. She'd broken her ankle on the trampoline once, when she was seven or so, and had refused Dad's help—she climbed down off the trampoline, gritting her teeth as hard as she could, refusing to even sniffle. She had hobbled on her own to the car and had refused a hospital wheelchair. At no point had she allowed so much as a single tear to fall. My second sister, Cassie, was much the same, but she was a little less stubborn about it than Lex. Cassie would show emotion, but explosively. She pent it up and kept it shoved down until one little thing would set her off, and she'd rage and stew, and then it would be over.

Lex? She was pure ice, all the time, at least when it came to pain, whether physical or emotional. She had very few moods: she was either happy and cheerful and energetic, or angry in an ultraliberated hardline feminist righteous kind of way, or even-keeled and focused, or a hypersexualized take-what-I-want party animal sort of way. Sad, scared, worried, nervous, frustrated...none of these applied to Alexandra Goode.

So, this call from her, sobbing and outright scared and borderline nervous breakdown? This was apocalyptic and very worrying.

And she refused to tell me a single thing over the phone.

Not one single detail.

A dozen scenarios ran through my head—most of them centered around the possibility of her being pregnant. I couldn't think of anything else that would cause this kind of panic in her. She was...adventurous, sexually, to say the least. Just don't use the "shame" word around her though, or she'll verbally flay the skin off your bones. She could make grown men cry with just a few words.

Mere mortals should stay away.

So, the point here was that she did what she

wanted and god help anyone who even thought of judging her.

Mom and I both have always worried that despite how careful she was about birth control and contraception she would eventually turn up pregnant. So that's where my mind was focused as I drove.

But I didn't want to assume—I couldn't afford to. If I were to show up at Sarah Lawrence with a brain full of assumptions Lexie just might, in her current state, disown me.

Or worse, unload both barrels into me, and I was dealing with my own crisis of identity and future, and I just didn't think I could handle a Lexie Goode tongue-lashing.

So I did my best to just focus on staying awake and getting to Sarah Lawrence in one piece with an open mind.

I finally arrived and navigated my way through the picturesque East Coast campus. As I got closer to where I vaguely remembered her dorm building being, I turned down the radio so I could see better. Ha ha.

I recognized her building—I have a pretty excellent visual memory, and this looked familiar. I'd only been here for a few minutes, once before, when she first transferred here from U-Conn.

I parked, consulted my message thread with Lex

for the building and room details and verified I was in the right place. I grabbed the coffees I'd purchased at my last pit stop, and headed inside. At her door, I knocked, three times, firmly.

A long pause.

A raspy voice. "Who is it." This, despite the peephole in the door.

"Lex, it's me." I peered at the peephole. "Charlie? Your big sister? The one who just made a three-hour drive in record time, *with* stops for coffee and pee breaks."

The only response was the sound of a lock clicking and the handle twisting, and the door opening a crack. A single mocha-brown eye peered at me.

I snorted. "What is this, Lex? You're acting so weird. Like, did you borrow money from the Mafia or something?"

"Shut up," she snarled. But she opened the door and allowed me inside.

I stepped in and she slammed the door shut, locked it, and her eyes went immediately to the coffee in my hand.

"Please Jesus tell me one of those is for me?" she whimpered.

I handed over her coffee, and frowned at her. "You look like shit."

She really did. Her hair was a mess, tangled and

snarled, obviously unwashed. She sometimes styled it messy, but this was just…a mess. She was wearing what had to be a triple-XL U-Conn sweatshirt that even Dad would have swum in at his heaviest.

Sorry, Dad. RIP. But you were not in great shape, there, at the end.

Probably she wasn't wearing a damn thing under that sweatshirt, either. She had the sleeves rolled a half-dozen times, and they still hung past her fingertips, and the bottom came to her knees, the neck hanging off her shoulders. If she'd been clean, it would have been a cutely endearing look. In her current disheveled and smelly state, calling it hobo-chic would be generous.

"My life is over," she muttered. "Personal hygiene can go fuck itself."

"Well, I'm not going anywhere with you until you shower."

She gave me the finger. Two of them. "Food."

"I have donuts in the car. But you don't get them until you stop smelling like a herd of goats took a poop on you."

She growled. Actually growled. "You're supposed to be supporting me in my time of need."

I shrugged. "I can't support you if I can't stomach being within ten feet of you." I wrinkled my nose. "Seriously. How long have you been holed up in here?"

"I lost track after the first week. My roommate has started sliding Lean Cuisines to me through the door. She's currently hiding out with her boyfriend off-campus because I'm, like, not safe to be around, according to her."

I shuddered. "Alexandra. Lean Cuisines? Really?"

She shrugged. "And whole pizzas."

I sighed. "Is that why your chin acne has its own area code?"

She blinked at me. "Wow, okay, Charlie. Why don't you go fuck yourself?"

I saw, then, that she was blinking back tears, and I leaned into her. "Sorry. But it's hard for me to help or support you when I have no idea what's going on. And when I can't breathe through my nose while hugging you. I love you, girl. I woke up at three thirty in the morning, listened to you cry on the phone, and then drove three hours to get here. So I'm here. I'm supporting you. But for the love of god, please, take a damn shower."

She pulled the crewneck of the sweatshirt away from herself, stuck her nose into the opening, and sniffed. And promptly yanked her head away, gagging. "Okay, yeah. Yep. You're right."

"You lost track after the first week?" I said, as she headed for the bathroom. "For real, how long has this—whatever it is—been going on?"

Ignoring me, she peeled off the sweatshirt and tossed it aside, rummaging in her dresser—and yeah, she was naked under it. Good thing none of us girls are squeamish about being nude around each other.

She'd obviously fallen victim to the freshman fifteen and never lost it, and maybe a little extra over the years since her freshman year. This I decided to keep to myself, though. She wore it well, at least, most of the extra weight being in her butt and thighs, which worked for her. Weight went to my butt and thighs, too, but I was already genetically predisposed to being curvy, so that extra looked like a LOT extra on me, whereas on Lexie the same amount of extra weight just looked like she had a bangin' booty. On me, I just looked like I couldn't muster the gumption to run off the junk in my trunk.

Not fair.

Sigh.

I was being judgmental, and I told myself to stop.

I turned my attention to the dorm room. One bed was neatly made, with a few floating shelves on the walls decorated with pictures of her roommate with various family members, a few Beanie Babies, dancing and volleyball trophies. The half of the room around this bed was spotlessly neat. The half around Lexie's bed?

It looked like a bomb had gone off.

I saw the evidence of her recent dietary mal-feasance piled everywhere—pizza boxes and Lean Cuisine trays stacked one atop the other in a top-pling tower. Soda bottles in the twenty-ounce and two-liter variety. More than one empty wine bottle—contraband on campus, I was sure. Empty boxes of Cheez-Its.

Ugh. Lex. Baby. You need help.

Lexie emerged from her rampage through dresser drawers and bins under her bed, a stack of clothing in hand, which she tossed on her bed. Wrapping a towel around herself and grabbing a toiletry kit, she scowled at me.

"Donuts," she snapped. "Need donuts."

"What you need is intermittent fasting and some salad," I muttered under my breath.

"What?" She peered at me through narrowed eyelids. "I missed that, Char. What'd you say?"

I shook my head. "Nothing. Go shower. I'll get the donuts. But we're leaving, yes? Shower, dress, and pack."

She shrugged. "Moira said she'd pack for me and ship it all to me in Alaska. I'm not coming back here. Ever."

I frowned. "You've been talking about going from U-Conn to Sarah Lawrence since you were in eighth grade."

"Yeah, well…sometimes dreams die," she said, and left.

I cleared a space on her bed and sat down, pulling my phone from my back pocket. As I did so, it began to vibrate: *Mom*, it said, accompanied with a thumbnail photo of Mom.

"Crap," I muttered. Warily, I answered. "Hello?"

"Charlie," Mom said, breezy, happy. "How are you doing, sweetheart?"

I sighed, not knowing how to start. "I…um."

"Oh shoot," she murmured. "What now?"

"Have you talked to Lexie?"

A pause. "Lexie? What's wrong with Lexie?"

"Um. I don't actually know. And I don't want to say too much, you know how she is."

"There's a crisis, though?"

"Yeah. I'm with her in New York right now, actually. She called me, hysterical, at three thirty this morning. But I have no clue what's going on—I mean that, I really don't know, so don't try wheedling it out of me. I just got here."

"So what's the plan, then?"

I sighed again. "I'm going to take her on a road trip. We'll eventually end up in Alaska, I'm guessing. Somehow, at some point. Hopefully along the way I'll be able to help her figure out whatever her issue is." I bit at a fingernail. "And my own, I guess."

"So you're not calling Poppy?"

My youngest sister, Poppy—Mom had been after me for months to get together with Poppy, since we were both going through crises of life and work and men, but I didn't get along with Poppy very well under the best of circumstances, and these were far from that, so I'd been avoiding doing so.

I growled. "Mom, god. I'm dealing with my own life crisis. Now I'm here with Lex, and she was *crying*, Mom. Begged me to come get her."

"Lexie was…*crying*?"

"Worse than Poppy cried when she burned herself on the bonfire that one summer."

"No," Mom breathed, in utter disbelief. "You're serious?"

"I wouldn't joke about a thing like that."

"No, you wouldn't. You don't joke about anything," she teased.

"Oh shut up, Mother. I do too. Just not about Lexie crying."

"She's pregnant, I bet."

"Mom!"

There was a silence, and I could all but see her rubbing the bridge of her nose. "Okay, okay. I won't push. Just…" She seemed to be trying to figure out what to say.

"Mom, we'll figure it out. I'll call you when I can, okay? But don't hold your breath."

"If you need me, I'll be there."

"I know." I could hear Lexie's voice in the hallway. "I better go. If Lexie hears me talking to you, she'll go apeshit."

"Yeah, she's weird about people talking about her."

"She's weird about everything," I said. "Also, I did talk to Poppy. She's not leaving Columbia yet. She's not ready to quit, mainly because she doesn't know what she *does* want so she's not quitting until she's figured out a plan."

"Well, that's logical enough."

"Well, on the surface of it, yes. But really, she's just scared of what she actually does want, which is to be a full-time professional artist."

"I know that, and you know that, but she has to decide that for herself."

I sighed. "Yes, Mother. Which is why I'm not road tripping with her, but with Lexie. Because Lexie needs me right now, not Poppy."

"Don't act like you're not relieved though. Poppy drives you crazy."

The doorknob turned. "Gotta-go-bye," I muttered, ended the call, and slid the phone back into my back pocket moments before Lexie walked in.

She rolled her eyes at me. "How's Mom doing?"

I laughed. "I don't know. We didn't talk about her."

She narrowed her eyes. "Yeah, she wanted to talk about me."

I nodded. "Well, yeah. And I told her what I know…which is nothing."

She shut the door, locked it, and dropped her towel on the floor. "Which is why I haven't told you anything yet—I knew she'd call, and I knew you'd tell her. And I'm not ready to talk to Mom about this yet. I'm not sure I'm even ready to talk to you about it, even though you're here because I begged you to come."

"Why don't you want Mom to know?" I asked. "And why call me, not her?"

"Because Mom would lecture me, and I can't handle a lecture." She glared at me as she started dressing. "And if you lecture me, I'll never talk to you again."

"I already promised I wouldn't judge you, hon, and I won't. I won't lecture. I really am here to help, okay?"

The mask she was maintaining cracked, just a lit-tle. Turning away from me, she stuffed her legs into a pair of baggy, blousy, breezy linen pants—something Aladdin would wear, it looked like to me—white, low-waisted, and tight at the ankles. She wore a thin maroon shirt with it, which left her midriff bare from below her navel to just under her breasts.

No underwear, no bra.

She did put on socks, and then knee-high tan leather boots. She faced a small mirror she had hung on her wall next to her dresser, put some product on her palm, and styled her hair into an artfully messy look, longer black strands draping across her forehead and into her eyes, other strands brushed back, some to the side.

I frowned at her. "You're annoying, you know that?"

She blinked at me, baffled. "What? Why?"

I gestured at her. "You can go from looking like a dirty hobo to...*that*, in fifteen minutes. Also, no bra, no panties? With white pants?"

She shrugged. "I don't give a shit. It's comfortable. I bend over, or the sun shines on me just right, sure, someone may get a little glimpse at the goods. I bend the wrong way and you may see some of my titties. So what? I genuinely just don't care. Someone wants to shame me for it, let them. I'll rip 'em a new asshole and go about my day happy as a fuckin' clam. Don't get at me about what I wear or don't wear." A glance at me. "Why is it annoying?"

"Because you actually pull it off."

She snickered. "You couldn't go without your plain white *brassiere* and granny panties for five fucking minutes, could you?"

I glared at her. "My bra is not white, and I am *not* wearing granny panties. And what's wrong with them, anyway? Sometimes they're just practical." I flicked my fingers at her chest. "Besides, you're gonna end up with saggy boobs when you're older."

"So? They sag, they sag. Not my problem."

I frowned. "How do you figure? They're *your* boobs, Lex."

"Yeah, but *I* don't care what they look like, and I don't care what anyone else thinks about what I look like, either. Some guy looks at me in fifty years and is like, ew, yuck, her titties hang down to her kneecaps, I'm gonna be like, motherfucker, if you don't like 'em then don't look at 'em."

I laughed. "Fair enough, I suppose." I frowned. "What if it's your husband?"

She shrugged. "He better love me for me, and not for the shape of my titties."

I shook my head. "Why do you call them that?"

"What, titties? It's fun. It's a fun word. And if you think about them objectively, titties are kinda funny. Like, they're these big bags of fat that just hang off your chest jiggling like fuckin' Jell-O with every move you make, and are largely useless for the vast majority of your life."

"They're not *just* fat, Lex."

She rolled her eyes at me. "Well *thank you* for

that helpful anatomy lesson, Charlotte, because I've *never* taken an anatomy or physiology course in my life and have absolutely no clue what my breasts are made of. Whatever would I do without your invaluable insight?"

I cackled. "Still got the sarcasm, I see."

"Why yes, I am the holy mother of sarcasm, Char-Char." She wiggled her fingers at me. "I dare you to go a whole day without a bra." She stuck her tongue out at me, and wiggled it side to side. "Double-dog dare you."

"What are we, five?"

She grasped the hem of her shirt, lifted it, and shook her boobs at me—and, annoyingly, despite being only three years younger than me, hers were perkier *and* bigger than mine. "Come on. Off with that titty-prison. Try it."

"No! I don't find it comfortable."

"What's the longest you've gone without a bra, aside from sleeping?" She asked.

I frowned. "Why? What's that got to do with anything?"

"Because you're probably just not used it." She rubbed her breasts in her palms, under her shirt. "You know that feeling of taking off a bra at the end of the day? Imagine that feeling, but *all day long*. It's amazing. Try it."

I sighed. "You know what? Fine. We're just going to be in the car all day, so why not?"

I slipped my arms out of the sleeves of my T-shirt, unfastened my bra, slipped it off, and put my arms back out. And boy was that weird. Loose, airy. Jiggly.

I shrugged my shoulders, wiggled my torso. "That's just odd. I don't mind it at home, but I'm going to be self-conscious as hell if we go in anywhere."

She just waved. "Because no one has ever seen a woman's nipples through her shirt before. Oh, the horror. The everlasting shame. It's NIPPLES. Whichever unlucky soul sees you might pass out from sheer scandalized mortification, because they saw your titties."

I sighed. "Are you done?" I dangled my bra—yellow, as a matter of fact—from a finger. "I took it off—happy? Now can we go? I thought you wanted donuts? Also, I need a real breakfast."

She tugged my shirt up with a finger, baring my boobs. "Also, when I said 'unlucky soul,' what I clearly meant was damned fortunate soul, because *girl*, you got some nice titties."

I yanked away from her. "Lex. Are we *quite* finished talking about breasts, yet? I feel like this conversation has gone on for a very long time."

She just grinned at me, and went about yanking clothes out of her drawers and bins, placing them into stacked outfits. "What? You have really nice boobs, Char. A nice firm C cup, round, a little pointy, not too far apart and not to close together."

I cackled. "What, are you boob expert, now?"

She continued laying out clothing, along with a pair of well-worn Birkenstocks, a pair of TOMS, and a pair of sneakers. Some underclothes, including two actual bras. Most of her clothing was…as unusual as the outfit she was wearing—unique, colorful, wild, daring.

"Yeah, I guess I am. Or, I'm just trying to build you up. You're self-conscious because you keep them imprisoned all day every day." She quirked an eyebrow at me. "I bet you've had sex with a bra on, haven't you?"

"I'm not telling you that, Lex." I rolled my eyes at her.

"Because you *have!*" she shouted, laughing. "You totally have, or you'd just deny it."

"So? So what, Lex?"

"So what? So what's the point of fucking if you don't get your titties sucked on, Charlie?"

I blushed so hard I thought my face would catch on fire. "Alexandra Rochelle Goode. That is inappropriate."

"Oh shut the *fuck* up, *Mother*." She flipped me off, both hands. "You are so fucking uptight."

"And you are a serious potty mouth."

"And *you* are a serious Goody Two-shoes. Loosen up. Drop an F-bomb. Fuck a dude without caring whether he liked it or not, and don't call him the next day. Get hammered before noon—just because."

I hissed. "That last one I *have* done. More than once, and recently."

Lex clapped a palm over her mouth. "No, you have *not!*"

"I have too!" I started helping her stack the piles of outfits together, and then shoved them into her hard-sided four-caster suitcase. "You're not the only one in crisis mode, Lexie."

She set a pile of clothes down on the bed, tilting her head and staring at me. "You? Really?"

"My life is not as neat and orderly and perfect as you girls all seem to think it is." I fixed my eyes on the suitcase, fixing the piles of clothing so they were more neatly stacked. "It's kind of upside-down right now, actually."

"So this road trip is for you, too." She stuffed shoes willy-nilly into the suitcase, which I then promptly began rearranging to fit more neatly.

"Yes," I answered. "I need this, too."

"So, here's the deal," Lexie said. "We are officially the no-bra, man-hating, day-drinkers road trip club." A broad, giddy grin. "Membership, two."

I shook my head. "That's a terrible idea."

"It's a great idea. It's completely irresponsible and stupid, which is exactly why you, more than anyone, need it most. You've been the epitome of a good girl your whole life. Four-point-oh every semester from eighth grade to graduation. Valedictorian. Three-letter athlete all four years of high school. Accepted to every school you applied for, including at least two Ivy League schools that I know of. Full athletic and academic scholarship to Yale, where you double-majored in business and law." She yanked my bra out of my hands and tossed it into her suitcase and zipped it up. "You dated the same lame dickbag all *five* years you were at Yale. Right out of college you got a zinger of a job at a big hoity-toity real estate law firm, a classy apartment with your lame dickbag boyfriend…"

"Okay, you think Glen is a lame dickbag and I'm an overachiever. I get it." I huffed and rolled my eyes. "No need to rub it in any further."

"My point, sister of mine, is that you have done exactly *everything* in your life correctly, by the book. You dot every i, cross every t, never speed, never swear, never drink. Glen was the one serious boyfriend you've had in your whole life. You probably gave him your V-card, too, I bet."

I glared at her. "Are you trying to upset me? Because it's working."

From the back of the nearby desk chair, she grabbed a chunky, cable-knit saffron cardigan with giant wooden buttons and slipped it on. "No, Char. I envy your ability to do things that way. But I just can't. I'm not built to be that kind of person, and I often wish I was." She grabbed my hand and the suitcase handle. Paused—glanced around and snatched a small hard-sided black ukulele case hand-painted with daisies and dragonflies and thorn bushes and poetry lyrics. "What I'm saying is, you deserve to take this time, this road trip with your irresponsible wild child of a sister and get a little crazy. Cut loose. Break a few rules. Be a rebel. Do dumb things. Then, when we get to Ketchikan with Mommy and Cass, you figure out the next phase of your life as an upstanding, morally aligned, socially responsible adult with an Ivy League degree and an impeccable resumé." She winked at me. "And fantastic tits."

I rolled my eyes at her, but my heart was a little warmed. "You're not an irresponsible wild child, Lexie."

"Ohhh yes I am. Just wait till I tell you my fucked-up train wreck of a story, girlfriend. You're gonna wanna slap me silly." She headed for the door, pulling me with her.

I tugged her to a stop. "Um, Lex?"

She glanced at me over her shoulder. "Um, Charlie?"

"Purse? Phone? Toiletries? Charger? Laptop? Makeup? A jacket?"

Lexie bit her lower lip and made a "derp" face. "Oh. Right. Those minor details."

I cackled. "You're such a space cadet, Alexandra."

"I am not," she said, archly. "I just get caught up in things and overlook details."

"Yeah, well, you know what Dad used to say— the devil is in the details."

She turned into a human hurricane, dumping all the aforementioned items and a host of other random items into a big duffel bag, shoved her phone and charger into her purse—a huge, battered, scratched, worn, leather sack-type purse she'd had since high school. All this done, she smiled at me eagerly. "Well? Is that everything?"

I shrugged. "I don't know, Lex, is it?"

She cackled and headed for the door. "Hell if I know. I was about to leave without a purse."

"Do you want to do a quick checklist?" I asked, hiding a smirk.

She stuck her finger into her mouth and faked a gag. "I'd rather have a vodka enema."

I blinked at her as I exited her dorm room. "That's vile."

"Exactly. So no, Charlotte, I do *not* want to do a quick checklist. If I've forgotten it, it's not that important. But, just to make *you* happy: I have several changes of clothes, I have my purse, my wallet, I have a cell phone in case I have to call the police, I have my favorite Berks, I'm wearing my ass-kicker boots, I have my favorite cardigan...and I have makeup in case I feel like seducing someone hoity-toity." A mischievous grin. "*And* I have a family pack of assorted size condoms, because I plan on being a very, very bad girl."

I just sighed. "You do not."

She arched an eyebrow at me, opened her purse, dug around in it, and came up with a fifty-pack box of assorted size, style, and flavor condoms. "Do too."

"And do you have your birth control as well?"

Her breezy, humorous composure wilted for a moment. "Yeah, I do. I've got an IUD."

I eyed her. "Lex?"

"In the car. Later. Okay?"

I nodded. "Okay, whatever you want."

"What I want is for you to have a bottle of hooch stashed somewhere."

I snorted. "Hooch? Lex, come on. No one outside of Kentucky says *hooch*."

"I say hooch. I also say cooch. And lady bits. And I have been known to call a man's dick his wiener.

Frequently. Because it's funny. And if I'm around someone who takes issue with me swearing, I say things like gosh-darn. Any other questions?"

I followed her out of the building. "Wiener?"

She laughed. "Yep. Pro-tip: Guys don't appreciate their sacred penis being referred to as a wiener. Which is why I do it."

"You are absolutely ridiculous."

She nodded primly. "Yes, yes I am. Thank you. Ridiculousness is my second major."

"What's your first major?" I asked.

"Well, it *was* women's history with a focus on sexuality."

I hesitated. "Was?"

She spied my car—a black Mercedes-Benz C-Class. "Let me guess, that's yours?"

"You sound awful judgy, there, Lex."

She just shrugged. "You're twenty-four. How do you have a freaking Benz?"

"Because I drove Mom's hand-me-down '96 Corolla all the way through high school *and* college *and* when I started at Denoyer and Whitcomb. I sold it and took the bus or the train or walked everywhere, and I saved every penny I could. I bought my Mercedes used, and I own it outright. It's my baby, and I love it, and I will not apologize for it. I worked my ass off to own a Mercedes by the time I was twenty-four."

She nodded. "Fair enough."

I popped the trunk, helped her shove her bags in next to mine, and then we were settling into the seats. Moments later, we were cruising away from Sarah Lawrence College and heading for I-87.

Silence, for about fifteen minutes—Lexie was staring out the window. Despite her outward calm and usual humor, it was obvious, at least in this quiet moment, that she was far from okay.

"Lex…"

She rested her head against the window. Her shoulders lifted as she heaved in a deep breath, let it out. "I've been awake for forty-three hours, Charlie. Can you just drive for a while? Please? I swear I'll tell you everything. I just need to rest."

I patted her thigh. "Sure thing, honey. Whatever you need." I paused. "How about this—I won't ask again. You tell me what you want, when you want. For now, I'll drive and you sleep. Later, if you're up for it, I'll even let you drive Miss Ginsburg."

She wrinkled her nose at me. "Miss Ginsburg? Your car is named Miss Ginsburg?"

I nodded. "I thought you would appreciate the fact that I named my car after the one and only Ruth Bader Ginsburg."

She huffed, a quiet laugh. "Yeah, that's pretty B-A."

"B-A?"

"Badass, Charlotte. It means badass. RBG is the OG B-A." A pause. "O-G is gang slang, means original gangsta."

"I know that one."

Her eyes were closing, and her words were slower in coming. "Sure you did."

"You didn't even eat your donuts, Lexie."

She didn't answer for a long time. When she did, it was muzzy, drowsy. "Ass is fat enough as it is. Later, maybe."

And then she was snoring.

Good grief. What did she get herself into? She was obviously working overtime to pretend she was fine. But the moment she slowed down, it all just seemed to hit her, weighing on her.

I wanted to fix it, to be the big sis and make it all better. But I knew Lexie well enough to know she'd dole out the story in little pieces. Bit by bit. I'd find it all out, and she wouldn't let me do anything to help. She just wanted me *there*. Just be her sister. Her friend.

Which meant...

I was officially joining the two-person no-bra man-hating day-drinkers road trip club.

I was going to indulge my sister, and do things I'd regret. I could see it coming.

But the hell of it was...she was right, too. I'd

done everything by the book my whole life. I was out of a job. No apartment. No plan. No man. Not even a checklist for getting back on track. I'd just been wallowing in self-pity for the last several weeks. It was time to do exactly what Lexie said I should do: Cut loose. Have fun. Be dumb. Maybe even a little irresponsible.

And as these thoughts tracked through my brain, I eyed my sleeping sister, wondering what on earth had she done.

TWO

Crow

I STOOD JUST OFFSTAGE, WATCHING MYLES SHRED THROUGH the guitar solo in "Pillow Talk," and waiting for the cue to bring his next guitar out to him. I'd tuned it, and had stuck an extra pick in the strings, because he tended to drop his picks during guitar changes. His fingers flew down the fretboard, making the notes squeal higher and higher, until he got to the final shrieking moment, which he drew out, hitting it with the whammy bar. Then, with a dramatic slug of the strings on an open chord, the lights cut to black and I rushed on stage, keeping my eyes on him and the glowing X taped on the floor where he stood. I handed him the guitar and took the old one.

"Dropped my pick," Myles muttered.

"No shit. You always do. There's an extra pick in the strings."

"You're the best, Crow."

"No shit." I kicked at his foot. "You fucked up that last note."

"Shut up. It was fine." He plugged the cord into the new guitar. "You only get to critique if you get your ass on stage with me."

"Nope."

"Then shut the fuck up and get off stage, asshat."

Jupiter, the drummer, was thumping the kick drum in a slow throbbing beat reminiscent of a heartbeat—*thud-THUD…thud-THUD…thud-THUD*.

Nothing but that beat for a good thirty seconds.

Then, still bathed in darkness, Myles bellied up to the microphone as I watched him offstage.

"Here in the dark, sweetheart, it's where we got our start, you and me, baby, just makin' sweat, makin' love, we got it down to an art…" he drawled the words in a low growl which he somehow managed to make sound predatory and seductive and syrupy all at the same time.

Ladies and gentlemen, the annoyingly talented, stupidly good-looking, disgustingly charming, the one and only Myles North. My best friend, currently my employer, and world-famous, globe-trotting,

chart-topping, record-smashing bro-country super-
star. Luke who? Jason who? Sam who? Nah, son.
Myles North, that's who. Triple platinum debut album. Third person ever to get the Big Four at the
Grammies, and for that same debut album—album,
record, song of the year, and best new recording artist. And now, another album of the year for his four-
times platinum sophomore album.

Yeah, he's fuckin' annoying like that.

Especially because he's also the nicest, most
genuinely kind person I've ever met, down-to-earth
despite his bonkers amount of talent and charisma.
I want to hate him for being so goddamn annoyingly
perfect, but I can't because I just love the idiot boy so
damn much.

Don't tell him I said that, though. I got a reputa-
tion as a hard-ass to maintain.

I tuned the Gibson for the next time he needed
it, which was in four songs. He had the red Fender
next and after that was Betty-Lou, his favorite and a
family heirloom, an antique Martin classical acoustic signed by Willie Nelson, Johnny Cash, and Merle
Haggard. Vocals only after that, and then the Gibson.

I checked the tuning on the Fender for the
third time, because that song, "Whiskey and Lace,"
is his biggest hit, and the crowd always goes nuts
for his big solo in that one, so the tuning has to be

keyed in right. Betty-Lou I didn't touch—no one but Myles himself was allowed to so much as breathe on Betty-Lou.

It was sacred, and rightly so: Myles's grandfather had been a small-time country singer; mostly dive bars and honky-tonks in the area of Texas where we'd grown up. But over the years he'd shared a dive bar stage with Willie, drank beers with Johnny, and smoked pot with Merle, and gotten his beloved guitar signed by each of 'em. And then, years later, Myles's dad, also a local dive-bar circuit singer, had lent it to Waylon Jennings for a whole set at a show, once. So that guitar had serious country music mojo attached to it by the time Myles inherited it, and since then, Myles has shared the stage with that guitar with quite an impressive roster of big names, and while he'd not added any signatures to the holy three already on there, he, being superstitious as hell, figured just having it on stage added to the mojo in the thing.

I had to admit, you felt something shivery in the air whenever you heard that guitar start singing.

The next few songs went off without a hitch, and the crowd here in—where the hell were we? Pittsburgh, maybe? —was going bananas. The rowdy, rollicking songs that had made Myles North a household name within a matter of a couple years took a backseat whenever Betty-Lou made an appearance. The moment the houselights dimmed, the crowd hushed, instantly went dead silent, expectant.

My best friend picked up the guitar from her stand near the drumkit, sat on the stool I brought him, settled the guitar on his thigh, adjusted the mic, and then grabbed my arm before I could vamoose offstage. "Hey, ya'll, how about a fine Pittsburgh how'd'ya do for my best buddy, Crow?" He clapped me on the back, forcefully pivoting me by the bicep to face the crowd. "Little known fact about this sexy motherfucker here is, he can play guitar better'n I can. Fact of the matter is, he taught *me* to play. You also may or may not know that he writes the music for damn near all my songs, always has. Maybe one of these days I'll get him to stay for a few minutes and regale us with his rendition of 'Sing Me Back Home'."

I smiled tightly at the crowd—I could only see the first few rows, the rest being lost in the glare of the lights—and waved, once, as the crowd screamed and whistled and clapped.

"Not fuckin' likely," I muttered. "Gonna kick your ass for this, Myles."

Myles just laughed and let me go. "He's got a wicked case of stage fright, ya'll. He's threatenin' to kick my ass for puttin' him on the spot like this. Now, he *could*, you know, him bein' a barroom brawler from way back, but he won't, 'cause he loves me like a brother, and he knows this pretty face is keepin' him employed at the moment."

I cackled as I thankfully regained my place out of the spotlight and behind the curtains. I gave Myles the double bird. "You're an ugly piece of shit, Myles!" I called, more confident now that I was offstage.

"Hear that?" Myles said, laughing. "Ugly piece of shit, he calls me. Mighty big words from someone *offstage*. Come back out here and say that to my face, you big damn sissy."

"Just play the fuckin' song, toolbox," I yelled back.

"Toolbox," Myles echoed, laughter fading. "Been his favorite insult for me since we were just kids." He picks the strings with his first two fingers and thumb, adjusts the tuning, continues picking out the melody to his crooner ballad, "If I Could Stay."

Damn the man, he could move from joking with me to killing the crowd with that tearjerker ballad without missing a beat, and the crowd ate it up. Of course, the way he sang it, every woman in the joint was wishin' it was her he was singing it to, and every man was wishing it was him singing it.

I went back to work, retuning, checking, and making sure I had strings ready in case he snapped one. By the end of the show, Myles was drenched in sweat and exhausted, but flying high as a kite on adrenaline. He'd done not one, but two encores, the last encore being mostly him doing bits and pieces of outlaw country requests shouted from the audience. Finally, he strode offstage with Betty-Lou in hand, grinning from ear to ear. He beelined for Betty-Lou's custom-made case— bulletproof, crush-proof, waterproof, fireproof, and biometrically coded to his thumbprint, with embedded GPS tracking. He locked Betty-Lou away, and then that case went into another separate wheeled, foam-padded, locked case. Yeah, he took the security of that instrument more seriously than he did his own life.

That done, he clapped me on the back. "That was a hell of a show, buddy."

I just glared at him, unmoved. "If you didn't have a show tomorrow, I'd break your fuckin' nose for that stunt."

He just grinned, clapping me on the back again. "Crow, my friend, one of these days it'll happen."

"No, Myles. Not any day. I don't perform. I just play for me, for fun. You ain't ever gonna get me on the stage in front of people. I don't want that attention."

He shook his head as we went through the argument we'd been over a million times. "You have God's own talent with a guitar, Crow. Shit, if you don't want attention, you could be a session musician in Nashville.

Everybody from John Mayer to Rihanna would suck their own dick to get you to play on their albums."

"Pretty sure Rihanna doesn't have a dick, dick."

He just shoved at me. "What if you faced away from the crowd and just played?"

"No. We been over this a million times, Myles. I'm content being the tech. Quit askin'."

"I ain't askin for you, I'm askin' for me. For the world. Talent like yours oughta be shared, man."

I went to work packing up the rest of his guitars. "Well, you and the world are gonna have to suffer without me, because I—do—*not*—perform."

He leaned against a stack of sound equipment cases. "I'll figure it out. One of these days."

"You been tryin' for years, Myles. Give it up."

"Never." He laughed. "I did get you to play once, remember?"

I snorted. "Yeah, once, and look how that turned out."

"Hey, that wasn't *my* fault. You were shitfaced."

"I was so shitfaced it was a miracle I could walk. I'll never forget that, by the way. Most embarrassing day of my life. One of those days I wish I'd blacked out."

"Thank god for us both it was in a dive bar in the middle of...where the hell was it? Kentucky? Alabama?"

"Fuck if I know, man," I said. "It was a couple years ago, and we were both obliterated."

"I think it was Alabama. Tuscaloosa, maybe? Honestly, it's a wonder there's no video of that. I keep expecting to pull up Twitter or YouTube and see someone's posted some grainy-ass footage of that night."

"Well, let's pray that never happens, because you fell on your ass, as I remember, and I couldn't even see the strings enough to manage a basic chord. Crowd laughed their asses off, though. They were as drunk as we were."

"Good times, man." He gestured out at the dispersing crowd as he guzzled another bottle of water. "Far cry from that, these days, huh?"

I finished snapping the last guitar case closed, and then began arranging them in their dedicated storage box. "Yeah, it sure is. You've come a long-ass way, brother."

He grabbed me and I straightened; the jokester, the charming Texas grin was gone, a rare serious moment with Myles. "*We've* come a long way, Crow. You've been with me since the day this shit started blowing up for me."

"I got your back, Myles. You know that."

He shook his head, frowning. "I couldn't have done any of this without you. I wouldn't be here if it wasn't for you." A pause. "Literally."

I sighed. "The bridge doesn't remember waters long passed, Myles."

He laughed. "The fuck does that mean, Confucius?"

"It means that shit is history, man. Not worth remembering."

"Yeah, it is. It's well worth remembering, to me."

I started coiling cords. "Myles..." I just turned away, went about my work. "What's our next stop?"

He consulted his memory, glancing up and to the right, grinding the toe of his boot against the floor. "Um. Illinois, I think. A festival near Chicago."

"Who's all there?"

"Everybody, bro. Sam Hunt, Luke Combs, Dustin Lynch, Kane Brown, Miranda Lambert, Old Dominion, Parker...somebody new on the scene, can't remember his last name, but he's pretty good. Single is 'Pretty Heart.' Shit, who else? Fuckin' a bunch of acts. Gonna be a good time. We go on Friday, and don't have to be in Denver till Tuesday. One of the little breaks we've got built into the schedule."

"Nice."

I had the last of his personal guitars, cords, and amps stowed away the way I liked them, and that was it for me—the rest of the crew would break everything else down. We'd been doing this together long enough that Myles was already heading for the bus as

I clicked the latches on the last of the crates, knowing I'd be right behind him.

He stepped up onto his bus, and I was only moments behind him. We splayed out side by side on the couch, and just sat for a few moments, soaking in the silence.

This was a ritual.

After the setup and mic check and rehearsal, after the opening acts and the side-stage drinking and bantering, after the show was over and the crowd was largely gone, we both needed a few minutes of just... quiet. Stillness.

Me more than him—he'd sit here with me a while, but inevitably he'd head out to find where the crew was partying, and there'd always be a few girls, and he'd have some fun. Me? I wasn't much of a partier, these days. I'd have some fun now and then, sure, but I liked my solitude, my privacy. Myles? He lived for the spotlight, lived to be the center of attention. He just drew the eye, wherever he was. He came alive when there was a crowd around him.

He reached up over his head, blindly opening the cabinet above the window, and pulled down a bottle of sixty-year-old scotch. Handed me the bottle, and reached up again for the glasses. Found them, and I poured us each a couple fingers.

"To another good show on the books," he said.

"Closing in on two hundred and fifty shows, now, you know."

I sipped. "You in this for life, Myles?"

"What, touring?"

I nodded. "Yeah. This it, for you?"

He sighed. "You know, I don't know. I'm just milking it for all it's worth, right now. Dad, Granddad, they loved this shit, you know? They'd be fuckin' stoked as hell to see me successful like this."

"They see, brother. They see you."

He eyed me. "You believe that? For real?"

I hesitated. I didn't like talking about this shit. But this was a moment you didn't ignore, a time you couldn't puss out on saying the real shit. "I mean, yeah, man. You know how I was raised. Who raised me. I didn't have much to believe in, those early days. Then I went to live with Mammy and River Dog and all that shit. So yeah, I believe our ancestors are watching."

He was silent. Absorbed. He knew I rarely ever discussed my past. Or myself at all, really. "I like that idea, I guess. Dad and Granddad watching over me. With me on the road, on the stage with me. They never got to see me blow up, you know?"

I nodded. "They're with you, Myles."

"What about you?"

I growled in my chest. "What about me?"

"Are your ancestors with you?"

I shrugged. "Yeah, they are. Dad's are, at least. I see them in the mountains, the trees. The rivers. The road itself, in a way, I guess. My dad's people lived in all those places and I believe they are still there. Never knew too much about Mom's side of things. I guess I get that from her—she never talked about herself or her past. Her family, none of that shit. Don't know jack."

"She was Native American, too, though, right?"

I nodded. "Comanche. Dad was Apache."

We finished our scotch, and Myles leaned forward. Took my glass from me, rinsed his and mine, dried them with paper towel, and replaced the glasses and the bottle in the cabinet, secured against the movement of the bus. This, too, was ritual—I worked for him on stage, brought him guitars and tuned them, kept them maintained. Replaced strings and all that. Then, in these quiet moments, he always served me scotch. Reminding himself and me, I think, that we were equals. Brothers.

He eyed me. "Coming out?"

I shook my head. "Nah, I'm good."

He just huffed a laugh. "Yeah, you're way too melancholy anyway. You'd kill the mood."

I kicked at him. "Get the fuck out of here. Go, have fun. I'll see you later."

"You riding with us, or riding your bike?"

"I'll ride the bus till we stop, probably."

He nodded, exiting the bus. Paused at the bottom of the steps, slapped the doorway. "Crow?"

I eyed him. "Yo."

"You belong on stage, man. You're the most talented motherfucker I've ever met."

I shook my head. "That's your thing, not mine. I'm happy the way things are."

He sighed. "Waste of fuckin' talent, man."

"How about I write something, and you can tell 'em it was me?"

He grinned. "I need new material anyway."

I reached across to the couch across from me, where my guitar lay. Snagged it. Strummed. Felt something bubbling up, and let it out.

I stopped, glanced at Myles. "Get out of here, man. Can't feel it with you watchin'."

"Think you can have it done in time for the festival? It'd be fun to debut a new song there."

I nodded. "Probably, yeah."

"Sweet." He smacked the doorway again. "Well, you have fun."

I just snorted. "I'm stayin' my ass on the bus. You're the one going out partying."

"Lame-ass."

"Party boy."

He left, then, cackling, whistling. I noticed he had a Sharpie in his back pocket, as always, which meant he was heading for the front gates where hangers-on tended to gather, hoping he'd make an appearance for photos and autographs—he usually did show up, most nights, and his fans knew it, which is why there was always a crowd gathered, waiting.

He'd sign autographs and take photos, hug and shake hands until they were all gone, and then he'd finally head off for wherever the after-party was, and he'd find a friend and a bottle.

I didn't envy him—but I was happy for him.

I had what I needed, and it was enough.

Most nights, at least.

There were times when the loneliness got the better of me, and I'd follow Myles off to the party, and assuage the loneliness with a pretty, willing, friendly face for the night. That would tide me over for a while, but it never lasted long.

In the end, you see, it was always how it had always been—just me. Old Crow, off by himself, stoic as the mountains.

I snorted at my own melodrama, but put it into lyrics and let it be.

I fell asleep at some point, with the guitar on my chest and the notepad on the floor. When I woke up, the bus was rumbling, and I heard Myles back in his room, making noises I didn't want to think too much about.

I went back to sleep knowing, when we stopped for coffee in a few hours, she'd be gone and we'd be back on the road for Chicago.

THREE

Charlie

"CHARLIE."

I was lost. Stuck in sludgy darkness, dream-time tar wrapping me up in syrupy-slow lucidity. I knew I was dreaming, but I was drowning in the dream. It was a dream of nothing—just me, in the dark. Wandering. Someone behind me, trying to pull me backward—someone ahead of me, needing me. It was recurring, maddening, meaningless.

"Charlie."

The darkness was shaking me. What do you want? I couldn't speak, couldn't form thoughts—it was a whisper of a thought, a breath of an idea, but the dream-sludge had my mouth fused.

"Charlotte. Charlotte Grace."

Insistent shaking.

What? What do you want from me?

"Charlie!"

Smack!

My eyes flew open, my cheek stinging. Lexie was in the driver's seat, eying me warily.

"There you are." She reached out and palmed my cheek. "You okay?"

I sat up, touched my cheek—looked in the mirror: my cheek was pink. "Did you...*slap* me?"

"You were screaming bloody fucking murder, Charlie."

I blinked. "I...I was?"

"Thrashing around, screaming, kicking. You almost hit me in the face—while I was doing eighty-five on I-90."

I looked out my window, and realized we were on the shoulder, emergency flashers on. It was eight in the morning, and I'd been asleep for two hours. We'd switched after four hours, stopped for gas and a quick meal, went another four. Shared a bed in a sleazy no-tell motel somewhere in Pennsylvania, slept a few hours, and gotten back on the road around dawn. I could tell Lex was antsy to put as many miles between us and New York as possible, so I'd pushed us along. Now, though, I could tell she was getting ready to talk.

The quality of her silence was different. Pensive, restless, thoughtful.

"Where are we?" I asked.

"Close to Chicago." She glanced at me, and then checked traffic, accelerating and merging. "I need coffee and an omelet and shopping."

"Sounds good to me," I said.

Thus, in another forty-five minutes or so, we found ourselves parking on the street outside a breakfast place in Chicago. We got coffee, ordered omelets, and relaxed.

I let the silence breathe, knowing she'd start talking eventually.

We were in a corner booth, and the restaurant was crowded, noisy. This was the best place to have a private, sensitive conversation.

Lex stared into her coffee, leaning over it. "I broke all my rules. I don't have many, but I broke them all."

I held my tongue.

"The rules." She ticked them off one by one, tapping a finger on the table for each. "No one more than ten years older than me. Never be the other woman. Never let a man dictate or pressure me into doing something I don't want to. Never be a secret."

I bit my lip. "Oh god, Lex."

She nodded. "Yeah. I broke every single fucking one. All with one guy."

I waited.

"Professor Marcus Tyne."

"A professor, Lexie?"

She nodded. "Yep. I'm that bitch." A sigh. "It's hard to talk about."

"Well, I may express surprise, perhaps even be upset, but just know that I love you, and that I will not judge you or think less of you, and that I'm here for you. I'll do whatever I can, and we'll get you through this."

She sipped coffee. "Thanks."

"Just tell me what happened, okay?"

"I'm not sure I can dump the whole story all at once. It's too much."

"Understandable."

Our food arrived, and we dug in, both of us ravenous. After a few minutes, she started talking again between bites.

"He taught a class on sexuality through history. My favorite course. He wasn't...gauche, or lewd. Matter of fact, and a wonderful lecturer. Eloquent, and a great storyteller. He could tell all these historical anecdotes off the cuff." She chased a piece of sausage around her plate. "He was...I don't even know how to describe him." Her eyes closed. Pain filled her features. "Tall, really tall. Like six-four, six-five. Strong, fit. Not a dad-bod, but not, like, an athlete. Dark salt-and-pepper hair, a neat beard. His voice was this silky magic. He had the hot, sophisticated professor look down pat—chic round-framed glasses, tweed or wool blazers with actual patches on the elbow. Wore real oxfords."

"Wow. Sounds like a caricature of a professor, really."

She nodded, laughing. "That's Marcus." A bitter sigh. "It happened the way it always happens, I guess. I wrote a paper, he gave me a shitty grade. I disagreed, went in to argue with him about it."

"Of course you did."

"It was a good paper! I had sources, and a logical development of my thesis. I was articulate. He just didn't like my position, I guess, so he gave me a shit grade. We fought. It got ugly. Finally, he agreed to let me rewrite it, so long as I, and I quote, 'toned down the hard left feminist vitriol.'"

I winced. "Ooh, I bet that went over well."

She bit her lip, holding back laughter. "Yeah, not so much. I rewrote it, all right."

"And let me guess…the hard left feminist vitriol went on afterburner."

"Yeah. I tripled my sources. Wrote an additional eight pages. When I turned it in to him, he called it inflammatory rhetoric of the worst sort. But, he gave me a decent grade."

"And that was that," I said, smirking.

"I wish. But no. Once that class was done, he emailed me, asked to see me."

"Oh dear."

"It was innocent enough. At first." A long pause. "He said he'd been doing his job as a professor in the grading of my papers, but that he admired my passion. Got me a gig writing for an underground campus paper. We'd meet once a week in his office to talk. He was…smart. So smart. Interesting. He knew so much—he could talk off the cuff with absolute authority on everything from the Boxer Rebellion to Stoic philosophy to the hippie movement of the sixties. We could talk for hours, and we did."

"And then?"

A shrug, a shake of her head. "And then nothing. That was it, for months. We just talked. Emailed. It was all on the up and up."

"But?"

"I fought it, Charlie. I fought liking him. He was a professor. He was *married*. He had kids, three of them, not that much younger than me." She rubbed her forehead with a knuckle. "But he was so *interested* in me. When we talked, it felt like I was the only person on earth. I liked that. I'd never felt that way before, you know? Most of my relationships, before him, were, honestly, mostly just casual sexual liaisons, at best. Louis, in high school, but that's really it."

"He paid attention to you."

She nodded. "You could hit that with a pretty heavy psychoanalytic hammer, if you wanted. I talked about Dad, how he had been gone a lot, and not really *there*, despite being there."

"Now *that* I understand completely."

"You too?"

"Oh yeah." I touched her hand. "All of us have that stuff. But that's a different conversation."

"Yeah, it is." Another long silence, as Lex dredged through her memory. "Shit went down kind of unexpectedly. I was at a party, off-campus. I'd ridden with friends, but then we all got hammered, and we got separated, and then Tanya, who'd driven, went home in someone else's car, and Leah was off chasing dick, and I was bored. The only hot guys at the party were the most cliche fucking douchebag jock frat bro assholes, and dumber than a bag of hammers, which is just a turn off. So I was just bored. So I left. Alone. On foot."

"Oh dear, not a great move."

A snicker. "No shit, considering I was smashed out of my head and had no idea where I was. Not a great part of town, and dressed like a skank."

I arched an eyebrow. "You go apeshit if anyone says that about you."

"I can slut-shame myself, but no one else can.

And I really was dressed pretty slutty. Basically, I may as well have been carrying a sign that said 'please rape me.'"

"And cue Professor Marcus Tyne to the rescue."

"Not quite. Sort of. I emailed him. I didn't have his phone number, just his email address. I don't remember how it happened, but he emailed me back like, tell me where you are. So I told him I had no fucking clue. I think I gave him my phone number, and he FaceTimed me. Triangulated my location based on who the fuck knows what, and next thing I knew I was in his car."

"Drunk, dressed like a slut."

"Yep. Gold sequin miniskirt so short the bottom of my ass cheeks hung out, a see-through gauzy white half-shirt. Like, nothing under it. Tits totally visible. It was fun, actually. Guys would all but shit themselves trying to get a better look."

"Oh my god, Lexie."

"Yeah."

"And how did Mr. Professor respond to the outfit?"

"He gave me his jacket. And I thought then that it was just because I was cold. Later, I realized it was his attempt to keep himself from wanting me."

"Did it work?"

"Nope. Well, in that moment, yes. Later, not

so much." A pause. "He took me home, back to the dorms. Total gentleman."

"So…"

"So get to the juicy part?"

I sighed. "It's not gossip to me, Lex, it's your life." A slight smirk. "But yeah."

"Well, he had my phone number. So we started texting. A lot."

"You knew he was married?"

She frowned down at her coffee. "Yes. I can't excuse it. I knew then I shouldn't be texting a married man. But mostly, it was just innocent stuff. Just talking. But still, I was a twenty-year-old college student, and he was a professor. It wasn't appropriate. Knew it then, know it now, and I'm not going to pretend otherwise. But he was funny. He made me feel good. I looked forward to every text he sent me, and spent a lot of time perfecting my responses…or I'd fire off whatever I was thinking without filtering it."

"Sounds dangerous."

"Yeah." Her fingertip traced circles on the table. "Then, one night, I got tipsy and started drunk-texting him."

"Ohhh dear."

"Oh dear, especially because he was drunk too. Admitted it. His wife was out of town for the week with their kids—we'd just finished finals, and he was buried in grading, so I guess she always took the kids to her sister's for the week of finals grading. Gave him time to grade without interruption, and then some time to unwind, and then he'd meet up with them—they lived in the Poconos, I guess."

"And here it is."

"Yep. Drunk Lex, drunk professor home alone for a week with nothing to do but grade papers." She sighed, long and bitter. "I have no memory of it, but I went to his house. How I knew where he lived I still am not entirely sure. But I was drunk and horny, and so was he. He let me in, and we got even drunker, together. Important note, I walked to his house, by the way. I never drove under the influence."

I arched an eyebrow. "Well at least there's that?"

"So, anyway. He cooked food. We kept drinking. Grading papers. Talking. His sweater came off, and then my shoes. His button-down, my cardigan. I mean, it was just so *hot* in that house, you know?"

"Ohhh, Lexie."

"I ended up naked, dancing in his living room to Miles Davis." She closed her eyes, and it was obvious this memory was...bittersweet. "He touched me first. Granted, I was dancing to get his attention, and it worked. But he grabbed me, and kissed me, and... Charlie, it was...*fuck*. The kiss of a man his age, who knew what he was doing? Fucking amazing."

"I bet," I managed.

"And he could use that mouth for a fuckuva lot more than just kissing. Oh god, so good."

"Lex, I don't need the details."

"Yes, you do." She squeezed her eyes shut. Kept going. "We didn't leave that house for four days. We fucked *so many times*. On the couch, on the kitchen counter, on the dining room table, on the floor, on his desk—apparently that was his big fantasy, bending me over his desk in his study."

I blushed. "Lex, come on."

She just laughed, poking at me. "You come on, you silly prude. Have you never made a man's fantasy come true? There's nothing in the world like it."

I thought about Glen—practical, considerate, and knew one sex position: missionary, in bed. Had I ever done it any other way, any other place, except with Glen, in a bed, missionary? I didn't think so.

I'd certainly never made his fantasies come true. What were his fantasies? Did I know? If he had them, he'd never shared them, and it had never occurred to me to ask.

She was watching me. "You haven't, have you?"

I shrugged. "So?"

"So, bucket list, Charlie. Make it a top priority— get a man to tell you his deepest, darkest, dirtiest fantasy, and do it for him, as long as it's within your parameters of safety."

"What if his fantasy is something messed up, like…I don't even know. Rape, or a golden shower, or something gross?"

"The whole point is to make it something hot, and kinky, but fun. More for him than you, but I guarantee you, if it's with the right person, you'll enjoy the hell out of it. With Marcus, it really was just the desk thing. But with *me*. His wife couldn't have fulfilled that one for him, even if she'd been willing to. That's the kind of fucked-up part about that, I guess."

"Yeah, kind of."

"So, four days. Fucking all day, all night. Eating, hanging out, him grading papers, and fucking."

I couldn't help the crimson blush. I could never talk like her, never, much less do what she'd done. "Four days?"

She nodded, shrugged. "Not my record for sex marathons."

I blinked, eyes wide. "Jesus."

"That would be…" she paused for effect. "Jimmy Nawrocki, sophomore year at U-Conn. We rented a hotel for a week, and never left it. Ordered room service, binged Netflix, got hammered, and fucked literally until I physically could not tolerate it. My poor pussy was so sore I could barely walk by the time we were done. But fuck, was it worth it. That boy was a *god* in the sack. The things he could do with his mouth? And that dick, man, it was—"

"Alexandra!"

She just grinned. Held her hands up, indicated an improbable length, and then made an improbably wide circle with her middle finger touching her thumb. "Like that. A fucking kielbasa, is what it was. Similar curve, too, now that I think about it."

I hissed at her. "Alexandra Rochelle."

She just laughed out loud. "Oh shut up. You're just jealous because all you've ever had is Glen freaking Twinkle Mouse the plaid wonder lad."

I snorted. "The *what*?"

"Me, Poppy, and Torie all called him Twinkle Mouse."

"Why?"

"Because when he thought he was being funny, his eyes would twinkle. And he looked like a mouse, and acted like one. Those ears, and the pointy face. The big teeth. Twinkle Mouse."

"That is not nice," I said, but I was laughing, because now that she'd pointed it out, I couldn't unsee it. "But true."

"Right?"

"Who came up with that?" I asked, expecting it to be her.

"Oh, Torie, I think. The first time you brought him home, she was stoned out of her head, like always, and was like, 'He twinkles. And he looks like a mouse. I shall call him Twinkle Mouse.'"

"Sounds like Torie," I said, still laughing. "God, now I'm gonna call him that."

"He was a Twinkle Mouse." She frowned at me. "None of us ever understood what you saw in him."

"That's a different conversation," I said, accepting a refill from the waitress and putting my card on the tray to pay the check.

"No, it's really not," Lex said, spinning her empty mug like a top. "You just tell me his redeeming qualities, and I'll destroy them one by one."

"He was nice," I said.

"Okay, and?"

I arched an eyebrow. "And what? No snarky comment?"

She shook her head. "I mean, nice is fine. Nice is boring as fuck, but I get it." She smirked. "But, if you want snark…they say nice guys finish last, but in my experience, nice guys usually finish *first*, and have no clue how to finish you off."

I sighed. "Yep, there we go." I shook my head. "Anyway. He was very, very smart. He knew what he wanted, and he had a plan to get it, and he was following the plan."

"Again, fine as far as it goes, but boring as fuck." She faked a gruff, dumb voice. "I have planned out every single moment of my life and will not deviate from this plan for anything. There will be *no* fun, *no* adventure, and *no* spontaneity what-so-fucking-ever."

I ignored this, because...well, again, it was the brutal truth. That was Glen to a T. "He was articulate."

She shrugged, made a face. "Can't knock that one. Continue."

"He was educated as hell. Stanford, and then Yale. He had connections he'd made himself, in the political world. His dad was connected, but Glen refused to use them."

"Again, not much to critique there, so I'll allow those."

"How gracious of you," I drawled, monotone, sarcastic. "He was easy to talk to. Good with money. Thoughtful. He always put the toilet seat down."

"Fine, fine, and very nice. Well-trained."

"Yeah, but I didn't teach him that. His mom did, I think."

"Ohhh, was he a momma's boy?"

"Oh, absolutely."

She nodded. "Makes sense." She cackled. "Did she call him every week?"

I sighed, rubbed my forehead, looking away. "Um. Well?"

"No. *No.*" She shook her head. "Every day?"

I nodded. "Yeah. On his lunch break, at noon. You could set your watch to it."

She rolled her eyes. "Did she cut the crusts off his sandwiches too?"

I blushed hard at that. "No, she did not."

Lexie studied me. And then blanched, pale, visibly nauseous. "You—did—fucking—*not.*"

"It made him happy, okay?" I ripped open a sugar packet and dumped it on my plate.

She cackled, and then the cackling devolved into hysteria. "You fucking cut the crusts off his fucking sandwiches!" She slapped her forehead. "He was fucking his mother through *you*! You do realize that, right?"

Me: Five-seven, black hair, athletically slender but with a little extra oomph in the hips and bust. Blue eyes, a recessive trait from Dad.

Glen's mom: five-six or seven, brown hair dark enough to be nearly black. Slender but with some curve. Light eyes.

Me: Given to nurturing. Authoritative by nature, being the eldest sister, but not a big fan of conflict. Not great at sitting still or being idle.

Glen's mom: See preceding.

Fuck.

Lex was watching me, and saw the penny drop. "Now you see it, huh?"

"Yeah, and fuck you for that."

She just laughed. "Ooooh, a swear. I really got you on that one."

"I'm totally a dead ringer his mom, even physically. I thought I was just nurturing and being a good girlfriend, but he was just looking for a replacement for his mom whom he could also have sex with." I hung my head in my hands. "I feel gross, now."

She reached out and awkwardly patted me on the top of the head. "There, there. There, there."

I blinked up at her. "Is that your version of comforting me?"

She shrugged. "Nurturing, I am not." She grinned lasciviously. "I've got one surefire way of helping someone feel better, and I really don't think you want that."

I shuddered. "Yeah, nope."

She wiggled her eyebrows. "I mean, you could probably learn a lesson, here, though. Next time you're wondering if a guy is interested in you or your nurturing qualities, just do what I do: whenever you feel like he's down in the dumps and you want to do something nice for him to make him feel better, just blow him. Don't make him a fuckin' sandwich, don't do his goddamn laundry, don't clean up after him, just suck him off. He'll feel better, and that sure as shit ain't nurturing. Save that shit for when you're really a momma."

I cackled, stifling laughter with my hands, and then spat laughter through my fingers. "Alexandra!"

"What, Charlotte?"

"You can't just dick-suck your way through relationships." I said this not quite *sotto voce*, but nearly.

"If I'm dick-sucking my way through it, it ain't a relationship, babe. That's the real secret."

"Secret?"

"To not getting attached. Keep it physical. Focus on the peen and the poon, and your heart stays your own."

I frowned at her. "You say that like it's a good thing."

"Worked for me so far?"

"Has it, though?"

And just like that, she was serious again. "Screw you, Charlie."

"Hey, I'm not judging. I was in a relationship I thought was serious, that meant something, but it wasn't, and it didn't. I'm no better off than you are."

"We are not in the same place, Char. Not even remotely."

"Why?" I asked.

She shrugged, staring at the table. "Because I've only told you part of the story."

"Ohhh my."

She nodded. "Yeah. And not even the worst part."

"You got caught, didn't you?"

She yanked the bill tray toward herself, scribbled a zero on the tip line and totaled it, tossed a generous cash tip onto the tray, and slid it back to me to sign.

She adopted a smooth, low, sultry, announcer-type voice. "Next time, in the ongoing saga of Lexie's Fucked-Up Life…find out if the wife and children caught her *in flagrante delicto* with the hunky professor, or will she get away with her sinful rendezvous? Also in our next episode we answer the question, is anal really worth it?"

I snorted. "Lex, jeepers criminy."

She sputtered a disbelieving laugh. "What…the *hell*…did you just say?"

"Jeepers criminy. I don't like taking the Lord's name in vain."

"Didn't know you were religious, Charlie."

"I'm not, really, but it doesn't seem logical to piss off a potential deity. Plus, it's just crass and unnecessary."

"God, you sound like Mother."

"Why thank you."

"Considering you're twenty-four, I'm not sure that's a compliment." She slung her purse over her elbow. "Come on. Let's hit the road." And so we left the restaurant, stretching in the sunshine with the towers of Chicago all around us. "You want to just walk a little bit?" Lexie suggested.

"Sure," I said. "Stretch our legs, maybe hit a couple stores."

And so we passed most of the day—shopping, walking, talking about anything but our messed-up lives. She told me stories about her various college escapades, I told her funny and embarrassing tidbits about Glen—such as how he once made an appointment for a massage, not realizing it was actually an illicit "happy endings" massage parlor slash prostitution front. That was hysterical, until he'd admitted he had actually, out of overly polite confusion, allowed the "massage therapist" to give him the happy ending. And that it had happened while we were together.

I had been less than pleased, but had chalked it up to him being naive and just too polite to tell her to stop.

Now, I wondered.

But I still told the story, because it was funny.

Lex told me about the time she went on three or four dates with this super-hot, beefy, charming Army officer on leave and in uniform…only to find out that he had an actual micro-penis, and hadn't been able to go through with sleeping with him for the gales of helpless, stunned laughter.

For which she still felt guilty, and claimed to have

actually tried to find him later so she could apologize and possibly even make up for it—to no avail, as he'd shipped back out.

"Like, god," she said, "it's not his fault—I know that now and I knew it then. Nothing he can do about what he was given by nature. And even teeny weenies need love. I should've been able to woman up and still have fun with him. But I was just so shocked, because everything else about him, including his hands, was just enormous. I was fully expecting a serious pocket python when he dropped trouser, but no. It would've fit in a damn Tic-Tac box, and I'm not lying. What was I supposed to do with it?" She held her index finger and thumb apart as if holding an invisible pencil, and mimed a vigorous up-and-down motion. "It would've been like this. Ridiculous."

"Lexie, you're still being mean."

She sighed. "I know, I know. I should have more compassion and understanding. But I just…I like big dicks, and I cannot lie." She glanced at me. "What was Glen packing? I've always been curious."

I bit my lip, half hiding a grin. "You'd probably be a little surprised."

"Yeah? Nicer than expected?"

I shrugged. "I mean, I have no frame of reference, because he's the only man I've ever had sex with."

She huffed. "We have *got* to fix that."

I shook my head at her. "I'm really not inter-ested in casual sex, Lexie. I'm just not. I don't say that to cast any judgment on you. I mean that. What you do with your body is your business, and as long as you're being honest with yourself and respecting yourself and sticking to whatever morals and con-victions you hold, then more power to you. But for me, personally, the idea of having sex with a perfect stranger just doesn't sound fun or exciting, it sounds terrifying and impersonal."

"That's part of why it's fun," she said. "But I get what you mean. We're just different people, I guess."

I hugged her sideways. "And that's okay. I love you for you, sister."

She shoved me off. "Oh stop being saccharine, Charlotte. It's gross."

I laughed, leaning in to plant a kiss on her cheek, a wet, sloppy one. "Oh come on, Alexandra. Don't be squeamish. I'm your big sissy!"

She cackled, pulling away, and then abruptly turned into me and licked my cheek. "There."

"Eeew! Oh my god you *licked* me!" I screeched, wiping at my face.

She just laughed, and wiped off her own cheek.

I had a thought, then. "You know, I would nor-mally never, ever, do this. But seeing as he violated my trust and broke my heart, and I need to delete them anyway…"

I dug my phone out of my purse and scrolled backward through my photos to March of the previous year, when Glen and I had had this brief, short-lived, and utterly unsuccessful attempt to "spice up" our sex life by sending each other nude pictures. I knew he still had some of me, but I'd only gotten as far as an awkward topless shot before giving up, so I figured hell, let him have it.

I still had these…and god, they were glorious.

Gloriously awkward, and funny as hell. Which was why I was showing them to Lexie.

I handed her my phone. "Swipe left," I said. "And behold the glory of Twinkle Mouse."

She took the phone, but her eyes stayed on me. "You have dick pics of Glen?"

"Yep."

"Why did he send you dick pics?"

I sighed. "We were trying to spice up our sex life."

She closed her eyes slowly. "And that, my dearest sister, is when you know the sex is shitty: if you're twenty-four and need to 'spice it up.' That's fine for a couple in their forties who have been married for like twenty years. People fall into patterns. Life weighs you down, and you get stuck in ruts. It's totally normal, and that's when you do something like that, to shake it up. But at twenty-four, you oughta be boning each other on the hood of the car just for the hell of it. You're a beautiful, funny, assertive, athletic young woman, Charlie. Sex should be fucking *wild*, honey!"

I couldn't look at her, because I knew she was right. "Just look at his dick and give me my phone back so I can delete the stupid photos."

She looked.

And burst into hysterical laughter. "Oh, my god. Did he Photoshop in a sun flare?"

I nodded, biting my lower lip. "Yes. Yes he did."

"Is that, in fact, a shag throw rug he's kneeling on?"

I nodded again. "A bearskin rug, as a matter of fact."

"And, correct me if I'm wrong, but…did he…*oil* himself down?"

I couldn't contain the splutter. "Yes." I had to focus on not losing my shit. "He took a whole series of these. With his professional grade Nikon DSLR, and a tripod, and a timer. He had a photoshoot with himself."

She swiped. "Wow. I mean, bonus points for going all out, but…*wow*." She pinched to zoom in. "You weren't wrong, though. He's bigger than I'd have thought. Smaller than what I would consider minimum for me to want a repeat, but I'd fuck it once."

I eyed her. "So, from your much broader range of experience, where does that fall in the spectrum of average penis size?"

She bobbed her head to one side, glancing at me. "Honest?"

I nodded. "I'm very much and very gladly done with him, so yes."

"It's on the small side. Length isn't that bad, but it's thin. Narrow. Pointy. Kinda weird looking. I mean, as a penis expert I can tell you authoritatively that is *not* a pretty penis. But, if he used it well, like you felt good with him and enjoyed sex with him and had yourself a nice little O when you were fucking him, then size doesn't matter. I've had giant dicks that weren't as fun and enjoyable to fuck as smaller ones that the man in question knew how to use. So, people say size doesn't matter, and others say size does matter—in my experience, both are true. It does matter, because there really is too big, and too small. But as long as it's inside the range of not too big and not too small, it really doesn't matter as long as he knows what he's doing." She swiped again, spewing laughter through a cupped hand. "Oh my god, so glamorous. The sultry look, the slicked-back hair, the oiled beer belly."

"Right?" I said. "That was the end of that experiment. I was laughing too hard to feel sexy when he sent them."

"Did you enjoy sex with him?"

I sighed, shrugged. "Well, again, I have no frame of reference. I've had plenty of sex, just all of it was with him. So I don't have any other experience to compare it to."

"But did you finish sexy times feeling satisfied?" She swiped through a few more. "Wow, I mean, wow." A glance at me. "How often did you feel the need to pop into the bathroom with a vibrator after he was asleep to finish the job?"

I blushed. "Um. I thought I was the only one who did that."

She cackled out loud. "Girl, you need to talk about sex more, if you think that."

We passed a group of women who all looked about five or ten years older than us. Lexie hauled me to a stop and waved them down. "Excuse me, ladies, sorry to bother you, but I'm hoping you'll help me out, here. My sister, my dear sheltered sister, has labored her entire adult life under the sad assumption that she's the only woman who has ever needed to sneak into the bathroom after sex to finish the job."

The women, six or eight of them, exchanged looks, and then clustered around Lexie and I, breaking out in the kind of deafening laughter only a large group of excited women can produce.

One of them, a woman of either Middle Eastern

or Indian decent, with an exaggerated New York accent, hugged me as if we've known each other for years. "Honey, I'd say you're in the extreme minority if you *haven't* done that at least once in your life."

"That is the damn truth," another woman said—this one was white and decked out in leather pants and a white silk shirt. "My husband left me like that at first, and then I decided fuck this, I'm gonna tell him has to up his game if he wants to keep fucking me, and he did, and now I get off at least once every time we go."

And then there was a barrage of advice and stories, and I couldn't keep it all straight. I've never in my life heard so much graphic sexual detail.

But, it did help, because I learned very quickly that mediocre sex is normal, and it's not until you find someone who really lights you up that you truly understand the importance of good sex, and what good sex even is.

Not that it would do me any good, because I had no intention of having any sex anytime soon. I needed to be emotionally distanced from Glen a bit more before I even thought of sex. And, honestly, I couldn't fathom what it would be like, to want someone else. There'd only been Glen, since I was seventeen. I met him my first day of freshman orientation at Yale, and never even thought about another man.

Five years at Yale, two years in Boston. Seven years, I'd given to him.

A lot of sex, but with zero variety.

Given the frequency of our sex, which was, honestly, a lot—two or three times a week, at least—there had been a pathetic number of orgasms for me. I know Lex would call that lame, barely enough to talk about. But to me it had seemed like a lot.

Because...

Well, because it felt like a chore, sometimes.

I didn't always look forward it. Or, I'd be all excited and horny going into it, but the reality would leave me disappointed. I'd imagine what the sex would be like in my head throughout the day, anticipating being with him, and then when we finally got to it, the reality would be a couple of lazy kisses, his hands groping my tits, a couple quick thrusts and a grunt, and that was it. He'd be asleep, and I'd be like, *well hell—what now?*

What usually happened was I'd wait until he was snoring, then dig my vibrator out of the old maxi pad box in the back of the cabinet under the sink, sit on the toilet lid, and finish myself off, biting my lip to keep quiet.

That's just what I knew. That was pretty much my sexual routine.

I couldn't fathom what else it *could* be. Certainly

not like Lexie's life. I could never let a stranger kiss me, let alone touch me intimately.

The group of women had said goodbye, hugged us all around, and went their way as we went ours—me lost in my thoughts.

Could it be better? How would I know if I wanted it? I'd never let myself be attracted to anyone else, or think about anyone else. How would I know what I wanted, and how would I know it'd be worth the effort of getting it?

What if mediocre sex was all I'd ever know? What if I only attracted mediocre men? I thought I was pretty enough, with a decent body, and I'd been hit on more than few times by some pretty hot men. But did that equate to being able to find, attract, date, and get into bed with a man capable of more than mediocre, half-hearted sex?

Was there, in fact, a man out there who would want me for *me*, and not just because I was a fuckable version of his mother?

At that moment, Lexie grabbed my arm, hauled me to a stop, and planted her fingertip on a flyer taped to a crosswalk/stoplight pole. "O-M-G! Charlie! Look!" It was a flyer for a country music festival, going on that same weekend. "Myles North is going to be there!"

Country music was one of the things we bonded over—none of my other sisters liked it, and even Glen had teased me about my predilection for country music. So, this was the perfect opportunity for Lexie and I to have fun together doing something we both loved, and shared.

"That will be fun. Myles North is pretty good."

She glared at me. "Pretty good? Pretty good? He's amazing!"

"His body, or his music?"

She grinned. "Both! I can appreciate the man for his sexy blue eyes and that rugged jawline, and that body...mmmm-god*damn* the man is fine. And he can play the guitar like fuckin' Santana, *and* he has a voice I could listen singing me to sleep every single night of my life."

I laughed. "Wow, you have a major crush on the man, don't you?"

"I mean, it's a celebrity crush, but yeah." She wiggled her eyebrows, shook her hips. "I may or may not have had quite a few sessions with Mr. Pickles, thinking of him."

I stared at my sister. "With *who* now?"

"Mr. Pickles. My vibrator."

"Your vibrator is named Mr. Pickles?"

She cackled. "Yep. He's long, and thick, and green, and covered in these delicious little bumps. And he looks like a pickle, and one time I was crazy fucking horny and had nothing in the dorm to help out except a jar of pickles and ohmy*god* do *not* try that. So I call him Mr. Pickles."

I closed my eyes. "There's so much there I *seriously* did *not* need to know, Alexandra. And you're telling me you've diddled yourself with Mr. Pickles thinking about Myles North?"

"Thinking about? Try looking at pictures of, and watching videos, and imagining him using those hands that play the guitar dancing all over my pussy, ohhh my. Yes. I have, in fact, diddled myself thinking about Mr. Myles Mackenzie North."

"You know his middle name?" I asked, half laughing.

"I know his favorite guitar is a fifty-year-old Martin signed by Johnny Cash, Merle Haggard, and Willie Nelson, and that Waylon Jennings himself played an entire set with that guitar back in the eighties, when it was Myles's dad's, and the guitar is named Betty-Lou, and she lives in a special case. I know his childhood dog was named Rollie, and she was a beagle, and got so fat that they started calling her Roly-Poly."

I shook my head again. "Wow."

She shoved at me. "Oh, shut up. He's hot, and I like his music." She eyed me. "Have you never had a celebrity crush?"

"Nah. I figured, I was with Glen, and I loved him, and I was going to marry him, so why entertain thoughts of anyone else?"

"Because there are sexy people in the world, and harmless crushes on people you'll never meet are totally innocent."

"I guess."

She just half sighed, half laughed. "We'll get you thinking outside the Glen box, Char-Char. Don't you worry." She tapped the flyer. "In the meantime, we're going to this, right? It'll be a hell of a good time."

I was already putting the address into a navigation app. "A little less than an hour from here. Let's go!"

She was giddy. "Yes! Myles North, here I come!"

"I don't think he knows or cares that you're coming, Lexie."

She just bit her lip and smirked. "No, but give me ten minutes alone with him and he'll know I'm coming, all right. More than once, if I'm lucky."

I groaned. "You're dirty."

"Yes, yes I am."

And so, we retrieved my car and headed for a country music festival.

And, honestly, I was excited too—and I resolved to keep my mind open, and really try to just enjoy the experiences, not overthink them, and have fun. No matter what form that fun may take.

And if fun came in the form of a hot guy and some innocent fun, so be it.

FOUR

Crow

GOD, WHAT A WONDERFUL CLUSTERFUCK THIS FESTIVAL was.

How the organizers had managed to book such big-name, high-dollar acts, I couldn't figure out. The main stage was tiny and rickety and scary as hell, the so-called "wings" were semitrailers backed up to the stage, the electrical and sound wiring was a godawful tangled mess, and the backstage area was only separated from the pit by a few paltry, handmade white sawhorses with "Do Not Cross" stenciled on with spray paint, and beyond the sawhorses, the equipment trailers were parked end to end.

The field was a giant open space, maybe a

hundred acres of old fallow field, with all the parking way off in back along a tree line near the county trunk line. There was, fortunately, plenty of what mattered: trash cans, porta-potties, food, and water. There were also a scary number of giant-ass bonfires—like twenty-foot high bonfires—scattered in regular intervals. But each one was maintained and secured by a trio of what looked to be off-duty cops or ex-military dudes, so I doubted anyone would fall in and die. There were tents in clusters all along the tree lines to either side, and in my prowling of the festival grounds last night and this morning, I'd seen and heard fornication in plenty. I saw no police presence at all, and people were wandering around with open bottles of liquor and smoking joints—it was reminiscent of what I imagined the original Woodstock had been with a quarter of the crowd. Which, to me, meant this would actually be fun, instead of a miserable fuckin' muddy mess. There were food trucks way in back near the makeshift parking lot, and wandering vendors charging an arm and a leg for sweating liter bottles of water, cans of beer, and mini bottles of booze.

I mean, there was a shitload of laws being broken here, but somehow the organizers had managed to make sure those who may've cared were looking the other way.

Women were dancing around topless, which I liked.

The sound was loud as fuck, but shitty, which I didn't like.

Overall, a good fuckin' time.

We were slated to go on later tonight, as one of the main acts. The festival was broken up into three days—yesterday, day one, was the day featuring the sort of acts who opened for the up-and-comers, with a well-known but not A-list act as the day one headliner; day two was the big day, when the top-draw headliners performed hour sets, opener acts doing twenty minutes in between headliners, fifteen to thirty minute breaks between sets, and the biggest draws going on well past dark, when people would be blitzed and wild. Day three, the closing day, was a sort of taper-off, with more lesser-known artists going on to round things out as people packed up and went home.

It was barely after noon on day two and things were just ramping up. I didn't have jack shit to do until at least eight tonight, when we'd have to start moving our shit around in preparation for setup, and then Myles and the guys would go on around nine. I had plenty of time between now and then to just kick back, have a few beers, and enjoy the show.

And by the show, I mean the crowd, which was

liberally salted with pretty women wearing a whole lot of nothing from the waist up, and even one or two dressed in less, as if it was Burning Man or some shit. I didn't mind. Eye candy, if nothing else.

I drank slow, and not much—I reserved my real benders for when it mattered, and the rest of the time, I tended to just nurse a beer over a long, long time. More for the taste and the appearance than any real desire to chase a buzz. I'd had enough of the party life by this point of my life, honestly.

But that was a different story.

Hour after hour, I prowled the crowd. Watched the acts, taking note of the newcomers and sorting them into worthy of playing with Myles and not so much. Enjoyed the scenery—the bright sun and warm air, the birds wheeling and singing, the trees in the distance waving their green arms, the wide open sky above and, yes, the half-naked women shaking their tits, and I let myself play a game of sort-the-tits, wherein I mentally assessed and categorized boobs by size and shape.

Not all the women were topless, though. Plenty were clearly just there to listen to country and get hammered in a big ol' empty field. You didn't have to drive anywhere, and there wasn't much by way of security, and no one was paying attention to what you did as long as you weren't bothering anyone. And the few times some drunk asshole tried to start shit, he was shut down by the rest of the nearby crowd, who just wanted to have some laid-back fun.

Dusk was lowering, the blue sky turning orange. I was due backstage in about twenty, and was enjoying the last of my beer—my fourth or fifth since this morning, and I'd timed them pretty damn perfectly to set me up with a nice mellow buzz. The act on stage was decent—a local trio, two men and a woman clearly inspired by Lady A but without that trio's insane talent quotient. They played a good foot-stomping set, though, and the crowd loved 'em. It was getting plenty rowdy by now, with pockets of people dancing, others just watching. I saw the bonfire security switch shifts, the new guys fresh and alert and watchful—so, if anything did get out of hand, at least there was something like backup presence. People were plenty wild, though. Staggering around in groups and pairs and alone, laughing, hanging on each other, toasting with red Solo cups. I saw a guy and his girlfriend making out near the backstage sawhorses, and by making out, I mean he had his fingers up what passed for her skirt, and I had a feeling in another few minute they'd be in the grass just going at it, and whoa, yep, okay, there they went, right there, her on top, topless and bouncing her shit for everyone to see.

I mean, damn, though. Good for them, but I couldn't imagine ever being so far gone I'd do that in public. Maybe I was just a private sorta guy, but that was plain weird to me.

I drew my attention back to the stage, and the rest of the crowd. Watching, assessing. I'd done security plenty of times, so old habits took over—a guy who looked like potential trouble, dancing loose and with eyes that said he was spoiling for a fight. But he had buddies around him who looked less like trouble, and I hoped they'd keep his ass in check, because I had no desire to ruin my buzz with having to throw down.

A foursome of girls in very short, ripped jean shorts, cowboy boots, and flannel shirts tied up under big tits, dancing like no one was watching even though everyone with a dick within fifty feet was watching, especially when things started to not so accidentally pop out, now and then.

A couple having a hell of a nasty argument as they headed for the porta-potties off to the sides, the woman stabbing her finger at him, and him stomping away trying to pretend he couldn't' hear her shrill shrewy-ass voice.

And…oh shit.

This wasn't good.

A group of dudes, rough lookin' ones, clustered

around someone, off in the shadows where the sawhorses and semitrailers met the porta-potties. Laughing, pushing. Nudging each other, leaning in and whispering. In a crowd, if you're whispering, you're up to no good.

And if you're around the worst of humanity like I've been my whole life, you learn to recognize a certain look, a certain kind of laugh. It's a low ugly laugh, a harsh bark. It's one that says you're getting enjoyment out of someone else's pain or fear.

That was how these assholes were laughing.

I heard a squeal, a cry, a shout. A feisty curse, and one of the guys staggered backward, holding his lip, and then lunged back in. I heard a smack.

Oh fuck, no.

I tossed my empty cup into a nearby trash can and jogged over.

When I got within twenty feet, I knew I had been right. These wormfuck assholes were harassing some poor chick. They had her ringed in against the saw-horses and trailers, so she had nowhere to go. Pushing her around, grabbing her ass, pinching her tits, smacking her enough to knock her off-balance. She was hammered to shit, and scared, but not backing down. She'd slam up against the barricade, try to shake off the alcohol in a way that said she was likely seeing double, if not triple. Then she'd rush at the assholes, only to get grabbed, pinched, licked, smacked...all at once and from all sides.

Her rage was something to behold. She was volcanic, and she was giving out as good as she could— kicking, biting, punching, and connecting, too.

Trouble was, she was just plain outnumbered, out-sobered, and had no fuckin' chance.

And way over here, where no one was looking, ten-to-one they'd end up dragging her off into the woods...

Fuck no.

I keep a close rein on my temper, which ain't pretty to begin with. It rumbles close to the surface on a good day and, even kept in check, it's an ugly fuckin' bitch of a thing. But a scene like this? I saw red.

Closed the distance.

Grabbed the nearest shithead, caught a fistful of the back of his shirt, yanked him backward, and smashed his fuckin' face in, hammer fist. Kneed his gut so hard he started retching. Kicked his balls in, and that fucker would never procreate again.

By that time the other five or six were on me.

Lousy cockroaches didn't stand a goddamn chance.

I was stomping faces outside of biker bars by the time I was eight years old, and had black belts in four disciplines by thirteen, plus an education in brawling from the hardest motherfuckers in four states, the kind of men you whispered about and hoped like hell they didn't look at you.

These little pissant mealworm shits?

They wouldn't even bloody my knuckles.

Block, arm-bar, knee, swing him into the other fella, kick a knee so it bent the wrong way, knife-hand to a throat and watch him gag on his own wind-pipe; break a forearm until I saw bits of ulna sticking through rends in the flesh. One of 'em managed a glancing blow to my teeth, but it hurt him more than me, and I returned the favor with an open palm to the side of the face, knocking some teeth down his fuckhead throat.

"I think you finished 'em off there, buddy," I heard a voice say. "You can stand down."

Five huge-ass security guys all in tactical black, each one with a bearing that said ex-military, and each with ice-cold eyes.

The speaker was the biggest, and meanest look-ing—with eyes so venomous and frigid they gave even my dead-ass soul a shiver. "We saw what was going on, but you beat us to the save."

I blinked. Looked around—I'd left six bloody messes. "These shitstains need doctors," I snarled.

The guy glanced past me at the girl huddled on

the ground, arms around her waist, fighting the urge to be sick while sobbing. "We got them, you get her."

I nodded, and turned away. Adrenaline was pulsing through me so hard my hands were shaking.

She was gagging, and sobbing. I crouched off to one side, close but out of spew range, and out of scare-her-worse range.

I kept my voice low, calm, like I'd talk to one of River Dog's skittish old half-wild Appaloosas. "Hey, now, darlin'. You're alright. Safe now, okay? Ain't nobody gonna touch you."

She stared, tear-stained eyes the same wild blue of the Mediterranean fixing blearily on me—scared stupid, seeing too many of me, trying to figure out what was going on. "They—they—"

"They ain't gonna bother you no more." I glanced over my shoulder, watched the security guys dragging the fuckers two at a time toward the woods. "Or anyone else, I suspect."

She saw that, frowned. "Where're they takin'em?" Slurred to hell, but a faint Boston accent.

"There's a med tent on the other side of the woods."

She eyed me. "You—" A blink, focused on not upchucking. "You did that."

"You're safe."

She shook her head. "Not safe."

"I got you. Won't let nothin' happen."

She closed her eyes, frowning. "God, I'm—I'm so…"

"Hammered."

A nod. "Yeah," she whispered.

"Not your usual scene?" I guessed.

She shook her head, which was a mistake. A long black braid snaked in an S-wave at her back—a complicated braid, and a whole hell of a lot of thick black hair. Those sea-blue eyes met mine again. Tear-stained, but drying. Firming up.

"Don't know where the hell I am." She tried to move, to stand up, but tipped over.

I caught her, and she was soft and light in my arms. "Why don't you just relax, all right, darlin'?"

Her eyes fluttered, unfocused, then she refocused on me, irritated through the inebriation. "Don't…don't call me darling."

I just laughed. "Whatever's clever, babe." I stood up with her long bare legs draped over one arm, and that thick black herringbone braid slung over her shoulder as she lolled her head against the crook of my elbow.

"Where'reyoutakingme?" she mumbled, slurring so bad it was nearly incomprehensible.

"Backstage."

She blinked her eyes open. "Lexie." Tried to sit up. "Lexie!"

I held her. "Whoa, now, darlin', just relax. I got you. Let me get you somewhere you can sit and sober up, okay? You're safe. I've got you. Nothin' gonna happen to you when I'm around."

"Sister," she whispered. Head lolled against my chest. "Lexie. Sister. Need Lexie."

She sniffed. Blinked. Realized her cheek was against skin; all I had on was my leather cut—my old, worn, AzTex MC vest adorned with the patch and other assorted pins and patches—unbuttoned over my bare chest, as it was a hot day and it was the way I felt most comfortable.

"Big chest," she murmured. "You're hard and soft at th'same time. It's weird." She blinked up at me, and fuck, those eyes could smolder and burn like fire and ice, blue and blue and blue and searing, even drunk off her ass. "Hi."

I laughed. "Hi there, hot stuff. What's your name?"

Her head wobbled, lolled. "Charlie." She bumped into my chest again, and she sniffed. "Soft skin. Feels nice. Smells nice. You smell clean. Are you clean?" Her hand wafted up, patted my chest. "You feel clean." Blinked, peered cross-eyed, smoothing her hand over my pec. Which, I admit, is not small, or soft. "And muscly."

I couldn't help a belly laugh. "You know how

to flatter a fella, don't you Charlie?" I was weaving through the bustle of offstage, between sound techs and stage crew and electricians and guitar techs and drum techs and security and singers and guitarists and drummer and groupies. "Got a last name, Charlie-darlin'?"

"Goode."

"Good?" I repeated.

"Goode. G-O-O-D...E. Good with an E. Like goodie, but don't say goodie. Lexie would kick your ass, if she was seven again."

"Charlie Goode."

She smiled, and managed to make a drunk smile look sexy as hell. "Yep. That's me, Charlie Goode, who hasn't, I'm not...I've never been as this drunk before."

"That wasn't even proper English, sweetheart."

"Derms of entearment...Terms of Denddearment...shit. TERMS of ENDEARMENT are non persona grata."

"I think you mean persona non grata."

"Shuh-up. Can *you* use Latin phrases this drunk? NO. You're too sexy to know Latin." She peered at me. "At least, you look sexy. I could have wicked bad beer goggles on, though. Too drunk to know for sure." She sounded enticingly Boston, just then.

"Say 'park the car' for me."

She blinked, made a face of extreme annoy-
ance. "Two years in Boston and this is what I get."
She huffed, rolled her eyes. "Paaaahk the caaaah,"
she drawled in a devastatingly cute Boston accent.
"There. Happy?"

"For now, yeah."

She rested her head against my chest. "Comfy.
Sleepy time?"

I laughed. God this chick was too fuckin' adorable. Trusting, and adorable, and sexy, and way too
innocent. "Not quite."

She peered at me. "I know your name, but you
don't know mine." A blink. "Wait, other way. *I* don't
know *your* name, but *you* know *mine*."

"Are you askin' my name, babe?" She gave me a
sloppy nod, and I rumbled another laugh. "Crow. My
name is Crow."

A blink, the pause I always get. "Crow?"

"Yes. Crow."

"Wow. That's super cool. Is that your whole
name?"

I keep my face blank. "Yeah."

"Crow. That's it."

"Yup."

Despite her colossal drunkitude, she seemed to
sense that this was not a line of conversation that was
going to play. "Okay. Crow. It fits you. You look like a

crow. I mean, you don't look like a bird. You look like a yummy man. Who somehow just seems like someone who would be named Crow."

"Yummy, huh?" I carried her up a rickety set of stairs to the stage, around into the back of one of the trailers, which served as side-stage wings. Settled her in a ratty old overstuffed suede couch they'd set to one side. "Now, just sit there, okay? I'm going to get you some water. Do *not* fuckin' move."

Her head wobbled unsteadily. "Yummy. Yuppers. You are yummy. I didn't know men could be yummy till I saw you, and I just know I'm going to regret this whole conversation once I'm sober. Assuming I survive the hangover I'm sure I'm in for." She patted the couch on either her side of the most mouth-watering pair of bell-curve hips I'd ever seen. "Not moving. Nope, nope, nope. I couldn't move, if I wanted to. Legs are all bye-bye. Bye-bye legs. No more walking for you." She patted her legs, encased in black yoga pants which highlighted every delicious curve. "I liked my legs. They were nice. Kinda fat, because I've put on weight since my asshole boyfriend-fiancé-dickhead decided to let me catch him cheating on me with my overweight middle-aged boss. But until then, I had pretty nice legs. Now they're just…" She squeezed her thigh. "Blub. Blub." Jiggled it. "Blub-blub-blub."

I grabbed her hand, pinioning her wrist. "Your legs are fuckin' perfect, Charlie Goode."

She frowned up at me. "Perfect is a strong word. Nothing is perfect."

I shrugged. "Maybe not, but from where I'm lookin', those sexy-ass legs of yours are about as perfect as legs can get."

She couldn't quite stop a smile. "Well. It's awful nice of you to make a drunk girl feel better. They're kinda jiggly though." She shook her thigh again. "See?"

I restrained myself, with great effort, from palming her thighs and showing her how those legs were meant to be touched. Instead, I pinned both of her wrists in one hand. "You always this self-deprecating when you're drunk?"

She sighed. "Never been this drunk before, so I don't know." She peered up at me. "Wait. You said sexy-ass legs."

I laughed. "Yes, I did."

"Sexy ass legs, like sexy ass and legs, or sexy-ass legs, wherein sexy-ass is one word hyphenated?"

I snorted. "Does it matter?"

"Yes. It does. I have to know what you meant. So I can remember this moment."

"What moment?"

"The moment in which I finally find a smidgen of validation that I am, in fact, still an attractive woman.

See, Twinkle Mouse, my ex, really fucked me up. Did a number on my self-esteem." She rubbed her beautiful face with both hands, frustrated. "God, you must really find this maudlin poor-me bullshit super sexy, huh? Really an attractive look for me, I bet."

I squeezed her hand. "Well, with any luck, you won't remember any of this tomorrow."

"Yeah, but you will."

"Everybody gets drunk and stupid sometimes, Charlie. No worries." I eyed the bustle going on in the side-stage area. "I promise you, I'll find you every bit as goddamn breathtaking when you're sober as I do now. But, I have to work. You stay here, and I'll check on you."

She nodded, and slumped backward, resting her head on the back of the couch. I fetched a couple bottles of water from a nearby mini-fridge, cracked one and put it in her hand.

"Drink this, yeah?"

"Okay." She sipped at it. "Hydrology is important."

"Hydrology?"

"Being watered."

I snickered. "You mean hydration?"

"Shut up. Just let me be wrong." She sipped again. "Go away. You have to do whatever kind of work a tall dark and handsome man named Crow does at a place like this."

"I'm the guitar tech for Myles North."

She perked up. "Ooooh. My little sister has a major crush on him. If she knew I might possibly meet him through you, she'd be super jealous."

"I'm sure I could set something up."

"Might not be a good idea. My sister eats men for breakfast and has moved on by lunch. She'd just chew him up and spit him out." She cackled. "Although I have a feeling she swallows."

I guffawed. "Wow, that was some serious shade, Charlie."

"She knows I love her. Plus, it's true." She looks around. "I need Lexie. She'll get into trouble without me."

Or you will, without her, I thought, but I didn't say a word.

"Her name is Lexie?"

She nodded. "Lexie Goode. She looks like me, but a slutty gypsy version. Shorter, bigger butt and boobs. Big ol' boobies. You'll like 'em. Just go out there and look for the slutty gypsy."

"I think gypsy is a derogatory term, you know."

"Well, that's the most accurate word for her look. It works for her, but that's just what I'd call it. You can't say slutty to her, though, or she'll skin you alive and eat your balls."

"Real ballbreaker, is she?"

"Yep. The breaker of many, many balls. Sweet, and nice, and funny, and smart, and so freaking beautiful it's annoying, but she's a major ballbreaker. So just mind your words."

She slumped back again; water precariously balanced on her knee, only loosely gripped in one hand.

"Do you have a phone?" I asked.

She nodded. Fumbling, she brought her crossbody bag around, laboriously unzipped it, clumsily hunted for a phone. Found it, took four attempts to unlock it with her face. Handed it to me.

"Too hard. I'm seeing, like two and half of everything. You call."

I hissed. I really had to get to work. But, I'd assumed responsibility for this chick, so…

I brought up her contacts, typed in Lexie, dialed. It rang until it went to voicemail, so I hung up and called back, again and again.

Finally, on the third try, it clicked, and I heard the concert from the crowd, and faint voice yelling. "What? Where the fuck did you go? I turned around and you were gone, you dumbass!"

"My name is Crow," I said. "Your sister got into some trouble, so I have her backstage. Meet me stage right—your right—between the two big semitrailers. I'll be in black jeans and a leather vest."

"Is she okay?"

"Yes, she's none the worse for wear, just very, very, very drunk."

"Shit. Okay, thank you. See you in a second."

"Yep."

"Wait, how will you know me?"

I laughed. "Your sister gave me a very detailed description."

"I bet."

"She used words she said you wouldn't appreciate hearing."

"Slutty gypsy?"

"Yup."

She laughed, not offended. "Well, it's accurate enough, even if gypsy is a derogatory and politically incorrect term."

And with that, she hung up, no goodbye. Okay, then.

I found a nearby stagehand from our road crew. "Hey, keep an eye on her," I said, pointing at Charlie. "Don't let her leave."

The guy, young, bearded, stocky, just nodded. "Don't think she can, but okay." He glanced at his watch. "You know he goes on in forty-five?"

"Yeah, I fuckin' know. He'll be ready."

Another nod, and then I jogged for the barricade. As I approached, I saw a girl who could only be Charlie's sister.

Shorter than Charlie by an inch or two, with curves for days. Black hair cut pixie short, buzzed on the sides to just above her ears, the longer top portion was twisted into a series of tiny knots on the top of her head in a wide mohawk-like row of little mini buns. Ears pierced from top of the shell all the way down to the lobes in plethora of gold and silver rings, studs at the top of the shell, dream catchers dangling from her lobes. I was still a ways away, but it looked like her eyes were dark as opposed to Charlie's blues, with dramatic smoky eye makeup. And yeah, slutty gypsy was the best description for her style: she was wearing a skirt made of patches and swatches of brightly colored fabric and squares of leather and corduroy, with tassels and feathers and strips of cloth dangling and fluttering—the hem swirled around her heels, but it was slit on one side all the way up her mid-thigh, so when she shifted, her leg up to her hip was visible, offering a tantalizing almost-glimpse of everything under the skirt, making you wonder what, if anything, she was wearing under it. Sandals wove in thick straps up around her calves to her knee. Her top was a scrap of gauzy red lace in the vague approximation of a half-shirt, leaving her belly bare, exposing a belly button ring and making it daringly, glaringly obvious that she wore not a scrap of anything under the shirt; and that, as Charlie had said, she had some seriously impressive melons, which were all but on display. Obscured just enough to tantalize, but only just barely.

I took one long look, and then put my libido in firm check—to be polite, for one thing, but also because as fine as this girl was, my mind was already captured by the long curvy legs and bangin' hips and ass of the drunk chick on the couch.

I kept my eyes on hers as I shook her hand. "Crow. You must be Lexie."

"Yes. Nice to meet you, Mr. Crow."

"No mister. Just Crow. Yes, it's my real name." I gestured for her to follow. "Sister is this way."

"What happened?"

"She was being harassed by some assholes. I took care of the assholes and brought her here."

Lexie kept pace with my longer strides, that crazy ass fuckin' skirt of hers fluttering behind her, one thick, tanned, smooth thigh peeking out every step. "You're leaving some shit out, I feel."

"Yeah. It was a bad scene. She was fightin' for all she was worth and not backin' down, but those fuckers were bad news."

"Did they…do anything…to her?"

"Nope. Pushed her around a bit, grabbing her, pinching, shit like that. Playing with her like a cat with a mouse. Would've been ugly, but I saw it, and I sorted the fuckers out."

"Not gently, I hope."

I gave her a glimpse at the violent wolf lurking inside me—I sensed this girl was far less innocent than her older sister in the dark and unfriendly ways of the world. "No. I was not gentle."

She paused, stared up into my eyes, assessing. As Charlie had said—there was a wild glimmering intelligence in those dark brown eyes. This girl was more than half-wild; a fey spirit, Mammy would have called her.

"Good," she said, nodding once, firmly. "I hope they piss blood for a week."

"Had to be dragged to the med tent," I said. "Pissing blood will be the least of their concerns."

She nodded again. "You have my approval, Crow. Thank you for taking care of my sister. She's going through a hard time. We both are, but she's not usually like this. Doesn't cut loose much. I took my eyes off of her for ten seconds and she was gone."

"No worries. It happens." I led her to the trailer, where we found Charlie passed out, the bottle of water about to fall out of her hand. "Here she is."

Lexie settled on the couch beside her sister, took the water from her, set it aside, and let Charlie slide sideways to lay in Lexie's lap. "Got her. Thanks."

I nodded. "Okay, you guys just stay there, yeah? There ain't really backstage passes at this disaster of a festival, but I'll make sure my guys know you're cool to be here. Just don't go wandering off."

She gave a two-fingered salute. "I will stay my ass right here, Mr. Crow."

I knew she was just goading me with the mister, so I ignored it. Charlie was slumped sideways, both hands pillowed under her cheek on Lexie's bare thigh. That long, thick herringbone braid of glossy black hair slipped sideways and dangled off the edge of the couch, until Lexie gathered it up, tossed it behind Charlie's back. Brushed at her cheek.

I had shit to do, so why was I rooted to the damn spot, staring at a passed-out angel? It could have been the way her breasts were piled up under her arm and about to fall out of the front of her plain black V-neck. Or the tender skin of her throat, pulsing with her heartbeat. Or the curve of her thigh rounding to hip and buttock. The soft breath, or the small hands curled under her cheekbone.

Innocent.

Made my heart skip, lurch, and then thunder.

Idiot.

I yanked myself around, forcefully, stomping off to work—I had to bust ass like a motherfucker to get all Myles's guitars unpacked, set up, plugged in, tested, and tuned, leaving Betty-Lou for Myles to take care of. I had cut it close, that was for fuckin' sure—I was still testing the Fender Strat, his latest acquisition, a pretty little classic black-and-tan number with beautiful sound when the stage manager notified us that it was two minutes to go time.

Myles was side stage, jumping up and down on his toes, slapping his hands against his thighs, shaking his head, humming scales and then singing them, high to low to high, warming up his voice. Shaking his hands. Rolling his shoulders.

He saw me, let out a short, sharp breath. "There you are, you lazy bitch."

I just slapped his back. "Kill 'em, buddy."

"Oh, I'll kill 'em." He smirked. "Just like you about killed those poor bastards."

"They were—"

He cut me off. "I heard." He craned backward, peering into the trailer. "Passed out, huh?"

"Yeah."

He turned to step a few steps closer, leaning forward, straining to see into the trailer. "*DAY-um*, though, who's the fine-as-wine rock star honey over there with your damsel in distress?"

"Her sister. Lexie." I debated telling him what Charlie had told me, but decided against it; let it play out naturally.

"Well. Do *not* let them go before I have a chance to say hi to that gorgeous piece'a sinfulness."

I laughed. "You fuckin' dog."

"I just wanna say hi. She looks like a firecracker."

I chuckled. "I only met her briefly, but I'd say that's about right. I don't know her from Adam, but from what I can tell, I'd step careful around that one."

He shook out his hands, ran wordless notes up to the top of his range and down to the bottom. Grinned at me again. "A challenge. I like it."

I shoved him toward the stage. "Get out there and break legs, Myles. Focus on the music for now, yeah?"

"Break a leg is theater, you idiot."

I laughed. "No, I know. I meant your own."

He flipped me off as he jogged backward on stage, and then the moment he hit the open stage, he spun around, lifting his hands over his head. The crowd went wild, deafening. Jupiter was thudding a steady rhythm on the kicker, Brand letting his fingers stroll around the bass frets, running low rolling licks to weave around Jupiter's kick drum. Zan let his Les Paul fade up into shrieking feedback as I brought Myles his guitar for the opening trio of numbers. Handed it to him, cuffing him affectionately on the back of the head as he shrugged the strap on, wiggled his shoulders, plucked the pick from the strings, winked at me, and then strode to the front edge of the stage, and his mic.

"Weeeeeeeeell howdy, Illinois," he shouted, drawling his accent into a thick South Texas twang. "Are you beautiful drunk motherfuckers having a good time out here in the middle of nowhere?"

Tens of thousands of gathered country music fans screamed and howled, the already deafening roar cranking up to a bone-rattling din.

"I *think* I heard you," Myles said, then paused to rifle off a quick, light, flicking riff. "But I got a feelin' ya'll can do better. I *SAID*—are you beautiful drunk-ass country music lovin' motherfuckers *HAVING A GOOD FUCKIN' TIME?*" This last phrase he shouted into the mic.

The noise was nearly unbearable, now, but Myles goaded them again. Another riff, this one longer, more complex.

*"I CAN'T FUCKIN' **HEAR** YOU!"*

Louder, and now the kick drum went faster as they transitioned seamlessly into the opening notes of the first song, a snare tap-tap-tapping, Zan laying a smooth chug, Brand thumping a steady chord, and Myles playfully toying with riffs, turning them gradually, masterfully, into the lead melody.

"Okay, I believe you, now," he said, his voice quieter, lower. "This is a fun little song, you may have heard it before. It's called 'I Can't Lie'."

The din of the crowd, which had been dying down, went nuts again.

And then he was off, rattling away the machine-gun-quick, not-quite rapped lyrics of the verse, and then Zan and Brand joined him at the mic to harmonize on the bridge, and then Zan and Myles played dueling riffs through the chorus, just Myles singing, using that low smooth baritone like he was promising every woman in the crowd the best night of her life.

Damn, the man was on fire. The band was always hot, but they drew off of Myles, and he was flying high tonight, ramped up and amped up, hitting every note, turning every solo into straight fire.

About halfway through the set, I glanced offstage as I tweaked the tuning of the next guitar—Lexie was clearly enraptured, eyes fixed on Myles, whom she could see in perfect profile.

Yeah, she had it bad. And judging by the way Myles looked right at her between songs, he was feelin' it too.

That oughta be interesting. Charlie had said Lexie chewed up most men for breakfast, but my little secret was that Myles was just about the same. I knew he set them straight on the way things were before anything happened, so they knew it was just fun for the night, but still he had a way of leaving half-broke hearts wherever he went, each new nightly conquest wishing she could be the one to tame the wild thing that was Myles North's bronco soul.

I wondered, though, if just maybe Lexie Goode could be the one to pull off that impossible feat. She'd struck me as every bit as wild, every bit as mare strong and mule stubborn and peacock proud.

What do you get when two wildfires met?

Crazy hell, that's what.

I rubbed my jaw, turned my attention back to the guitar. Brought it to Myles at the correct moment, and returned side stage to my little area.

And noticed Charlie was awake, somehow, sitting up.

Staring at me.

Toying with her braid, looking half-sober.

Thoughtful.

Damn, damn, damn.

I ripped my gaze away from those deep baby blues before I lost my soul in them.

Shit, this was bad.

The look in her eyes told me she remembered every word that had passed between us. God, why did she have to rally? Why couldn't she just stay passed out and forget I'd told her she was perfect?

But it hadn't been a lie, or even an exaggeration. Not at all. The truth was she was purely breathtaking, and that was the honest to god response my soul gave me when her blue eyes locked on mine, just for a split second.

Oh god, I'm so fucked.

I looked away first…

Because I had a job to do, which required my full attention.

Not because I was scared of what I saw in her half-drunk eyes.

Nope. Wasn't that. Not at all.

FIVE

Charlie

I MORE THAN HALF WISHED I'D BEEN ABLE TO STAY PASSED out. At least that way, I'd have been able to forget a little longer how I'd acted.

What had happened.

Those nasty men, their nasty hands.

Pinching, grabbing.

The memory of the harassment, however, as gross and nauseating as it was, was eclipsed by the arrival of Crow.

I will never, ever, for as long as I live, forget that moment.

One of my harassers was yanked backward as if by shepherd's crook in a Merry Melodies cartoon.

Yank. A massive, scared fist hammered down, and then hell broke loose. Bloody, wrecking hell disguised as a sinfully sexy man. If he was even a mere man. If he told me he was a shapeshifter from a Sherrilyn Kenyon novel, I would have believed him.

Six feet tall, broad shouldered, narrow hips and a wedge waist. Hard, heavy slabs of muscle sheathed in dark weather-leathered Native American skin—his heritage was written all over him. His short messy hair as black as a wing of his namesake, the hawkish angle of his nose, his cheekbones, his eyes. His bearing, his demeanor. Even his smooth low quiet powerful voice. He wore faded, tattered, tight black jeans over tall, thick black leather boots with silver buckles on the sides. A leather vest was unbuttoned and open over bare skin—and god, his body.

Now, my whole life I've read romance books. Since I was a preteen girl awash with hormones and budding body parts, I have devoured romance novels of all kinds. You read about the heroine seeing the hero for the first time and her mouth watering. Maybe even a phrase like "her delicate center coiling with low, insistent heat."

I always thought that language was melodramatic bullshit to make the story more interesting.

Nope.

It's real.

My mouth? Watering.

The delicate center at the apex of my thighs? Oh yeah, definitely coiling with low, insistent heat.

One look at him, and my legs pressed together. Heat gathered, throbbing dull and hot, pulsating—*NEEDneedNEEDneedNEED*.

God, I was still wasted, but at least there was only one of everything—if I focused and moved slowly.

Lexie, beside me, was still partially holding me up, but she had eyes only for the spectacle on stage.

"Lex."

"Mmm." A verbal response, but her eyes were on the singer on stage, tall and dark haired and lean, angled up to a mic like he was making out with it, belting a song I'd heard on The Highway a hundred times.

This must be Myles—Lexie's crush, and my savior's boss.

"*Lex.*"

"Hmm."

I palmed her face, turned her attention onto me. "Alexandra."

She blinked. "What?"

"I'm sorry."

She was fully with me now. Hugged me. "No apologies."

"I'm the older sister. I should be the responsible one."

She shook her head. "No. I told you, we're cutting loose. No responsibility. No older or younger, no roles. Just you and me, and whatever happens." She squeezed me hard. "Just next time, stay close."

"The crowd moved all at once, and I got swept away. Pushed and bounced around like a frigging pinball, and spat out the far side." I sighed, bitterly. "And then these guys started talking to me, surrounding me, and to stay away from them I backed up and ended up at the barricade. And they were...they were playing with me."

"I'm so sorry that happened, Char-Char."

"I was fighting them. But they were just laughing, even when I hit them. I was so scared, Lex."

She squeezed my hands in hers. "Baby, you're okay.

"I know."

I glanced over and saw him, my savior.

Off in the wings, a guitar strap looped loosely over one shoulder, a small tuner clipped to the headstock of a weathered classical acoustic guitar. His head was tilted to one side, eyes shut, ear close to the strings, plucking, twisting a tuning peg a hair, plucking again, glancing at the tuner to verify.

Done, he stood and waited, one hand on the neck.

God, his shoulders were so wide. Hard. Round, strong. His back was like a wall. Arms rippling with lean, toned muscle. His hair was messy, a pair of mirrored aviators slid back on his skull, long-since forgotten. Both arms featured full-sleeve tattoos, but it was too dark and he was too far away to see the details. I vaguely remembered my head flopping against the warm skin of his bare chest as he carried me—effortlessly, easily—and seeing on his right bicep part of a tattoo, a row of crosses, each one with initials. It was a vague, hazy memory, but somehow I could see those crosses as clear as day, in my mind.

The song ended, the stage lights dropped to black, and Crow strode onstage, traded the singer guitars, giving him the acoustic and taking the electric. Back off stage, he plucked a cloth from his back pocket and wiped the strings carefully and thoroughly, bringing it back into perfect tune and replacing it on the rack of guitars, stuffing the cloth into his back pocket again.

"He really hurt those guys, Lex."

She was quicker to give me her attention this time. "They deserved it."

"I mean, yeah—they'd have raped me for sure, if he hadn't stepped in. But he...he really, really hurt them. There were six of them, and he just..." I shook my head, visions of fists and feet and knees and elbows moving with surgical brutality. "He was an angry, avenging god, and they were pathetic little children caught up in his fury."

Lex snorted. "Wow. That's...a very specific image, hon."

"You don't know, Lex. You didn't see what he did to them." I shuddered. "He could have killed them. They're definitely going to have permanent disabilities."

"They were going to *rape* you, Charlotte." Her voice was hard. "Don't give those pieces of shit another thought."

"It was just so easy for him. He wasn't even breathing hard when he was done. I don't think they got a single hit in."

"Good for you. Bad for them, but you reap what you sow, right?"

I nodded. "Yeah, I guess."

She tilted her head. "What, Charlie? You're thinking something you don't want to be thinking."

How could she tell? My brain was swirling, whirling. Tumultuous and chaotic.

I ground my teeth, but the thought wouldn't dissipate or recede back inside, no matter how hard I tried to shove it down. "It's dumb."

She smirked. "I bet I know."

"You couldn't possibly."

"You think it was *hot*. You being in trouble, and

him saving you." She grinned wide and bright. "You think you should be more shook up by what happened, but all you can think about is *him*."

"Shut *up!*" I snapped. "You don't know that."

She just laughed. "Oh, I do now, girlfriend. You are turned on like a motherfucker."

"I am not."

She slid closer. "Own it, Char-Char. Nothing seriously bad happened to you. It was gross and scary, but he stopped it before it got bad. And yeah, he's fuckin' hot as hell, in a big bad wolf kind of way."

I let my head sink back against the couch cushion. Groaned. "It's so dumb." Another groan. "*I'm* so dumb. I was such a drunken idiot, Lex. The things I said, god, I won't be able to look him in the eye."

Lexie cackled. "Newsflash, darling, you're still drunk. How you're even awake right now, I'm not sure."

"Me either. I shouldn't be." I tested my legs, pushing against the floor, and got nearly to what my yoga teacher would call a sloppy version of chair pose. Fell back, dizzy from the effort. "Nope, I will not be upright any time soon." I held my head in my hands as the world spun like a top. "Still very, very drunk."

"Yeah, you're not sobering up that fast, baby girl. It just doesn't work that way."

I'd finished the water, both bottles Crow had

left—and even his name was sexy. It fit him: he was dark and sharp and intelligent and cunning and predatory and sleek.

"I wonder where he got the water," I said. "I want to be more sober faster." That didn't sound right, but I couldn't bring myself to care.

I had my eyes closed, felt something cold and wet pressed against my cheek. "Here." A low, powerful voice, smooth and dark.

I opened my eyes, and Crow was there, kneeling in front of me, his chest against my knees. Pressing a bottle of water to my cheek. His eyes were pools of inky darkness, swallowing me. I could just see his throat in the shadows, and could almost make out his pulse. Was it beating as hard as mine?

"Thanks," I said.

"How the hell're you awake right now? Thought for sure you were done for the day."

I shrugged. "I don't know. I don't sleep easily, even drunk, it seems."

"Don't fight it," he murmured. "Just let it all spin around you. You're safe."

"Don't like being out of control."

Lexie was watching the exchange, biting back a smirk, but remaining silent.

He nodded. "I know what you mean. Feel the same way." He glanced at the stage, listening. "Song's almost over, gotta go. Guitar change. Just wanted to check on you."

I just nodded, as gently and shallowly as I could manage, to keep the world from spinning off its axis. "Okay," I whispered, dumbly.

He went, and I watched him go. The man had a beautiful ass. The jeans wrapped around it, seemed to cradle the taut hard globes.

"Man's got a great ass," Lexie muttered.

I laughed, feeling myself blush. "Yeah. I noticed."

"Oh, I bet you did." She elbowed my ribs. "He's into you."

"He is not."

She ruffled my head, playfully condescending. "You'll understand when you're older, but when a man likes a woman, he looks at her a certain way."

"Oh shut up. You couldn't see how he was looking at me in this darkness."

"I could fucking *feel it*, Charlie. I know what a man looks like when he's digging on someone, okay? And that man *wants* you."

"He barely met me. I was stupid drunk—I'm *still* stupid drunk. He can't want me."

Lexie just laughed. "I think he saw enough to know what he likes."

I glanced down at my chest. "What, am I popping out of my shirt or something?"

She cackled. "No, dummy. It's just *you*."

"Drunk, embarrassing me?"

She side-hugged me. "Believe it or not, you don't hold your liquor well." She said this with her voice dripping sarcasm. "It's obvious you're not a hard drinker, and it's cute."

"Cute." I growled, an unladylike sound Mom would not approve of. "Cute is the kiss of death."

"No, cute can be super sexy. If you're cute *and* hot in a certain way, you end up with a combination men will go dumb-dumb for."

"And you seem to think I have that combination of cute and hot?"

"I mean, I'm into men, not women, and I'm your sister, but I think so, yeah."

"Well, bully for him. But as soon as I can move, we're leaving."

Lexie just laughed like I'd said something hysterical. "Oh Charlie, you silly goose. I am way, *way* too buzzed to drive anywhere, number one. Number two, we're in the middle of nowhere, and it's midnight, and I guarantee there's no hotels with vacancies within fifty miles of this festival. Number three, I'm sitting backstage mere *feet* from Myles fucking *North*. If you think I'm missing out on my chance to meet him, you're on drugs, babe."

"Meet? Is that all you want to do with him?"

"Hell no! I'd have the man's babies." She paused, and I felt her mood darken, go heavy. Then, as if the moment had never happened, she laughed, merrily. "I would let that man fuck me doggystyle on the stage, if he asked me to. Right there in front of everyone."

I sighed. "You would not."

She sighed, staring at him. "No, I wouldn't. The things I want to do to him are *wayyy* too X-rated." She laughed again. "Backstage is private enough. For starters, at least."

"Lex. Come on."

She shook her head, glancing at me, serious and brooding. "This is where you just have to let me be me, Charlie. If he comes on to me, I'm going with it. Judge me for it if you must, but I would absolutely let him have his wicked way with me backstage. It's Myles North. It'd be worth it."

I rolled a shoulder. "You do you, honey. That's not my way, but if it's yours, go for it. Just don't... well, never mind. You can take care of yourself."

She was silent a moment. Then spoke, her attention on the stage, but her words to me. "If your guy Mr. Crow was to hit on you, you're telling me you wouldn't let it play out?"

"I...I don't know. Yes, I'm attracted to him. But I'm confused by it."

"Confused? What is there to be confused about?"

"He scares me."

"And?"

"And being scared horny is just weird."

"He makes your pussy wet, doesn't he?"

I sputtered, "ALEXANDRA ROCHELLE GOODE!"

"He does, doesn't he?" She leaned closer. "He makes you want to do things you didn't know were a thing."

"Stop."

"Like climb up on that big hard body and make him forget his own fucking name."

"*ALEXANDRA*," I hissed. "Stop!"

I wriggled. Because the image of climbing on top of a man like Crow did indeed make certain portions of my anatomy, which I had thought were essentially atrophied at this point, get all gooey and shivery.

Lex was watching me intently, biting a thumbnail and grinning in the dark. "Ohhh, baby, you are *gone*."

"Shut up."

"Stop fighting it, Charlie. Just go with it. This is as safe an opportunity to go a little wild and get a little dirty without repercussions as you're gonna get. Stop overthinking it and just go with the flow." She tickled my ribs. "And if the flow lands you riding that man's cock, then all the better. You'd be a hell of a lot less uptight if you got boinked."

"Lexie, there's so much wrong with that statement I don't even know where to start."

"Let me guess, in order, you take issue with the words 'cock' and 'boink'?"

"Yes."

She leaned close, whispering. "I bet he has a huge, veiny cock. Thick, and throbbing and hot and hard as a steel fucking spike. Eight inches and thick as my wrist, or I don't know men."

I closed my eyes, refusing to let her goad me into revealing my runaway imagination.

"I bet that stubble of his would be scratchy and soft against your thighs as he ate you out…"

"Shut the hell up, Alexandra!" I lurched upright, away from her. "What the hell is *wrong* with you?"

My legs gave out as the world span crazily, and a big hard body pressed against me. A strong arm wrapped around my waist, holding me tight. "Got ya. Again." That voice, like a lion's feral snarl put into a human throat.

I put my feet under me, but he didn't let go. "Hi."

He stared down at me. "Gotta stop meeting like this, sweetness."

I swallowed. Heat—so much heat. Radiating from him, and billowing inside me.

What was happening to my body? A chemical reaction to too much alcohol, I bet. That's all.

He licked his lips, his eyes raking over my face. "Ever see a concert crowd from backstage?"

I shook my head. "N-no." Now, why did I stutter? I must be sick. The alcohol has pickled my brain and turned me into a stuttering moron.

Woman up, idiot girl.

Be strong.

He kept his arm around my waist, and I honestly don't think I could have walked at all, much less in a straight line. His hand was on my hip, or just above it, actually. Wildly intimate, but not *exactly* inappropriate. He walked me toward where the guitars were, stacked in a line, waiting. On stage, Myles, in profile, had his guitar slung around behind his back and was on his knees at the edge of the stage, reaching out to touch hands of the people below. Singing, grinning. Shaking a hand, kissing another, tapping fists, from one side of the stage to the other. Back and forth, never missing a beat, a word.

I blinked against the brilliance and heat of the stage lights along the top, and then squinted through them and saw the crowd. It was one thing to be lost in a sea of humanity like that, but seeing it like this? Wow. Just...so many people. Too many to make out an individual face, except for the first few rows. How many? Ten thousand? Twenty? Thirty? Smaller than Coachella, which I went to with Cassie once, a couple

years ago, at the end of college before I started at
Denoyer and Whitcomb. But still massive, especially
for what seemed to be a pretty lax and last-minute,
barebones sort of thing. The focus was on the music,
and providing enough infrastructure for the amount
of people they hoped to bring in. No frills. It was…
dizzying.

"How does he not get nervous?" I asked.

He laughed. "Hell if I know. He's been perform-
ing on stage since he was a kid, though. His gramps
was a honky-tonk legend in South Texas, and so was
his dad, and my boy Myles there has been playing
guitar and singing on stage since he was old enough
to do either. Just in his blood, I guess." He brought
his hand from my hip to my shoulder—I was relieved
and disappointed at the same time. "He gets nervous,
though, but he just channels it into excitement. I just
feel like I'm gonna puke whenever I go out there."

"Not a performer, huh?"

He shook his head. "Nah. Not my thing." Onstage,
Myles finished the chorus, and moved to the middle
of the stage, brought his guitar around, and launched
into a dazzling solo. "Look at the fucker showing off."

"He's amazing. I see why Lexie loves his music."

"He's talented all right. What most people don't
realize is that he practices hours a day, every day. He's
got a lot of innate talent, a lot of exposure to music of

all kinds, growing up on tour and onstage the way he did, but his skill with a guitar is just that—a skill. He's not a dazzling virtuoso. Couldn't play for shit as a kid, just had that voice. But he learned, and he practiced, and he keeps practicing. That's why he's so good."

"Impressive." I twisted to look up at him.

Didn't know what to say, I just…it seemed surreal that I was here, side stage, watching Myles North, with a man's arm around me. Sure, it was just because I couldn't stay upright on my own, but still.

He glanced down at me, smirked wryly. "What?"

I looked away. "Nothing."

He stared down. Nodded, after a moment. "Yep."

I frowned, tilted my head. "Yeah, what?"

"Yeah, I still find you goddamn breathtaking."

Gulp.

Beat, stupid heart. Beat, damn you. There it was, gone nuts—*THUMPTHUMPTHUMPTHUMP*—like the kick drum on stage.

I swallowed, barely. "Oh."

He reached, tugged a handful of my braid, but ever so gently. "Just in case you'd forgotten."

"Nope."

Weird. A million thoughts were banging around in my brain, but precisely zero of them were exiting my mouth. I just couldn't seem to manage words. Or intelligent thoughts.

And really, those million thoughts in my head were mainly—meaning entirely—focused on the odd rhythm of my heart when I was around Crow, and the way my thighs kept wanting to press together to relieve myself of the aching heat between them. And his eyes. And the way his hand had felt searing through my clothing to my skin as it rested on my shoulder, and how I wanted it back on my hip.

I must still be super-duper drunk, because I couldn't figure out why I was so bizarrely and strongly affected by him.

It was new. I didn't like new. I liked predictable. I liked order. I liked to-do lists and checklists and schedules. I liked knowing what to expect. I liked knowing what to feel, what to say, what to do.

I didn't like having zero freaking clue about what I was feeling, why, or what it meant. Why did my sex ache? Why did I feel like I was empty inside? Why did I feel this inexplicable need to touch, to be touched?

This was not mere horniness, or at least not as I knew it.

This was something far, far wilder, deeper, and more dangerous.

It scared me stupid. Probably why I couldn't form a coherent thought.

"Hey, Earth to Charlie." He was grinning at me.

I blinked. "Um. What?"

He arched an eyebrow. "Been staring at me like I was somethin' to eat for nearly a minute, babe. You hungry or something?"

Or something. "Uhh, sorry?"

He turned away from the stage, tugging me with him. "Maybe you oughta sit down. Not sure you're totally with it yet."

Hand—big, rough, strong, warm. Folding around mine, enclosing it.

I wanted to sit down.

On him.

OHMYGOD. What was *wrong* with me? That was a Lexie thought, not a Charlie thought.

Dumb drunk Charlie needed to go to bed before her alcohol-loosened libido got her into a situation she wouldn't want to be in, sober.

Like in bed with Crow.

I blushed, thankful for the darkness which hid my burning cheeks. In bed? With Crow? Like that would happen.

I bet he has a huge, veiny cock…

I heard stupid Lexie's stupid whispered, taunting words thundering through my head, on repeat.

Huge, veiny cock.

No, no, no.

I didn't want to know, didn't want to know, did *not* want to know how big and veiny his cock was.

Stop thinking that word, Charlotte Grace. Stop.

"You want a cock or anything?" I heard Crow ask.

I blinked at him. "Excuse me?"

He chuckled. "I said, you want a Coke or anything?"

I realized we were back in the trailer. I shook my head. "No, I don't drink soda. Another water would be great, though."

"You oughta eat something, soak up the booze."

I blanched. "God, I couldn't possibly. Not yet."

He shrugged. "Later, then. You'll get hungry, if you stay awake long enough." A pause. "Well, I gotta get ready to put Myles's guitars away. Ya'll just hang tight here. Shouldn't take long."

"Okay," I said.

He didn't leave, though. Just smirked at me with an arched eyebrow. "I need my hand back, sweetheart."

I stared my hand, which was locked around his. "Oh." I unclenched my hand from his, shook my hand. "Silly thing. Must have a mind its own."

Crow snickered. "Don't they always?" He strode off toward the stage, where Myles and the band were finishing their encore, waiting for Myles to exit the stage so he could take the guitar.

Lexie was grinning at me like the cat who ate the canary. "You want his dick."

"Shut up."

"You do."

"Shut *up*, Alexandra."

"You do realize saying my full name doesn't actually contain any magical powers, right?" She made circles with forefinger and thumb of each hand, stacking one hand atop the other, and mimed an up-and-down stroking motion. "Cock, cock, cock," she sang, falsetto and pitchy, "you want the cock!"

I shot her the evilest, ugliest, most death-inducing stare I could summon. "I will leave you at the next hotel, Alexandra Rochelle. I swear I will."

She just snorted. "Oh stop being so damn uptight. Say the word, woman. Cock. It's not bad. It's not dirty, it's just a word."

"No."

"I will shout it as loud as I can."

I glared. I knew she would. "Don't."

"I play that game in the cafeteria with my friends all the time."

"You do not."

"I silenced the entire cafeteria once. I shouted 'big fat cock' so loud it echoed. Got reprimanded by the dean, who was eating lunch in the cafeteria at the time."

"You are twenty-one years old and still playing the penis game?" I asked, incredulous.

"The penis game is for amateurs."

"You're impossible."

She grinned, shrugging demurely. "Yep." She booped my nose. "Now. Quit being an uptight, stick-up-the-ass Goody Two-shoes and have some fun."

"I did!" I snapped. "And look at the trouble it got me into."

"Oh, that was just bad luck, bad timing, and assholes being assholes. And you not being used to drinking." She wiggled her eyebrows. "And that's not the kind of fun I'm talking about."

"I'm not saying that word, Lex. I can, and have, but I have nothing to prove right now."

"Not what I'm talking about either. I'm talking about a certain tall dark and handsome drink of very fine water. Whom you are absolutely bonkers for."

"I'm not bonkers for anyone."

"You wouldn't let go of his hand."

"I'm still very woozy. It's made me forgetful."

"Sober enough to know you have to let go of someone's hand."

I pinched the bridge of my nose. "Can you get off my case about this?"

She leaned forward, elbows on her knees, chin in her hands, watching Myles as he paraded backstage, shirt off, sweaty, high-fiving his bandmates, and taking swigs from a bottle of something. "When was the last time you had sex?" She asked, turning her face toward me but keeping her eyes on her prize.

"Six months, two weeks, and four days ago," I answered, the words tumbling out without even having to think about it.

She blinked rapidly, turning a stupefied stare at me. "How the fuck are you alive right now?"

"You do realize sex is not actually literally essential to being alive?"

"It is if you're doing it right," she said. "And was it good?"

I shrugged. "It wasn't the best sex Glen and I ever had, but it wasn't the worst."

"Did you come?"

I flushed, because I apparently run hormone-high, now. "No."

"Was there foreplay? Did he go down on you? Did you at least sneak into the bathroom after?"

"No, god no, and no."

"Wait." She turned her body to face me, grabbed me by the shoulders and held me in a death grip. "You said 'god no' for the middle question, which was the one about him going down on you. You said 'god no' as if this was a foregone conclusion, which leads me to the worrisome conclusion that our not-so-esteemed Señor Twinkle Mouse did not, in fact, provide you with regular and enthusiastic cunnilingus.

Hi-Myles-I'm-so-excited-to-meet-you-I'm-Lexie-please-can-I-kiss-you-even-just-once."

This last all in one rushed breath, because Myles had sauntered up at that moment, grinning like a fool, sweat running in rivulets down his lean, ripped torso, a white towel around his neck, a bottle of water in one hand and a bottle of Jameson in the other.

He wore black leather pants like he'd been born in them, shit-kicker square toed boots, and a worn, curved-brim gray Coors hat that looked like it had been chewed on by a dog, set on fire, and then attacked by an angry cat.

He was a rock star god, is what he was.

Lexie was staring up at him, open-mouthed, now that she'd barfed up her hero-worship ode.

"Just once?" He dropped to his knees, wedged his waist between her thighs, set his bottles on the floor, wrapped one hand around the back of her head, and kissed her absolutely stupid.

As in, when he pulled back, she blinked like a scared fish, and then sucked in a frantic breath.

He took a swig of whiskey but didn't swallow it, held it in his mouth, grinning. Yanked her against his mouth, and she whimpered in surprise, and then the two of them did something ridiculous and complicated with the mouthful of shared alcohol.

Again, he pulled away, but only an inch or two.

"Jesus, woman. With a mouth like that, you can kiss me till the cows come home."

"Moo?" Lexie breathed, inanely.

Myles laughed, and then grunted in surprise when Lexie smashed her mouth against his and took her turn kissing him like she owned him.

"Okay then," I said, and carefully levered myself to my feet. "Time to go."

They ignored me, kissing like long-separated lovers.

I stumbled out of the trailer and in search of Crow.

I found him backstage, leaning over a crate, clicking guitar case latches. He saw me, and smiled. "Hey there, beautiful."

Like he'd known me forever. It made my gut do something flippy-floppy, and my heart do pitter-patter nonsense.

"Hi," I mumbled. "Am I in the way?"

He glanced around in a broad gesture—the area was empty but for part of the drum kit, a few monitors, and piles of cords. "Nah, babe. Park that sweet ass on the crate there and tell me a story."

Sweet ass.

What?

I swallowed, not sure how to process the way he spoke; no one had ever spoken to me the way he did, and I wasn't sure if I loved it or hated it or some baffling combination of both. Moving carefully, balancing precisely, I hopped up on a chrome-and-black sound equipment crate, kicking my feet like a child.

"Tell you a story?"

He winked at me. "Yeah. Talk to me."

He had another guitar in hand, looking it over carefully, examining each string, the bridge, the neck, the frets, the tuning pegs, the headstock, the backside, and the little bar thingy on the front. He wiped it down with the cloth from his back pocket, settled it in the case, snapped it closed, and fit the case in the crate with the others.

"Um. I'm absolutely mortified at my behavior."

He didn't look up at me from his work, but snorted nonetheless. "Don't be. We've all been there."

"You have?"

He nodded. "Yup."

"Most embarrassing drunk moment, then," I said.

He propped the red-and-gold electric guitar on his knee, foot braced on the crate, and twiddled the strings as if playing a solo, though without amplification the strings produced nearly no sound. "Hmmm. Okay, so. I'm twenty. Eight years ago, that'd be. At a bar in…Yuma, I think it was. Me, Mo, Panther, Zoom, Crutchy, and Clint were all bellied up to the bar."

I shook my head. "Wait, who?"

"Nicknames, babe. My brothers from the club."

"Club?"

He reached over one shoulder and patted his back. "The MC. Keep up, shorty."

I shook my head again. "I'm a very sheltered upper middle-class white girl from Connecticut."

He laughed. "Well that explains a hell of a lot. MC means motorcycle club." He turned so I could see the patch: "AzTex" in one semicircle on top, "Texas" in a semicircle underneath, with a serpent in a recognizably Aztec style in the middle.

"Aztecs?" I read. "You're in a motorcycle club?"

God, can I please stop acting so boneheadedly stupid? Please? I'm faster on the uptake than this, usually, I swear.

"Founding member, sort of." He fiddled with the guitar. "My pa and uncle were founding members, ma was an old lady, aunt was an old lady. Cousins and I were all raised in it."

"Old lady," I repeated.

He snickered. "Don't take offense. It's the just the term."

"So who's your old lady?"

He frowned at me. "Don't have one, never had one. And I'm more or less retired. You don't really ever retire from an MC, but being that Pa and Uncle

Snake were the founders, I get special dispensation to sort of do what I want."

"Uncle Snake." I laughed. "And your friends are Panther, Zoom, Crutchy, and Clint. And you're Crow."

He nodded, and set the guitar in the case. "Yup."

"Anyone with a normal name?"

"Well, sure. They all had normal names. Mo was really Morris, Panther was...Mike, I think. Zoom was Ezekiel, so not normal, but normal-ish. Crutchy was...well, he was old as dirt and older than the hills when I was a little tyke, so I don't know his real name—not sure even Pa or Snake did, matter of fact—and Clint was just Clint."

"What was your dad's name?" Why was I so curious?

"Coyote." He said it with a decided accent—*coy-OH-tee.* "Coyote Crow."

I blinked. "Wait, that means Crow is your last name?"

He shrugged. "It's complicated."

"Your name?"

"Yup. I'm half Apache, half Comanche. My family had traditional Western Apache names, a few generations back, but somewhere around the turn of the century one of my grandfathers decided to... whiten...our names, in a weird way. To fit in off-rez

better, I guess, I don't know. I've been called nothin'
but Crow since I was in diapers."

"I see. But you do have another name."

He looked at me then, dead-on, eyes not really
humorous anymore, and I shivered. "Not tellin',
Charlie. Nothin' personal, just not into sharing my
full name."

"Okay, sorry." I swallowed. "Hope I didn't offend
you."

"Names have power," he said. "You people go
around giving out your whole name to everyone.
Not our way."

I thought about that. "Yeah, you're right."

He grinned, that easy humor back as fast as it
left. "Myles find your sister?"

I leaned backward, glancing into the dim interior
of the trailer—now that the show was over the lights
were lit and the backstage area illuminated, but it
was still shadowy inside that trailer. I saw something
moving, writhing, and I looked away.

"Yeah, I'd say he did."

He sidled over to the crate I was sitting on,
leaned against it and lifted up onto his tiptoes—his
hands braced on my thighs, and he was so close I
could smell him, and it made me dizzy and mushy
inside, the pungent man-smell of beer and sweat and
leather.

"Oh, yeah, he found her alright."

"I think they found each other," I said.

He eyed me, hands on my thighs still. "That so?"

"He took a pull of whiskey and spat it into her mouth, or something. And I think she liked it, judging by the way she kissed him back."

He laughed. "You gonna stop them?"

I shook my head. "No. She's a big girl. She can make her own choices. And she told me she'd go along with pretty much anything he wanted, if she had the chance."

He chuckled wryly. "That's a dangerous thing. Myles is awful fuckin' creative, and ain't super big on giving much of a shit about what people think."

"You just described Lexie."

His thumbs moved in circles on my leg, and I worried my skin would burst into flames where he was touching me, even though I had on leggings and he wasn't touching skin. "So they're a perfect match, it sounds like."

"That or they'll kill each other," I said, my voice faint. I looked down at his hands. "You're rubbing holes in my legs."

He followed my gaze. "Oh. Whoops." His thumbs stopped. Then his hands slid a little higher. The movement resumed, and his lips curled in a sly grin. "New spot. Better?"

I nodded, dumbly, and then realized what I was saying and put my hands on his, intending to stop him, but instead just ended up with my hands resting on his as he kept rubbing my thighs with his thumbs.

"Silly things," he said, "must have a mind of their own."

"That's my line," I whispered.

"Stole it."

I looked down—his hands were well up on my thighs now, getting kind of daring. Close to parts which were beginning to sit up and take notice at the promise of attention.

Down girl, I told myself.

I felt my nipples disobeying, going firm, hard, aching.

Why was I even letting him touch me this way?

Oh, right. Because it felt like he was setting me on fire, and that was new, and I didn't like new.

But I liked this new.

I liked being on fire, as long as he was doing the igniting. Didn't I? Seemed that way, but it was all new to me, and I wasn't sure how I felt.

Or what I was feeling.

Was my vagina supposed to tingle when he wasn't even touching it? Should I feel this ridiculously damp and hot down there?

Apparently I'd had no real understanding of true desire, or need, or sexual arousal...until now. Not until Crow.

This was inconvenient.

Disconcerting.

And deeply, intensely difficult not to act.

SIX

Crow

SHE WAS GOOD. TOO GOOD. JUST SWEET AS SUGAR AND sexy as sin, but something told me she'd sort of lost track of feeling sexy at some point in her life. Damn shame. But the good girl, the girl who didn't know how to talk to me, couldn't hold her liquor, got uncomfortable the closer I got, and went stiff and tense as a board when I touched her...was fuckin' impossible to resist.

I wanted to see if some of the squeaky clean would rub off on me. Get her just a little dirty.

I shouldn't, god, I really shouldn't. She was just genuinely a good, decent person.

One who didn't seem to know what to do with the goddess body she had.

Good and holy fuck, did I want to show her.

I craved her curves, her skin. More of her. All of her.

Stupid of me, but I did. She was too good for an old road dog like me—sure, I was only twenty-eight, but I'd packed several lifetimes of hard living into those years, and felt every bit of a thousand years old, most days. Looking at the pale creamy skin around the V of her shirt where I got tantalizing glimpses of mouth-watering, resistance-melting cleavage, I wanted nothing more than to bury my face there…on my way south. She wasn't wearing a bra, I was pretty certain. Just those big beautiful tits of hers pressing against soft cotton, the shape of them outlined, nipples peaked.

I bet she'd moan so sweet when I take those lovely things in my mouth…

Shit.

Stop, Crow.

She wasn't a one-hit wonder. Not a groupie or backstage bunny to tumble with in the corner of the bus, when no one was looking. This was a woman you fought for and held on to, a woman you kept as long as she'd let you. A woman you stayed up all night hoping she'd be there in the morning.

She was just staring at me, eyes wide, a little glassy. Head was weaving—exhausted, now, rather than blasted.

"How long you been up, shorty?"

She glanced upward. "Uh. Since like, six. Then I fell asleep in the car for a couple hours."

"Road trip?"

"New York to Alaska."

I whistled. "Holy hell, woman, that's clear across the damn continent two ways."

She frowned. "Huh? Two ways?"

"East to West, and South to North?"

"Oh, right. Duh." She rubbed her face with both hands. "I swear, Crow, I'm actually a very smart person." She laughed. "I have two degrees from Yale."

I cocked an eyebrow. "Two?"

"Double major, business and law."

"Damn, girl."

"So, I'm not this airheaded, normally. Promise."

I squeezed her thighs—fucking mistake. Juicy, soft, tender, strong. I wanted them bare, and wrapped around my neck. Gritting my teeth, I shoved the lecherous thoughts away.

"I never thought you were airheaded."

"I'm acting like one, though."

I laughed. "Alcohol can turn the smartest person into a fuckin' dweeb."

She was gazing up at me, soft blue eyes searching me like she had a billion things to say and couldn't make any of 'em make sense. I knew the feeling.

She didn't seem to mind my hands on her thighs, although I could tell she was intensely aware of them. I wanted to curl my hands into the stretchy black leggings, into the waistband, yank 'em down, get my lips all over that creamy skin.

Fuck, what was wrong with me? I've got more control than this. She was still drunk. Not in the place to make smart decisions, and a girl like her—gorgeous, two Ivy League degrees, and smelling like the innocence of all Heaven's angels—had no business knocking around with a scarred-knuckle, bar-brawling nomad like me.

She'd regret it in the morning, and if a woman was gonna regret me, she was gonna damn well remember every sinful second of it. And I wasn't entirely sure her brain was recording at the moment. She seemed lucid enough, but you never knew.

I forced my hands off her thighs. "Gotta finish up a few things. Sit tight, yeah?"

She just nodded.

I made quick work of Myles's amps, cords, and other shit, checked the area over for anything missing, checked all the cases and crates so I was triple sure I wasn't forgetting anything, and then turned back to Charlie.

…Who looked like she was about to pitch off the crate, her eyes drooping.

I curled an arm around her waist and helped her off the crate. "You need to crash, darlin'."

"Uh-huh." A belated nod. "Suddenly super tired." She leaned against me, and I was tortured silly by the soft press of her breast against my arm. "And hungry."

I laughed. "Told ya."

I had to hold her up, so I just kept my arm around her waist, and damn me if she didn't just fuckin' *fit*, right there, where my arm could sling low over her hips like a gun belt. Like it belonged there, even though I knew it didn't.

"Where're we going?" she asked, all but laying against me, letting me mostly carry her.

"Bus."

"Lexie?"

I cast a glance around. Saw Myles on the couch, Lexie sideway, legs tossed with familiar ease across his—they were sharing the bottle of whiskey and chatting like they'd known each other forever. "With Myles. Just talking and drinking."

"'Kay."

"You're crashing on the bus tonight, all right? You got my bunk. You can figure out your next step in the morning."

"Car?"

"In the lot?" I asked, and she nodded. "Keys?"

She patted randomly about her person. "Purse."

It was tangled around behind her. I grabbed it, brought it around front. She peered at it. Clumsily unzipped it. Dug in it. "I almost feel drunk again."

"Yeah, that happens. It's exhaustion hitting you. You get a second wind and feel sober, or sober-ish, and then the booze leaves your system and your body is like, fuckin' nope, we're *done*."

She found a bundle of keys attached to a big yellow sun made of floppy, broken-in leather, with a long strap and a key ring. Several keys for various locks, a PO Box or condo mailbox key, and a key fob for a Mercedes Benz. Handed them to me.

"That's my baby," she murmured. Then a worried glance. "Are you driving her? Where is she going?"

"You think I'm leaving your side in this state? Nah, babe. I'll have someone from the crew follow us in it."

"Follow us?"

"We got a show in Denver Tuesday, so we're driving all night. You're on the bus, and a crew member will be driving your car."

She straightened, eyes focusing on me, and her fists grabbed the edges of my cut. "That car is my *baby*. You have to pick someone you really, really trust. This is serious."

I patted her hands, prying them off the leather. "I got you covered, Charlie. The guy I got in mind used to be a limo driver. He's a pro. He'll take good care of your car. Now, where's it parked?"

"Way, way, way back. Far back left corner." She leaned into me again, woozy. "Oof. Can't tell if I'm more hungry or more tired."

We reached the bus, and I helped her up and in. She stopped a few stumbling steps inside, and blinked. "Whoa."

I laughed. "First time in a tour bus?"

A dumbfounded nod. "This is a freaking *bus*?"

I tried to look at it with new eyes—tricky, since I'd helped him design it. The front lounge wouldn't be out of place as the living room of an upscale Manhattan condo—and for similar size and style, you'd be paying seven figures, easy. Clean, sleek, black and white and chrome, modern lines, with a pair of overstuffed scarlet leather couches facing each other. Right now, being parked, we had the slides on each side popped out, creating extra space between the couches. A full kitchen with a pair of diner-style booths featuring seating for eight to ten, and plenty of storage above and below everything. A pair of 60-inch flat screens on either side instead of windows, each connected to a server system containing a boggling number of movies; the whole bus was wired with theater quality surround sound. Four bunks, oversized and fitted with charger-wired nooks for phones and tablets and laptops, dim lights for reading, five sides baffled for sound protection, with sound-deadening curtains across the opening.

Myles's master suite was, of course, over the top. King-size bed, his own flat screen and sound system, full bathroom. The ceiling overhead was a giant window made of electronically dimmable glass, so he could watch the sky at night and have sunlight during the day.

The whole bus was wired with satellite-fed 4G Wi-Fi, and Myles's suite could be turned into a mobile recording studio—the bed folded up and out of the way, another wall hid a mixing board, with amps and mics built into the walls, stowable as needed.

The bus had been paid for through his sponsoring partners, Fender and Harmon, the latter of which provided most of our sound equipment as well; Myles had pimped it out with his earnings from that first gangbusters album and the subsequent arena-busting eighteen-month world tour.

I knew all that, but now, with Charlie's eyes bugging out, I saw it for what it was—a ridiculously lavish mobile luxury estate. Especially considering it was home to just people—Myles, Jupiter, Zan, Brand, and me.

She turned around to take in everything. "This is crazy. I've never seen anything like this before."

I laughed. "Yeah, but it's home to us."

"This is nicer than my condo back in Boston. By, like, a *lot*."

"He's sponsored by some big companies, and that comes with pretty nice perks. Like this bus." I helped her to a couch. "So. Let's get something to eat. Something quick, or something elaborate?"

She slumped back, holding her head in both hands. "I'll take whatever will make the world stop spinning."

"Greasy, or healthy?"

She eyed me sideways. "I usually eat pretty healthy, but right now? Fatten me up, buttercup."

I laughed. "I got you." I pulled a skillet from a cabinet, set it on the induction stovetop, pulled out fixings and turned on the heat.

She watched. "Mmmm—my spider-sense tells me you're making grilled cheese."

I grinned. "Kind of. I do it my own way, though."

My grilled cheese recipe included cream cheese on the inside, ghee coating the pan, liberal amounts of sliced cheese in four varieties, a sprinkle of parmesan, and a thick layer of deli-sliced turkey. I made one for each of us—I was hungry as hell myself. As they cooked, I pulled out blue corn chips and homemade guac.

She dug into the chips and guac, eyes widening

as she tasted it. "This is the best guacamole I've ever had."

I performed an elaborate bow. "At your service, m'lady."

She frowned. "You made it?"

I nodded. "My grandfather, River Dog, lived most of the year way down in Mexico and the rest of it in various parts of the Southwest. I lived with them after my folks passed. He's the one who taught me to cook, and that old man could cook the best Tex-Mex on the damn planet."

"River Dog, huh?"

I nodded. "My grandfather is the sole reason I'm alive right now and not in jail. He was a great, great man, and I miss his leather old ass every damn day."

She was watchful, thoughtful. "Tell me about him?"

"River Dog. It was the only name anyone called him including Mammy—my grandma—Mom and Dad, the guys from the club, my uncle. It suited him, too. Not sure where the name came from, honestly." I flipped the sandwiches, letting my memory wander. "He was one of those old guys who was just ageless. To me, he looked about the same my whole life. About my height, but thin in that lean, leathery way, you know? Not sure I ever saw him wear a shirt, and his skin showed it. Barefoot, always. He could walk barefoot across scorching sand, blacktop, over gravel. Him and Mammy, up until my parents died when I was ten, eleven lived nomadic. Following the old ways. And I don't mean to sound all mystical or shit, but they were just...people out of time. They wandered for decades, just lovin' each other, following the wind. They'd go down into Mexico, hang out on the beaches of the Yucatán. Wander up into Texas, Baja, SoCal, into the Four Corners region. They had a truck and an old Airstream, and that was all they ever owned."

She shook her head, grinning. "Really? You're not making this up to sound cool?"

"Every word of it is the truth. I worshipped River Dog and Mammy. Every spring, Mom and Dad would pack me up and we'd head out to look for River Dog and Mammy, and it always felt like an adventure, trying to find 'em. Usually around spring they'd be down in Mexico on the beaches only locals knew about, far away from the tourists. We'd spend days and days in the saddle, just riding."

"Horses?"

I laughed. "Naw, bikes. Motorcycles. I rode in a sidecar with Dad." I sighed. "He had a 1946 Indian Chief. I lived for those trips with them, and then I'd spend the summers with River Dog and Mammy. Riding horses, swimming, not doing shit-all but just relaxing and eating and playing with local kids."

She was enthralled. "Sounds magical."

I nodded. "It was. Best years of my life."

Her brow pinched. "And then?"

I shrugged. "Ehh, you don't wanna hear the 'and then,' babe, ain't a lot of fun in the tellin' of that old misery."

"Try me."

I flicked off the heat, plated the sandwiches, and sat next to her on the couch, our thighs touching. I handed her a can of sparkling water I'd grabbed while cooking, and a pair of ibuprofen. We ate in silence— except for Charlie's groans of delight.

Each one of which shot straight to my cock like lightning. To get my mind on another track I forced myself to think about Sister Maria, the old-as-dirt nun I'd lived with between Mom and Dad dying and then going to live with my grandparents; she was wrinkled and had a sour horse-face, like a mule that had swallowed a lemon. Ugly as anything but still, to this day, the quietest, most patient, most compassionate human being I'd ever met.

Sister Maria faded my arousal enough that I could think properly.

"So. I was ten, near eleven when Mom and Dad died."

"Motorcycle accident?"

I paused, staring my sandwich. "Uh, no. They

got tangled up in a big ol' mess with a rival MC." I bit, chewed, swallowed. Sighed. "They were shot."

She flinched. "Oh. Wow. Um…wow. I'm so sorry."

"Going on twenty years ago, now." I smiled at her. "At the time my grandparents were off somewhere, and I had nowhere to go. None of the others from the club, those who survived that fuckin' mess of a shootout, wanted me. Not full time, at least. So I lived at a little convent down in Monterrey, with an old nun named Sister Maria."

She was staring at me. Not quite believing. "By Monterrey, you mean the one in Mexico."

I nodded. "See, the thing is, I was born in a bathtub just this side of the Mexican-American border, outside El Paso. In a motel, during a shootout. Legally, I'm a naturalized American citizen. I have a driver's license and everything. But back then; I was more than half wild. When shit got hot for Mom and Dad up here in the States, they'd head south. Spend time with River Dog and Mammy while things cooled off. I never went to school. Didn't get immunized for anything till I was a teenager. I was just this crazy-ass outlaw kid, spoke a pidgin mix of Western Apache, Spanish, and English."

"Do you still know those other languages?"

I nodded. "Sure. Mom and Dad both spoke

Western Apache to each other almost exclusively, and Mammy and River Dog—Dad's parents—spoke a mix of that and Spanish. I didn't start using English all the time till I was sixteen. Had to sort of learn it from scratch."

She shook her head. "You had a crazy childhood, didn't you?"

I chuckled. "You got no clue, darlin'."

"Say something in Apache."

"*I wish you were sober, so I could get you naked and make you scream my name.*"

"What does that mean?"

"It means I think you're beautiful."

She frowned. "Bullshit."

I snorted. "How do you know?"

She leaned close. "I have a bullshit detector like nobody's business. You said something dirty, didn't you?"

I shrugged. "It amounts to what I told you."

"It does not. Tell me what you said."

I stared at her. I didn't dare tell her. So I repeated what I'd said, but in Spanish.

"I don't speak Spanish either." She leaned her shoulder against mine. "Tell me what you said, Crow. I won't be mad, no matter what it was."

I eyed her. "Count backward from twenty."

She did so, only faltering a couple times. "I'm

still pretty buzzed, but I'm not…insensible. I know what's going on and what I'm doing." She finished her sandwich, set the plate aside. "Now, what did you say, Crow?"

"You don't want to know." I felt my gut spinning. I shouldn't tell her.

But her eyes begged me to. That hint of cleavage begged me to.

My cock was insisting I whisper the translation in her ear and see how she responded.

"Yes, I do," she murmured. "It was something dirty, wasn't it?"

I just nodded. "Yeah."

"Tell me."

I caught her braid in my fingers, traced the complex pattern under my fingertips. Stared into her eyes and sought…something. I wasn't sure what.

I repeated the sentence in Apache. Tugged on her braid so her ear tilted toward me. Whispered. "It means 'I wish you were sober, so I could get you naked and make you scream my name.'"

She sucked in a sharp breath. Twisted her head so her nose brushed mine. Eyes on mine, so close she looked cyclopean, one big bright blue eye. "I'm sober enough."

"No, you're not."

"I can be the judge of that. I'm an adult."

I still had her braid in my fist, and I couldn't help but pull on it again, and this time, her face tilted, mouth falling against mine. Her lips were soft and wet and inviting, welcoming. I licked at her lips, and she moaned, pushed against me, gave me her tongue. Hungrily, she kissed me back.

Ohh shit, this girl was eager.

My cock sprang alive at the feel of her mouth on mine, and then she pressed her body against me and I felt her breasts crush soft and pliant against my chest, and I tipped back, flat on the couch. I brought her on top of me, one hand coiling her long braid around my fist. Her palm scraped against my cheek, across my stubble, and then she gripped my shoulder and pressed against my chest. She shifted forward, and fuckfuckfuck she was lined up on me, my achingly hard cock throbbing against her soft center, and I had her juicy ass in my other hand, palming and squeezing, kneading.

I delved under the elastic of her waistband and gathered a handful of soft warm silky skin, and I groaned at the velvet wonder of her skin, the firm heft of her ass. She writhed, needy, and whimpered into my mouth, pressing against my hand. I let go of her braid and took a double handful of sweet, tender ass cheek, playing with the softness and movement of it. I twisted her sideways, toppling her against the back of the couch, pressing her in with my body, not breaking the kiss.

My hand reached up under her shirt and I found out for certain that she wasn't wearing a bra. Just those gorgeous melons piled up in my hand. She gasped as I cradled one in my palm, brushing a nipple. God, so soft. Her nipple was a hard little nub under my fingers, and I tweaked it, toyed with it until she whimpered, and then I played with the other. She arched her back, and her tongue sought mine. Her hands curled between our bodies, splayed out, palms against my chest. Then her fingers dug in, clawing at my shoulders and chest.

I wanted her moans. Her sweet voice whispering, whimpering.

I became mindless, ravenous, a man of want and need—consumed by Charlie, by the soft perfection of her skin and the eager kiss of her lips and soaring scouring drive of her tongue. The plump squish of her tits in my hands, and I needed, needed, needed to feel more of her.

She refused to let go of my mouth, breaking for breath and then diving right back in. Scratching my pec, tracing my stubble and my jaw.

Shit, I was done for. No way I could resist sampling more of her delights. There wasn't one thought in my brain about denying myself the sound of her orgasming under my hands.

I slipped one hand down, teasing my way south. She huffed, forehead on mine, pausing in the kiss as my hand slipped into the front of her leggings. I paused, but she flexed her hips, and I kept going. Her mouth stole up against mine again, demanding I kiss her, and I did, because kissing her was how I kept breathing.

No underwear either? Fuck, this good girl was maybe not so good after all.

My cock throbbed harder with the idea that a girl as radiant with wholesome goodness as Charlie might be a sex-hungry nymph as well.

That break in the kiss told me she knew what I was doing, and the flex of her hips told me she wanted it.

Scratchy fuzz—trimmed close. God, she was like a drug. I stopped breathing, my mouth open, my lips on hers. Forehead to forehead. Throat closed, mouth dry. Gut trembling in anticipation, though I'd only just met her, barely knew her.

This desire, this need was sudden and it became *everything* to me. Slowly, I delved my middle finger into the slick wet softness of her slit. And ohhhh fuck me sideways, she made a sound that turned my cock into a fiery rod of rigid magma, swollen painfully hard at the desperate pleasure in her voice. There was a faint squelch of her wetness as I slipped my fingers through her essence, spreading it over her clit. Not that she needed it, god no. She was drenched for me. Lying on her side, she lifted her upper thigh to make room. To invite me, welcome me. I slid in, and she was fucking *tight*, even around my finger.

Out, then.

Slowly.

In, and this time I found her clit, and it was prominent and firm, ready for my touch. One soft flick of my finger, and she shook all over, flinching bodily, gasping a breathy shriek. So, *so* sensitive. Another flick, and she whimpered, gasped, and her hips flexed.

I needed more of her.

Twisting, settling her on her back, I straddled her. Her palm cupped the back of my head as I dipped kisses over her throat, and then pushed up her shirt to bare the most magnificent pair of breasts I've ever had the privilege of laying eyes on. Plump and firm, high, perky, big enough to fill my hand, wide round dark areolae and big pink thick nipples, sweet as plums and just as firm. I suckled her breast into my mouth and she cried out, arched her back, and cradled my head against her body, holding me there—as if I'd ever leave, now that I had such incredible tits in my mouth.

I palmed the one I wasn't licking and sucking, pinching her nipple.

My hand was still in her leggings. A finger inside her, slipping in and out, delving into her tight channel and spreading her slippery essence around her clit until she was moaning. Then I started a circle with my fingertips, just two of them, a gentle delicate touch, barely making contact.

She whimpered, gasped, cried out—her hips moved in time with my fingers, and I flicked my tongue against her nipple in synch.

Within sixty seconds, she was shaking all over, and I brought her over the edge and kept her there, and god love me, she was crying out, wordless, hips spasming, pushing. I needed more, more. I was greedy for her, now. I'd had a taste, and now I needed more. Needed to taste her sweetness on my tongue.

I slid down her body, bringing my hands to curl inside the waist of her leggings. She buried her fingers in my hair, and I glanced up at her. Her eyes were wide, wild. Lucid.

Still.

"Tell me you want it."

"Crow…" she breathed.

I tugged her leggings down an inch, baring the top of her pubis. "Need to know you're with me, Charlie."

"Ohmygod, *Crow.*"

Never heard my name said that way. Sultry.

Sensual. Desperate. Her voice was music, my name the melody and the lyrics. It made my already painful dick throb so hard I groaned at the searing pain of its rigidity.

"You with me, Charlie?" I gazed up at her, meeting her eyes.

Blue, azure and intense, fixed on me with a tumult of emotion. No denial, no fear or worry or doubt. She swallowed hard. "Y-yeah."

I heard the hesitation, but she closed her eyes, tipped her head back, and feathered her fingers in my hair—and that feeling of her hands on my scalp, fingertips tingling through my hair…it was more than I could take.

I tugged her leggings down further, and she lifted her butt off the couch to allow me to pull them past her butt, down to her knees. Now with her shoes off and her leggings tangled up between her knee and the couch she was splayed open, her sex was a delicate pink flower. I kissed the inside of her thigh, and she gasped, flinched—the tender silken skin melted under my tongue as I kissed closer and closer to her slit, and when I got there, I smelled her desire, a pungent perfume. I tasted her.

She whimpered as she presented her core for me.

I licked her, long and slow, using my tongue fat and flat, and then hard and thin and probing, circling around her clit. She whined in the back of her throat, a small sound of desperation. I slid a finger into her, curled, and she lifted her hips off the couch, demonstrating her need.

I breathed on her, a hot breath against her soft wet center. She wiggled, huffed a not-quite laugh. I licked her again, and then set a rhythm, fast and relentless. My neck ached, and my tongue too, but her moans made it all worth it.

After the first orgasm, the second was slower in coming, building gradually. A breath, a gasp. A whimper, a sigh. My fingers moved, my tongue slicked and circled. I pulled away and then used my fingers on her clit, until she responded, giving herself up to pleasure. Wanting to please her, I devoured her again with my mouth, taking my time, not hurrying her.

When her hips began to flex, I slid off the couch and pivoted to kneel on the floor, twisting her, pulling her ass off the edge of the couch, holding her aloft. Bringing her slit to my mouth, I gave her the speed and intensity she needed to get the rest of the way there.

She was whimpering, trying to flex, to move, but I had her at my mercy. She tasted sweet, so sweet. Her ass flexed taut in my hands, and her legs hooked around my neck, thighs quivering, pinioning. I welcomed them, letting her squeeze her thick strong thighs against my face, my neck. God, yes, it felt incredible.

She was writhing, now. I opened my eyes and watched as her big lush tits jiggled and swayed, falling to one side as she twisted, pushing her core against my mouth, trying to extract every bit of feeling.

"Oh-oh-ohgod*CROW!*" Shit, her voice was tight and hoarse and maybe a bit shocked.

I hummed, moaning my pleasure at the sounds this gorgeous woman was making. I held her in place, firm against my mouth, devouring her with every ounce of my energy, creating a rhythm that answered my insatiable hunger for her slick sex. Slurping her essence, the flexing bubble and swell of her beautiful ass in my hands, her soft thighs vise strong around my face, her hands boldly gripped in my hair, yanking me against her, wantonly grinding her slit against my mouth, forcing her rhythm on me.

The harder she demonstrated her need, the more I gave her, wilder and faster, until her hips were pumping and her breasts were heaving and her voice was lifted in a loud song of crazed luxuriation. Screaming, screaming, careless and heedless of who may hear. All lush bare skin and soft flesh sweat-smeared, fingers knotted in my hair, grinding and grinding against my tongue.

The buildup was so slow, from gentle movements to whimpers, to soft cries and then gently circling her hips, loud gasps of needy, thrusting sex, and finally to madly pumping hips and hoarse screams of orgasmic abandon.

"Crow, Crow, Crow—god, Crow fuck, yes, god yes, please please more please yes god please yes—oh fuck oh fuck oh fuck ohhhh fuck *ohffffuck!*"

The good girl had a potty mouth when she came. God, yes.

At the last, her eyes flew open and she curled forward, thighs locked around my neck and hands knotted in my hair, her whole body tensed and taut, eyes riveted on mine, wide and tearing up with fervent wonderment, with shocked ecstasy.

The orgasm was seemingly endless, and I tasted her release flood against my tongue, felt her slit clamp and spasm, felt her stomach tighten and her thighs go rigid. I growled against her sex as she came, held her up with one arm and slid three fingers inside her and curled them in a come-here motion, thrusting in and pulling out fast and faster, pushing her from orgasm to something beyond, to utter dissolution. Her breathless cry became a sobbing whimper, her eyes never leaving mine.

Those open, wild eyes. Blue as the sky and the sea, roiling with a turbulent flood of emotion—shock and wonder and incredulity and disbelief and something like relief but amped a thousandfold.

As if she'd never come before, or at least not like that.

"Crow, my god...what was...whatthe*fuck* was *that*?" She was gasping raggedly, sweating, as if she'd sprint a few hundred meters full out.

I slid up onto the couch and brought her with me, swiveling her around to cradle her. Clothed, she was breathtaking. Nude, she was...a goddess.

All pale skin and perfect curves. Heavy, swaying breasts and full hips, an hourglass waist. She obviously took care of herself, but I don't think she was obsessive about it. I think she ate well and exercised intelligently. Soft in all the right places, with just enough sweet tender soft extra something to sink my fingers into and, believe me, I wanted to devour each curve, each line, each morsel of her gorgeous body.

I just held her. Ignored the agonizing throb of my hot, iron-hard cock in my jeans, ignored the way it throbbed all the more painfully as I settled her bare ass on my crotch, feeling her buttocks split perfectly around it. I knew she could feel it.

I just held her.

She nuzzled against my chest, her head under my chin, hair smelling of lavender and roses. Her naked breasts pressed against my bare chest between the edges of my open cut.

She was shaking all over. "Crow...I—"

I cradled her in my arms. "Hush, Charlie. Close your eyes, relax."

"But—"

"I got you, babe."

She wriggled her backside. "I can feel what you need."

"Later."

She hesitated, silence extending. "I want you to know…what you just did? That was…an incredible gift."

I huffed a laugh. "Goddess like you, Charlie? Oughta have guys lined up around the block, begging for the opportunity to drop to their knees and worship that sweet pussy."

She inhaled sharply, tensing. "God, Crow." I felt her embarrassment. "You can't say things like that."

I laughed. "Sure I can. You're a goddess, and you have the sweetest fuckin' pussy I've ever tasted. How some lucky fucker hasn't locked you down with a ring already I do *not* understand." I felt my mouth running away from my better sense. "If you were mine, I'd never let you fuckin' go. Not for anything in the whole damn world."

Shit, that was way too much. Where had it even come from?

She was gonna get up and leave.

Instead of lurching to dress and run, however,

she sank deeper into me. "I don't know what to say to that."

"Nothin' you need to say to that, darlin'. I got you. Just relax."

"Gonna…pass out. Soon." She was muzzy, half-way there already.

"Good."

It felt for all the world like I was holding the woman of my life as she fell asleep in my arms. Like I had some bone-deep urge to protect this woman, to hold her, shield her, make her feel good and safe.

It made no sense—I didn't know shit about her life, or her past. I didn't even know her middle name. And she sure as shit didn't know some pretty fucking salient details about me. I'd told her a lot about my family, but there were some details which I just knew were going to be deal breakers.

But, for right now? I had a beautiful, naked, satisfied woman in my arms, and she seemed content to be there.

I'd take it…while it lasted.

Gathering her more fully into my arms, I snagged her clothing, shoes, purse, everything, and carried her and all of her stuff to my bunk. Slid her in. Covered her with my blankets, hesitated, and then said fuck it. I climbed in with her, and lay next to her, and knew we would wake up outside of Denver.

SEVEN

Charlie

I WOKE UP FEELING…OKAY, ACTUALLY. I WAS CLINGING TO the side of a bed, my eyes firmly closed.

A little woozy, a bit of a headache, but considering how drunk I'd been, I was not too bad. I had slammed several bottles of water, and I think there'd been some painkillers at some point. I'd had some food. God, delicious food. Such good food. That guac, that sandwich? So good.

Then, still with my eyes closed and no real comprehension of where I even was, I remembered the rest of what had happened.

Crow.

Kissing him.

Or, him kissing me, and then suddenly needing to kiss him like I needed my next breath. Needing him to touch me, to do things to me. And good god did he ever. He did things to me.

Dirty, delightful things.

I squirmed, remembering the scratch of his stubble on my thighs, and Lexie telling me exactly how good that would feel, and jeepers criminy, was she ever right. The feel of his tongue, his mouth, his lips all over my sensitive sex, driving me wild. His hands cupping my ass, holding me up like I weighed nothing at all.

But the way he looked at me.

That was *it*. That was everything.

No man had ever looked at me like that and it was more than I could handle.

The way he'd looked at me was...too much. Too intense, too wild. Too hot and hungry and primal. He wanted to do things to me.

And I wanted that.

I wanted to be overwhelmed.

Taken. Used. Needed.

Owned.

Appreciated.

Fuck, I must be crazy. Utterly crazy.

I had just met the man. Literally. Yesterday. I had let a man put his mouth on my vagina—a man I had met only hours before.

God, what was wrong with me?

Where was I, anyway?

I became aware of a gentle movement, a bump, and a sway.

I tried moving. Testing my body. I opened my eyes.

It was then that I realized I was naked, and in an unfamiliar bed.

I was, like, totally naked. Had he taken off my shirt last night? I remembered, with intense vividness, his hands on my breasts, his mouth on my nipples, his tongue slathering over them, making them stand up into diamond-hard points of sensitivity, but had he actually taken my shirt off? I didn't think so. I thought he'd just pushed it up. Now, I do, for sure, remember him taking my leggings off, but only on one side. But they were gone. Where? I would have to find them later.

I was aware then of something else—other sounds and movements.

I became aware of the motion of the tour bus and the quiet sounds of other activity. We were on the move, and I guess the next stop would be Denver. I think it was still dark outside, so I imagined we had a ways to go. Now, semiconscious, I couldn't believe Lexi and I had ended up on the Myles North tour, for god's sake. Not to mention everything else that had happened. But I was adopting a new mantra: just go with it, and so far that had worked out pretty well for me.

I heard a huff.

Soft, slight, gentle, snores.

I twisted slowly around, and saw him.

Crow, lying next to me.

As magnificent as I'd remembered him from last night. More so, perhaps. His hair was messy, thick and black, cut into a short, utilitarian, easy-to-leave-messy style. His skin was so dark, a gift of his heritage certainly, but evidence of a life lived outside in the sun and weather. Squint and laugh wrinkles on the sides of his eyes. A scar over his left eyebrow, partially bisecting it. Another along his jaw. Thick stubble, almost a beard but not quite. His mouth was a thin slash in his face, but his lips were…was it emasculating for me to say they were plump? Because they were. As soft-looking as I remember them feeling. I wanted to kiss them all over again. Right now.

Gahhh.

He was shirtless, and god, the body on the man was unreal. Hard muscles, firm, large, but not shredded by obsession or compulsion, nor bodybuilder swollen out of proportion. Just fit, strong, healthy. Faint abdominal definition, enough to make my mouth water as he flipped onto his back, his head turned toward me. One hand rested on his thigh, low. The other tossed up over his head.

Thick arms, powerful, and covered in tattoos.

I'd never been a fan of tattoos, but god, on him they were extraordinary. More than just decorative art, it was obvious, even to me, they were meaningful.

His jeans were still on, but unzipped and unbuttoned, slung low, showing a hint of tight gray underwear. A bulge pushed against the fabric, straining. I could clearly make out the shape of the head, the ridge, an inch or so of the shaft, and I thought about how hard it had been behind his jeans last night, clearly fully engorged with arousal, yet as I'd shaken and shuddered through my orgasm and the ripping afterquakes, he'd just held me. He'd obviously let me drift off into sleep, and then had gotten me into bed. His bed, I assumed.

I felt a warm rush of gratitude for that. Yet gratitude didn't seem like nearly a strong enough word for what he'd done for me—rescuing me from danger, feeding me, giving me two intense orgasms, and then allowing me to fall asleep and just be...

Taken care of?

It felt like heaven.

His bunk was a decent size, I realized. Larger than I'd imagined a tour bus bunk being, honestly, but this was no average tour bus. This thing was a luxury condo on wheels. There was enough room in this bunk to prop up on an elbow, but not to sit up. It had a flip-down TV screen in the ceiling, and a cubbyhole in the wall to plug in a cell phone and an iPad. There was also room for a battered black wallet, a small folding box cutter, and a much larger fixed-blade knife—that one was showpiece quality, the handle made of handworked antler, carved into an intricately detailed meadow scene with deer and trees, along with a leather sheath with an exquisitely detailed crow worked into the side. At the foot end of the bed, there was another cubby, this one was a bookshelf stuffed well beyond capacity with paper-backs—I saw sci-fi, fantasy, biographies, histories and historical fiction, and even a romance or two. All well-thumbed, dog-eared.

He snorted, shifted. His hips flexed, his ass tight-ening to push him upward.

I realized why.

The bulge was enlarging. Significantly.

I bit my lip, gnawing on it. Ohhh god, that was...gargantuan. As it hardened, it lengthened and thickened inside the gray fabric, straining against it, so clearly outlined it may as well have been uncovered.

And then, oooh wow, okay, wow. WOW.

It poked up out of the top of his underwear.

Pink tip, plump and round, with a tiny slit, peeking almost cutely, shyly, out of the elastic waistband.

I wanted to touch it.

He was asleep, though.

I shouldn't.

Really, really I shouldn't.

I should go back to sleep and forget I saw anything.

Yeah, right. Like that was going to happen.

Like I could ever, ever forget this. The monstrous size of the thing, so big it would fill my fist and then some, thick and so long, fat and hard.

Soft, I bet.

Yet rigid. Steel sheathed in silk.

I want his steel sheathed in my silk.

I snorted out loud—I'd heard that in Lexie's voice.

But shit, it was true.

I wanted so badly to touch it. Run my finger over the pink tip. Pull the underwear down and bare the whole thing.

God, no. No. That was crazy.

I didn't know him. Last night had been a lapse in judgment due to my extreme impairment. Sure, when it had happened I'd been more sober than drunk, more exhausted than woozy.

I'd known what I was doing, what I was letting him do. I'd wanted it, and I'd just...gone with it.

That was then, though, and this was now. And I wasn't touching him. Not now, not like this. But holy crap, it was a hell of an effort.

"It won't bite," a deep, sleepy voice said, inches from my ear.

"No, but I might," I heard my own voice say; I surprised both of us with that comment.

"Well hell, woman." A wry, surprised smirk.

I blushed crimson. "Not awake all the way. I, uh—" I could not physically blush any harder. "I...I don't know what I was thinking."

His smirk turned wicked. "Hey, you wouldn't hear me complain, babe. Just maybe, you know, don't bite *too* hard."

I wanted to hide, but there was nowhere to hide, so I squirmed. Wriggled. That was a truth I didn't want to tell him. But the way I was not meeting his eyes, the way I was unable to speak, just stammering...

"That sounds, I mean—you're—I..."

His eyes narrowed. "You are *not* a virgin. No fuckin' way."

"No!" I protested. "I'm not, not at all. I was engaged, actually. With the same guy for five years."

"Then what's up?"

I shrugged. "What do you mean?"

He smiled, laughing. "Playing coy, huh?"

It was weird how *not* weird it felt to be in bed with him. It felt utterly natural. Strangely comfortable.

"I'm not playing coy," I lied.

He snorted. "Then you're full of shit, one way or another." He arched an eyebrow. "I was joking, and I don't think you were."

"Joking?"

"The biting thing." He indicated his still-hard member, the tip still peeking up over the top of his jeans. "How this thing don't bite, but you do."

"Oh, that. Ha, yeah. Just…just joking."

He sighed. "You wanna play dumbshit, fine by me, babe. Just know I see through it."

I sighed. "You want the truth?"

He nodded. "Always, babe. Hard, painful, or strange, the truth is always better, in my opinion."

"I'm not a virgin. I met my ex-fiancé in my fresh-man year of college. I was a virgin. I dated him all through college, moved to Boston with him after col-lege and we lived together. He proposed a year and a half ago, and I found out a few months later that he was cheating on me with my boss. I dumped him, quit my job, moved out of the condo we shared—pay-ing him for the rest of the years' worth of my half of the rent. I've lived off my savings since."

He quirked an eyebrow. "Okay. That dude was a

dumbfuck piece of shit, number one. Number two, what's your point?"

"The point is, I'm not a virgin." I sighed. I tugged the blankets up to my neck, suddenly hyperaware that I was buck naked underneath. "But…while I've had a lot of sex, there are some things I haven't done."

He nodded slowly. "Like a blowjob."

My cheeks flamed, my chest burned, and I couldn't breathe. My eyes went to his shaft, the pink tip drawing my gaze. "Right. Among other things."

"Like?"

"Why do you want to know? So you can make fun of me?"

He frowned, puzzled. "Have I made fun of you for anything so far?"

I sighed. "No, you haven't. I apologize. I get defensive, sometimes."

"You know, Charlie, there's a thing you're allowed to do. It's called telling me to mind own goddamn business. They just invented it yesterday, I heard, but I can teach you, if you want."

I laughed. "I feel like I owe you the truth, at the very least."

His fingers pinched my chin, gentle but firm. Eyes on mine, fierce, unrelenting. "You don't owe jack shit, princess."

"But, I…last night. You…"

"Had the unbelievable privilege of putting my hands and mouth on the most beautiful fuckin' woman I've ever seen. I got to watch you come underneath me, watch those big beautiful tits move around...*fuck*. What I did last night was *selfish* of me, Charlie. Make no fuckin' mistake about me—I'm a selfish, horny bastard, and I did what I did because I had no chance of keeping my hands off you. I feel a little shitty about it, truth be told, because I still ain't sure you were sober enough to know what you were letting me do."

Suddenly, breathing was difficult and I found it impossible to take my eyes off of him. His words lanced through my core. Dirty, filthy, crude, crass... and beautiful. Intoxicating.

"I knew what I was letting you do, Crow. I was drunk enough that my inhibitions were very, very relaxed, but I was in control of my mind, and able to make informed decisions."

"Swear that's the truth, Charlie?" His eyes betrayed worry and guilt that he'd done something untoward.

"Yes, I swear. I..." I was lost, my mouth and mind disconnected, my body feeling strange intense fluttering disorienting new things I couldn't process or identify, but they were all focused at the nexus of my thighs and low in my belly. "I really, really, *really* liked what you did."

"Well, good to know I got it right."

"Oh, you got it right. I've never felt that way before." I knew my eyes betrayed that secret too.

"Never?"

"Nope. Nothing like it." Let him guess from that.

"That's one of the other things you never did with your ass-bag of an ex," he surmised.

I nodded shallowly. "Yeah," I whispered.

He let out a slow breath. "So, what else haven't you done?"

"Anything that's not...regular sex, I guess."

"What's regular, to you?" he asked, not quite smirking.

"Missionary, I think they call it."

He had his fingertip on my temple, pushing back flyaway hair, then down my throat, over my shoulder. Nudging the blanket down with his finger. Centimeter by centimeter, he bared my skin, and I held my breath and let him.

"That's it? That's all you and that dude ever did? Him on top, you on bottom, wham-bam-thank-you-ma'am?"

I swallowed hard. "Yeah, basically. When we first started dating, there was some, like, going around the bases kind of stuff. Heavy petting, touching under clothes. Then sex, and we never really tried anything else."

"So, you've never…" he paused, shifted a little closer—he was on top of the blankets, I realized, and he'd likely done it to make me more comfortable. "You've never gone down on a guy. Never felt him losing his shit, and knowing you have absolute control over him. Last night was the first time a guy has ever *taken care* of you, too. Showed you what feeling good is supposed to be like. Just made you feel good and left it at that."

I wanted to breathe, really I did, but I couldn't. He was taking my breath away. Moving closer, that single fingertip sliding down the outside of my arm. Bring the blankets with it, baring me. The upper swell of my breast was bared, now.

"That would be correct."

"And you've never taken a good hard pounding from behind either." He smirked. "Never gotten on your hands and knees and felt him just…*fuck* you, like you're all there is on the whole planet and if he doesn't fuck you as hard as he can, he'll just fuckin' die."

I swallowed hard. "N-no." Jesus. "Definitely not."

"Damn. Really missing out."

"This all sounds like things you particularly enjoy."

He nodded. "Abso-fuckin-lutely, babe." He kept brushing the blanket down—my areolae were exposed now, and then my nipples, and then all of my breasts, my nipples puckering in the air, under his bold, predatory gaze. "Why, do they not sound fun to you?"

"Fun? Not sure fun is the word I'd use."

"So, what would you say, then?"

"Intense. Exciting. Daring."

He laughed. "Daring? Babe, you been in a box your whole adult life. That shit ain't daring. It's how it *should* be."

"I'm realizing I have been in a box," I said.

"Someone's gotta get you out of that box, then."

The blankets were at my sacrum, then sliding down my hip, to my thighs. He left them there, my sex exposed. His eyes raked over me, devoured my body greedily, blatantly.

"*Fuck*, Charlie." He sounded almost pained.

"What?" I whispered.

He shook his head. "Nah, nothin'. Just you. Woman, you're incredible."

I shrugged, and the way his eyes followed my breasts told me he appreciated what that movement did for them. "Just me."

"Well, just you is fuckin' sexy." He ran his tongue over his lip, his eyes going from my eyes to my breasts, staying there.

His hand slid across the mattress. His eyes flicked

to mine, and I knew he was watching to see what I would do. Cover myself? Stop his hand?

I did nothing.

My nipple was peaked, hard. I remembered his touch from last night and wanted to feel it again.

Crazy, yes. But I was naked in this bed, with this man. I was on a crazy road trip with my crazy sister. For the first time since I was seventeen years old, I was single.

And this man found me attractive.

Made me feel like…

Well…

As he just put it, he made me feel fucking sexy. And god, that was an addictive feeling. I realized I'd never really felt *sexy* with…my ex. I didn't want to think his name, not here, not now. I knew he'd wanted to have sex with me, sure. Some affection for me as a person, sure. But…not this all-consuming *need* which I saw in Crow's eyes.

Like, if he didn't get his hands on my skin right now, he was going to explode.

Or more accurately, perhaps, he was *going* to get my body in his hands no matter what, unless I stopped him.

I didn't stop him.

I watched him, my eyes on his. Slowly, his hand palmed my breasts, and I sucked in a sharp breath, held it. My eyes were wide—his hand was so big, so rough, so gentle. He just held me, for a moment. Then his hand twisted, his scratchy palm scraping my sensitive nipple, and he lifted my breast, held it in his palm, cradling it. Thumb brushing my nipple, making it sing with ecstatic sensation.

I bit my lip. "Crow."

"Yeah?"

I shrugged, shook my head, laughing softly. "Nothing, I just…" I swallowed. "I like that."

"Yeah?"

I nodded. I moved over onto my back, offering him both breasts. He levered over me. We both watched his hands as he caressed and cradled and kneaded my breasts, flicking the nipples, making them hard, achy.

The blanket was rucked down at my shins, and I kicked it off, spreading myself bare and open on the bed, and watched as Crow looked at me—his eyes telling a story.

One of awe.

Fierce need.

Appreciation—for me, exactly as I was.

I would do anything to keep being looked at like that—the intense wonder in his gaze. Did that make me desperate? Maybe.

But in that moment I decided I would just go with it.

Maybe I was sex starved. Not for the act of sex, but for the things which, according to Crow, were supposed to go with it. The need, the desperation, the fiery ache.

And Crow made me feel those things.

Right now, I wanted another orgasm. I wanted his face in my thighs, his tongue in my sex. I wanted to come apart, to look down and see his big hard body between my legs, feel his scratchy stubble sandpapering against my inner thighs, his tongue lashing me to screaming climax.

I wanted it. Fuck, I wanted that.

I felt dirty. I felt wanton. I felt…sensual. Sexual. I felt needy.

He'd given me something last night. Unlocked something in me, and now I couldn't put it back in its cage. It was out, and it demanded that I let it run wild.

His hand left my breast, stole down my sternum, over my belly. Teased my belly button, and then moved down further, hesitating inches above my sex, toying with the line where my pubic hair started, trimmed close but not shaved bare.

I instinctively felt the urge to bat his hand away, the reaction of a lifetime of…prudery. No, that wasn't right. I wasn't a prude. I enjoyed sex—that was the problem, really. I had always wanted *more* out of sex than I ever got, and had never possessed the requisite courage to demand it, ask for it, go get it. I wasn't a prude, I was…sheltered. Repressed.

Undersexed.

His gaze softened, the sharp edges of sexual fervor gentling. "You're thinkin' a lot of deep thoughts over there, Charlie Goode."

I nodded, but shrugged too. "Yeah, I guess."

"Want my two cents?"

"Sure."

"There's a time for thinkin', and a time for feeling. Gotta know which is which, and keep the two separate." He paused. "Feeling, I mean physical feeling. But emotional, too. Thinking ain't got much to do with either one, in my experience."

"I'm a classic Type-A, overthinking, overachieving, check everything five times, schedule my whole life a year in advance, manage my days with checklists kind of girl. So to say I get lost in my head would be an understatement."

"What do you want, right now?"

"What do I want?" I repeated.

"Yeah. What do you want?"

"With you? Or…?"

He just shrugged. "Don't think about your answer, just blurt out the first thing that comes to mind."

I laughed. "That's hard for me."

"Yeah, I'm realizing that." He brushed hair away

from my forehead, mouth, eyes, brushing it aside; my braid was coming loose, and he stripped the ponytail holder off the end, tossed it into the cubbyhole with his phone, and deftly freed my hair of the braid, spreading out like a cloud of ink on his pillow. "Damned lot of hair, girl."

"I've never cut it, not significantly."

"Fuckin' beautiful." He touched my eyelids ever so gently. "Close your eyes."

I did so. Felt his breath on my shoulder. "Okay?"

"Don't think about nothin', just lay there and be you. Just float in your head."

I snorted. "That's like asking water to stop being wet."

"Try."

I focused on nothingness. Forced thoughts out of my head. Darkness, and nothing but Crow's presence, his heat, his breath, his body.

"Now. Gonna ask you again, and this time, just… run your mouth. Don't think, don't filter. Just tell me…Charlie, what do you want?"

I spoke before I had a chance to stop myself. "I want you to go down on me again," I blurted. "And I want you to be my first blowjob."

He inhaled sharply through his nose, and my eyes flew open. "I think I can handle that."

He was already climbing over me. I scrambled

further up the bed, to give his big body room. I worked with him, curling my legs toward my belly so he could fit between my thighs, and then let my heels rest on his back. I slid my fingers into his hair—this, I remembered, too. His hair in my hands. Coarse, thick.

He didn't dive right in like I expected. He took his time. Breathed on me, kissed the tenderest inner part of my thigh, an inch or two away from where my thigh met my hip, then over, just above my slit, to the other thigh. Teasing me. Huffing hot air on my sex. Then a finger dragged up through my slit, and I gasped. His fingers touched my clit, and I was struck by searing lightning. It coiled low in my belly, pushing through me, pulsing. His tongue found me, and I exploded, hips lifting already.

"God*damn*, woman. So fuckin' sensitive. So fast to come."

"Didn't—didn't know I *could* come more than once at a time."

"Yeah, you can. Twice last night—wanna make it three times?"

"Oh god, I might die," I whimpered.

He laughed, and then kissed my nether lips. "Maybe. Be a good way to die, though." Another kiss, to a different spot, lower.

"You're teasing me," I said. Glancing down at him I added, "I don't know whether to love it or hate it."

"Making you wait makes it more intense when you do come. It's all about the buildup."

"Then tease me till I can't take it anymore," I said, and wondered who that was speaking with my mouth. Saying such crazy things.

"Oooh, lady, you're askin' for it, now." I heard the grin in his voice. "You sure about that?"

I nodded. Toyed with his hair. "I wanna know."

"You asked for it."

And so began the most insane few minutes of my life, thus far. He would lick and lick, and just when I started to rise, to push against his mouth, he would slide a finger into me and stimulate me a different way, getting me closer that way all over again, and then when I started to really enjoy it, he would change again. Go back to using his mouth, but not the same way as before. Different rhythm, different feel of his tongue. Again, and again, I got close, and he would change.

It made me crazy.

The need to come was building to frantic intensity, and I was gasping, huffing, whimpering, lifting my hips, seeking the edge I needed.

Closer, and closer, each shift of technique bringing me nearer the edge than last time, with consummate skill. He knew my body, intimately, exquisitely, knew my reactions and could read them perfectly.

"How do you…oh fuck, how do you always know when I'm getting close?" I asked.

He waited to answer until his tongue circling my clit had me flexing, pushing against his mouth, and then he added two fingers and used those and his mouth together to make me ride the closest to the edge I'd been yet.

"You are the most responsive, sensitive woman I've ever known. I touch you, you gasp. Lick you, you flinch. Get you going, your hips start moving. Get you close, and you just start makin' these noises, the sexiest goddamn fuckin' noises I've ever heard. Get you close, and fuck, man, I'm *done*. So fuckin' hard it hurts. When you come, the noise you'll make, I may just come in my pants like a friggin' schoolboy."

I squeezed my eyes shut tighter. "I've always been self-conscious about the sounds I make."

"Don't. The noises you make are the most sensual music in the world."

And then mouth and fingers together, again, and I rode up to the edge, hips rocking, belly taut, breasts quivering. I flicked my eyes open, looked down my body, saw Crow, his wide deep dark eyes shining, smiling, eager, watchful. Eyes that knew me, wanted me, more of me, eyes that saw me, truly saw me in way I'd never felt seen before.

I was shaking all over, thrusting against him

nonstop now, and need was a wildfire inside me. Raging, demanding.

Silence was no longer an option.

"Crow…"

He pulled his mouth away enough to speak, but kept his fingers kept working. "Yeah, babe. Talk to me. Say anything."

"Need…I need to come."

"Yeah?" A swift hot lick. "Now?"

I pulled at his hair, drew him closer, thrust myself against him, wanton and greedy. "Yeah, now. Please, now."

Another lick, a circle. Fingers flying. Pumping in and out, driving. Maddening. Nearly enough, but not quite. "You wanna come?"

I curled forward, hooked my heels together around his neck and lifted. The only way to put it is that I fucked his mouth. "Yes, fuck, yes, I want to come, I want to come, Crow. Make me come. Please, fuck, please."

"Love when that sweet, innocent mouth gets dirty." He licked again, and sunburst heat flashed through me, and I knew I was close. So close. He could put me over the edge in an instant. "Would you do anything to come?"

"Yeah, god, Crow, yes, I'd do anything. Please." I rode his tongue, but he kept it light, teasing. "No more, I can't take it anymore. I'm so close, so fucking close. I need to come so bad it hurts."

A slow fat lick, hard against my clit. It felt divine, but it wasn't good enough. A slow circling of his pointed, firm tongue, but it wasn't enough. His fingers slicked wet in and out, making me ache for something bigger and harder and thicker and more *him*.

Nothing was enough.

"Not sure you want it bad enough."

I growled, so feral and rabid I didn't recognize myself. *"Crow!"* I squeezed my thighs around him. "I'll crack your head like a melon if you don't let me fucking come!"

He laughed, as if the feel of my thighs crushing around his face was the best thing ever. And he just kept going, slow and steady and maddening.

I was so frustrated, then, so wild with need, so crazed with the need to reach the edge that everything just broke inside me, and I started crying.

"Fucking let me come, please!" I whispered. "Please!"

He stopped, everything, all at once. Grinned up at me. *"Now* you're ready. Now you fuckin' *want* it."

And he thrashed me with his tongue, drove three fingers inside me in a fast hard rhythm, and I soared. Sky high, to outer space, past Mars. I flew, ecstasy a mad skyrocketing blush taking over my whole body, staining my soul with the flood of beauty. God, I flew.

Arching off the bed entirely, I pressed against him. Only my shoulders and head touched the bed, the rest of me was suspended, bridged upward, against his mouth. And he was taking me there, wild and fast and vigorous and unrelenting, and I felt a hoarse whispering escape my throat in a raw whistle.

I couldn't even scream.

Stars burst behind my eyes and inside me. My core exploded, and I was seized by lightning, like I'd stuck a fork in an outlet. My heels scrabbled at his back, and his stubble roughened my tender inner thighs, and his tongue drove me to utter madness.

How long?

I have no way of knowing how long that orgasm lasted. It destroyed the concept of time within me, leaving me shaking. Trembling helplessly, boneless.

After a time, I was able to open my eyes.

A while later, I could start to move.

Crow had his chin propped up on his hands, still laying awkwardly between my legs. Gazing up at me with an expression of complicated emotions I dare not try to parse.

"Hey there," he muttered, smirking. "Back with me?"

"Yeah." I blinked. "I think."

His grin was pleased. "You, Charlie. You're...so fuckin' incredible. Watching you come, making you come, god*damn* if ain't the most amazing thing I've ever gotten to experience."

"Did...did I pass out?"

He nodded. "For a couple minutes, yeah."

"Wow." I laughed, a soft breath. "Didn't know that was a real thing. Just thought it was for fiction."

"Guess not." He crawled up over me, lay beside me. "So. Hungry?"

I nodded. "Starved."

He tugged his zipper up, not without difficulty, however. "I'll rustle us up something while you get dressed."

I grabbed his wrist. "That was only half of what I wanted."

He stilled. "Charlie, you—"

"So far, I'm the only who's gotten anything."

He shook his head. "Ain't in this to *get* anything, Charlie. I just can't help but want to do things to you. Got a woman like you, classy and smart and beautiful as all hell, and you want to let me make you feel good? Well, shit. I'd be a fool to pass that up."

I looked at his groin—he was about to break the zipper, he was swollen so hard. "Crow. You asked me what I wanted, and I told you. It was the honest truth of what I wanted." I was less sure I had the courage to do this, but god, I wanted to try.

Him making me feel good in all new ways was incredible.

What else could I enjoy? What else was there which I'd never experienced? Making him feel things? Touching him? Exploring this body?

Yes, please.

I grabbed his wrist, pulling it away from his crotch. I turned onto my side and braced on one elbow. Unzipped his black jeans. Hooked two fingers in each belt loop on either side of the fly and tugged down. He lifted his butt, and the jeans came off inside out. He kicked them off, left them tangled at the other end of the bunk. His cock was outlined fully by the tight stretchy fabric, and it was...monstrous. A quarter inch of the tip was poking out the top, pink and leaking clear fluid.

I curled my fingers in the elastic on either side of his cock, feeling it brush the outside of my fingers, and pulled down. Another lift of his hips, and he was kicking those off, too, and ohhh shit, oh shit, oh shit.

What in the world had I gotten myself into? His cock was...

Beyond any scope of comparison. Seeing it outlined in the underwear hadn't done it justice. So long, so thick. Straight as an arrow, lying flat against his belly, the tip at his navel.

I just looked. "Oh...my...god." I turned to stare into his eyes.

He just gazed back levelly. "Whatever you want, Charlie. Everything or nothing at all."

"It's..." I bit my lip. Grinned helplessly. "Crow, your penis is colossal."

He laughed. "You know how to make a man feel good about himself, Charlie-girl."

I reached out, because I had to touch him. Had to feel him, to know how he would fit in my fist. Soft delicate heat, skin stretched thin against his shaft, the veins blue-purple. I wrapped my fingers around him and he flinched, his cock twitching. I glanced at his face, and he had his eyes closed, but flicked them open in that moment, to watch my hand on him. A single slow stroke downward, my fist stuttering lightly over his veins. My mouth was dry, my tongue sticking to the roof of my mouth, heart pounding—I was doing this. Touching this man. Simply letting go and allowing him to go down on me was one thing—that felt like an out-of-body experience. Passive, in a way, *allowing* something to happen to me...something delicious, incredible, every fantasy I'd ever had come true. But still, a passive event.

This was something I was *doing*.

Very, very different. In my sex-starved little brain, at least. I mean, it had been months since I'd had sex, and even flying solo, my Os had been lackluster at best, because apparently I lack any kind of imagination. I had even tried porn a few times, but everything just seemed so stupid and contrived and silly—and I sampled a little of everything. Plain fucking? Gross, who wants to watch fifteen minutes of ultra-close-ups of a giant hairless penis entering a surgically enhanced hairless vagina—both disembodied? Not me. Um, how about the more "female-oriented" stuff? Still just an actor and an actress pretending. Not as many extended closeups of body parts entering body parts, but it just didn't turn me on, watching two people have sex. Oral scenes? A little better. I had no experience with giving BJs, so that didn't do anything for me, and I also just had this feeling giving a blowjob was for *him,* not me, and that I would find it fun to watch him enjoy it, but that I wouldn't personally get much out of it. The only thing that ever really got me going even a little was videos of girls getting eaten out.

Because god, I wanted that.

Just for a man to want me enough, to care about me enough, to put me first long enough to just give me pleasure.

It was that fantasy which got me going, not the

contrived sounds and elaborate displays of position, all the arching and writhing and screaming.

Now, having experienced Crow's oral skills, I realized that maybe, just maybe, some of that wasn't entirely contrived.

"Charlie?" Crow's low, amused voice.

I started. Realized I'd stopped, just holding his cock in one hand, and had been spacing out.

I grinned sheepishly. "Sorry."

He just chuckled. "You really get lost in your head, don't you?"

I nodded. "Yeah, I do. I've turned overthinking into its purest art form."

"Just be here, now." He snagged my wrist. "And don't do anything you don't want to."

I sighed. "I *do* want to," I said. "That's the thing. I really want to...try new stuff. And you're...I guess you seem like a safe person to try it with. But...I'm just fighting a lot of...mental conditioning, I guess."

"Maybe instead of getting lost in your head, you just talk it out?" He pulled my hand away from his member.

I shook my head. "It wouldn't be sexy to hear me going on and on, like some sort of messed up hormonal female version of *Ulysses*."

He snorted. "Not sure what that means, but you'd be surprised what would be interesting to me."

"Interior monologue. *Ulysses* is a novel by James Joyce, who more or less invented the idea of what he called stream of consciousness, where the narration of the story is the interior monologue of a person."

"Sounds boring."

"It's not boring, per se, but hard to follow, if nothing else. It's a book a lot of people like to say they've read to sound more erudite than they really are."

He caressed my back, fingers tickling and tracing, following the angle of my extended shoulder blade, the curve of my spine. "Well, this ain't James Joyce, and I am interested in hearing what's going on in your head." He gathered a handful of my hair, running it through his fingers. "You don't have to be doin' nothin' to me, either."

I bit my lip, tracing his rugged, brutally handsome features with my eyes. "Crow, I know I don't make any sense. But I do want to touch you. I want to…" I swallowed. "I don't how to put it."

"However it occurs in your head, babe. No filter, don't worry about sounding cool or shit. Just say it like it is."

I felt his eyes pulling me in, deep dark wells of intelligence and kindness and complexity and desire and a million things I couldn't even begin listing. I let myself fall into his eyes, let my mouth run, just let the words tumble out unbidden, unfiltered, raw and weird and maybe incomprehensible.

"I just...I've always done the right thing. The good thing. My mom has a super strong moral compass—we're not really a religious or spiritual family, but my mom was always like super into being the best version of yourself. Doing the right thing, always, no matter what. *Being* good. *Doing* good. Sounding articulate and intelligent and sophisticated and cultured and proper. No swearing, no crude jokes, don't use fillers like 'um' or 'like' or whatever. I'm the oldest, so I got it the worst, so to speak. She was the strictest with me. Had the highest expectations for me. So I was always the absolute paragon of virtue, morality, rightness, and achievement."

I stared into his eyes, relaxing my tension, letting the whole dumb story fall out, because for some bizarre reason he was *listening*. As if he cared. As if I was the only thing in this world worth looking at, worth listening to, and it was genuine and it just drew words out of me like a clown pulling on a trick silk tie.

I let my fingers dance on his firm skin, over his belly, on his thighs. Just touching *him*, not sexually, just...male skin, reassuringly real and warm. He didn't move, didn't stop me or urge me anywhere, just kept his own hands busily moving on me, tracing continually from shoulder to spine, hip to side to clavicle, never touching me sexually, just...*touching* me as I was touching him. So weird, to be this comfortable with a near-perfect stranger. I didn't dare examine that too closely—just went with it.

I kept talking, my voice pitched low. "I never cut loose. Never partied with my friends. I stayed home and did homework, helped Mom at home. Watched my younger sisters, did chores. Book reports, just for myself, for fun. Boring, nerdy, ridiculous nonsense. I had friends, and we'd go to the mall together or hang out and do each other's nails or hair, girl stuff. But I didn't drink, didn't smoke, didn't sneak out. Never had a boyfriend in high school. I kissed Scott Pruitt under the bleachers during a football game my sophomore year. Kissed Al Crenshaw in the limo on the way home from senior prom. He wanted to go further, tried to cop a feel, but I wasn't having any of that and told him so. I just...I couldn't have messed around with him and then faced Mom. She'd have known, and would have disapproved. Even though I know now that she wouldn't have disapproved as long as I was in control of myself and the situation and wasn't being pressured into anything, especially senior year, it was this ingrained idea that I had to be perfect, and messy physical relationships felt imperfect to me. Letting a boy touch my boobs felt wrong. Letting him touch my privates felt wrong.

Me touching him? Even more wrong. Dirty. Nope—
not happening."

"Wow. Mom was a powerful influence for you,
huh?"

I nodded. "Yeah. No kidding."

"So then you get to college…" he prompted.

I sighed, grinned a little. "Yeah, then I got to college. Straight As, with extra GPA points and a ton of
college credits by graduation from taking a bunch of
courses at the community college on a transfer pro-
gram through my high school. Nearly perfect SAT
and ACT scores, accepted to pretty much any college
I wanted. I even got an offer from Cambridge."

"Like, the one in England?"

I laughed. "The only one, yeah."

"And you didn't take it?"

I grimaced. "Yeah, no. I should've. But it was too
scary, moving that far from Mom. So, I chose Yale.
It was a toss-up between Yale, Harvard, and Brown,
but Yale just sounded…I don't know. Cooler, to me.
Probably pretty shallow and stupid reason. But it's
where I went, and I met Glen the first day during orientation. We sat together during the initial meeting,
and stayed together for the whole tour, hung out af-
terwards, and never really separated." I swallowed.
"We dated for six months before I worked up the
courage to let him kiss me. Another month before

I felt confident enough being away from Mom and making my own decisions to let things progress. Poor guy was very patient with me, I have to give him that much. It took nearly a full year of dating before we had actual sex. A lot of messing around, and me getting used to that. Just kissing and stuff. All the stuff I think most people do in high school, I was doing in college. He never rushed me or pressured me."

"Good for him, for that much at least."

"But he was also not…" I sighed, not sure how to put it. "Excited, I guess. By me. By us."

He stared at me, eyes narrowed. "You're filtering."

I groaned. "Yeah. So, it's weird to say these things out loud, but…he clearly was aroused by me, because when we started kissing he'd get an erection. And… before we had sex, yeah, I…you know. We did things with our hands."

"Just fuckin' say it, Charlie. We're not kids, here. Not gonna be weird for me to hear you tell me you jerked off your college boyfriend."

I blushed. "Yeah, well, there you go. I jerked him off." I laughed. "A lot, actually. He, um. He would never… do anything. He wouldn't make a lot of noises or move, he'd just sit there and watch, maybe his butt would clench a little as he got close, flexing a little. A sigh as he…you know. Came. And that was it. Clean up, and we were done."

"And then he'd return the favor, right?"

I shrugged. "Not usually. He'd touch me, a little. But he wasn't...um...good at knowing how to tell what I liked."

He frowned. "Was he fuckin' blind? Reading your body is like reading a large-print book."

I laughed, but it was a little bitter. "So, he'd...he'd start, but I'd get impatient and take over, and he'd just watch me finish myself. And for quite a few months, that was our sex life. Me jerking him off, him watching me masturbate, essentially."

"Wow. That's...shockingly shitty, babe."

"I guess so. It was all I knew, and I got frustrated sometimes, but I thought that's just how things were, and he was nice to me, and easy to talk to. Our relationship was...cerebral. We could talk about heady, sophisticated things. Philosophy, politics, economics, literature. He was smarter than me in a lot of ways, and I felt mentally challenged by him."

Crow smirked. "Ain't gonna get conversation like that with me, I'm afraid. I ain't even got a fuckin' GED."

I frowned. "Crow, you may not have a lot of formal education, but I think you are one of the smartest people I've ever met."

"How the fuck can you tell that?"

"It's obvious. Intelligence shines out of a person's

eyes, and your eyes just...*burn* with intelligence. You can read people, you understand situations." I pointed at his bookshelf. "You read widely, and a lot. You're curious, I can tell. So, sure, perhaps you've never read *Ulysses* or Kafka or—or Hemingway, or whoever. But that's just exposure. Anyone can read a book. Being curious isn't something you can teach."

He frowned, and his eyes left mine, thoughtful, following my curves, pausing at my breasts, continuing to my hips. He spoke without looking at my eyes. "Thank you for that, Charlie."

"Hey, I'm just callin' 'em like I sees 'em," I drawled.

He laughed. "Anyway. You and Glen."

I shrugged, and traced my fingers from his shoulder over his pec, dimpling the hard muscle, down to his abs sheathed a layer of what I would just call the insulation of a life lived. He was still mostly erect, but fading.

I didn't want that to happen.

I wanted to touch him. I felt my brain going into overthink mode—thinking of all the times I'd done it to Glen, how I'd tried different things to get a reaction from him, and never could, which made me feel like I wasn't doing it right. I gnawed on the inside of my cheek, pulling myself out of my head.

I wrapped two fingers around the head of his cock, and immediately felt it begin hardening again.

I kept talking, because if I was talking, I wasn't thinking. "Me and Glen. Sex was what you would imagine. Vanilla missionary, and nothing but. I told you this."

"And you left wanting more often than not."

"Right." I slid my finger and thumb down his length. He inhaled slowly, deeply, his forehead tightening. Feeling it. Responding. "Then I found him in our bed with my boss—twenty-six years his senior, overweight and unattractive and not even a nice person."

"Wow."

I winced. "That's not kind, I suppose. I shouldn't be mean."

"I'd say you're allowed to feel a little less than charitable toward her. And him."

"I suppose. Point is, that was it. I just...upended my life. Moved into a month-to-month furnished rental for super cheap in a not great part of town, lived on my savings, drank during the day and watched Netflix and gained an extra ten pounds, because without my schedule, I had no motivation to work out or shop for healthy food."

"Good for you."

I blinked. "What? No, not good for me."

"Yes, good for you. That's called being selfish. And after the way you lived, I'm guessing being as much a mom to that shiteater boyfriend of yours as a girlfriend or lover, and probably going above and beyond at work, and being a good daughter and a good sister and voting in all the local elections and helping the poor…you needed to be a little selfish."

I frowned. "I…" I laughed. "I worked overtime and only occasionally got the time-and-a-half I deserved. Volunteered at a soup kitchen once a week, and counted ballots during elections."

"See?"

I chuckled. "It's like you know me." I didn't quite look at him as I said that, focusing instead on the feel of him in my hand. The thick hard girth, the seemingly endless length. The way the fat round head seemed to strain as I caressed him, my whole fist wrapped around him.

"I wanted more," I whispered. "I would fantasize about…about what you did for me. Someone going down on me, just…just to make me feel good. I fantasized about…" the whisper became nearly inaudible. "About just being…desired. Seven years with Glen, and I never did, not really. He would want sex regularly, and we really did have a lot of it, but it was quick and not satisfying for me. It took a lot of introspection during my selfish time in that shitty apartment to come to grips with exactly how unsatisfying my sex life with him had been. And I'm still coming to grips with…myself, I guess. With letting myself really open up to…to who I am. To what I want. Because I think…" I paused to put this into the right words, no longer whispering. "I think I kept the true depths of my real…needs, and desires, sexually, physically, and even emotionally, under wraps. Repressed. Because I didn't think I could get more than what I had. That Glen was all there was. He fit my plan for my life and, more than anything else, I've defined myself as a person who follows my plans through to the end, no matter what. Move to Boston. Work my way up at the firm. Partner by thirty-five at the latest. Get my masters, maybe a PhD and lecture at a university. There would be kids and a two-story brick Colonial in an upscale Boston or New York suburb, and we would have sex every Saturday or Sunday, and then kids and life would get in the way and I'd probably just stop wanting it. That was…that was what I assumed would happen."

He shook his head. "Wow. You had that planned out to the last detail."

"I had kid's names picked out, boys and girls. Interior designs chosen. Dog's names. I knew the kind of curtains and fine china and silverware and linens I wanted in my formal dining room."

"Jesus, babe, what about, like, spontaneity?"

I snorted. "What's that? This road trip, getting

drunk, ending up with you, this is the most sponta-
neous thing I've ever done in my life. And it feels so,
so reckless."

He laughed. "I'll have to show you real deal reckless spontaneity. That'll open you up."

All the while, my one hand, loosely curled around
him, was sliding up and down. Lazily, almost, and he
was seemingly capable of ignoring it. But I saw the
corners of his eyes tightening, his jaw ticking.

I wanted to see more of his reactions. See him…a
little wild.

I closed my fist around him, gripping him.
Twisted my fist. Plunged it downward, fast. He sucked
in a breath, and his abs tensed. I watched his eyes, his
body—I loosened my touch and caressed him in slow
measured gentle movements, and his jaw fell open,
and his eyes went glassy. Yeah, he liked that. More
than the hard fast stuff, he liked the slow and gentle.

So I stayed with slow and gentle. I rubbed the
pad of my thumb over his tip, and he stopped breathing for a moment. Gave each upward stroke a twist
around his girth, and then at the top, shallow twisting
half-strokes, until he started flexing his hips.

"Fuck, Charlie. You have any fuckin' clue how
good that feels?" He snarled.

"Tell me," I whispered. "I want to know what
you like, what you want."

"You wanna know what I want?"

As I nodded I plunged my fist down to his root and squeezed at the base, and pumped him. "I really do."

He closed his eyes a moment, his breathing going deep and rapid. Eyes opened, focused on my hand, his cock. "I want your mouth, Charlie. I want to see those pink lips around my dick. Want to feel your tongue. Want you to fuckin'—to lick it. Want you to make my cock all sloppy wet with your spit and…shit, woman. I shouldn't say this, but I'm gonna. I ought to want to be inside you more than anything, and I fuckin' do, so bad. I want to sit you on top of me and watch you bounce on my cock until you scream. But right now, Charlie, all I want is to come all down your pretty fuckin' throat. Knowing you never done that before? Feel fuckin' dirty for this, but I wanna be the first."

I felt fire in my lungs, a burn in my sex. A flutter in my gut. I slid down, so I was lying mostly on his legs. My face near his cock, the huge thick thing bobbing with his rapid breath. Comfortable with it in my hand was one thing, but putting it in my mouth was another. I'd considered it any number of times over the years with Glen, but never had the courage to try.

Did I have the courage, now?

It felt like there was a mental block, a part of me telling me I shouldn't. That I wouldn't like it.

That *he* wouldn't. That I'd do it wrong.

I pulled his hot, silky-soft yet iron-hard cock away from his body. His stomach was pulled in, his eyes watching me. I could see him thinking, wanting to tell me to not do anything I didn't want to.

"Don't say a word," I said. "I want to, I just have to get over my mental block."

"Whatever you want, babe."

"I…" I touched the tip of it to my bottom lip. Soft, so soft. Tender. Springy. I licked my lips and tasted skin. "I just…I need…"

"What, Charlie? Tell me."

"I want to know what you're thinking. How it feels. If I'm…" I swallowed, feeling stupid for saying this. "If I'm doing it okay."

He chortled. "You can't get it wrong as long as you don't bite me, honey."

"I won't bite," I said, giggling a laugh. "Is it stupid I'm so nervous? That I'm so insecure about this?"

He shook his head. "No, not at all. Nothing stupid about it."

I drew the tip through my lips, and then again, and then a third time. I let my tongue touch him and tasted skin and something salty and liquid. He sucked in a breath.

"Fuckin' killing me, girl," Crow snarled.

"What?"

"Teasing me." He grinned. "It's good. No hurry, no worries. It's just...beautiful fuckin' torture, that's all."

"I'm not trying to tease you. Just...working up the courage to put my whole mouth on you."

Growing up on the East Coast, we'd had oysters a lot, and the flavor of his cock, his pre-cum, tasted a bit like oysters. Not unpleasantly, as a matter of fact. I ran my tongue over the tip again, and he flinched, bodily, groaning. Salty liquid smeared on my tongue, and I grinned at him.

"I like how you taste."

"Feeling is mutual, I fuckin' promise you." His eyes met mine, hot and boiling with barely restrained need. "You taste like sugar. Can't want to get my mouth on your sweet fuckin' pussy again."

I stroked him, root to tip, and then held him upright again, and drew a deep breath, parted my lips... tasted pre-cum, and then flesh, and then his tip was sliding along my tongue and I pressed my lips around him and he was in my mouth and I was swallowing hard, because he was huge and thick and holy shit, any more and my jaw might crack, but he was groaning and his hips were pushing up and his eyes were crossed and rolling back in his head, and that was reason to keep going.

I pulled away, a string of my spit connecting my mouth and his cock.

"Fuck, Charlie." He met my eyes, swallowing hard. "You are making it so damn hard to not just blow my load right now—"

I palmed his heavy balls, cradled them, caressed them, and he sucked in a breath. Fisted his length with the other hand, and stroked his cock and caressed his balls, and then added my mouth and did all three at once, and he went from speaking to just wordless gasping breathless wondering groans of pure bliss.

"Oh shit, oh shit, Charlie, god, you're fuckin'— so fuckin' good. So, so fucking amazing, what you're doing." He reached down and touched my hair, gathered it in his fists, held it, the long shimmery mass of black. "Fuckin'—god, oh god, oh *shit.*"

Tasted him, salt and skin, and felt his belly tightening, felt him twitching, his cock jerking, his balls pulsing.

And then, right then, as I knew he was nearing the edge, there was a jerk. Not from him, but from the bus.

I'd forgotten we were on a bus.

"Fuck—no, no, no, not now," Crow snarled. "Goddammit, not now."

"What is it?" I asked.

"Shit—I think we just blew a motherfucking tire." He thumped his head backward. "Goddamn it, I was *so* fucking close."

"So close. I could probably…" I went back down, put my mouth on him.

A voice shouted from somewhere near the front. "Myles! Crow! Major problem."

He caressed my face. "Gonna have to pick this up later."

I felt…disappointed. Achy. "This sucks."

He hissed, gently pulling away from me. "You got no fuckin' clue, babe. Gonna hurt all fuckin' day."

"I'm sorry. I shouldn't have taken so long."

He cupped my cheek. "Nope, don't take this on yourself. It's just shit luck. I'll be fine." He lay still, closed his eyes. Focused. He somehow ran through some sort of mental gymnastics, and I watched as his cock slowly subsided.

"Crow!" I heard the voice yell again.

"Coming!" he shouted. "Or not," he muttered. "Gimme five fuckin' seconds, dammit."

I handed him his jeans and underwear, and he wriggled into them. Tugged the blanket up over me, covering me, and then yanked the curtain aside and slid out, fastening his fly and tugging on his cut over his naked torso as he moved barefoot and messy haired and beautiful toward the front of the bus.

"The fuck is the problem?" I heard him snarl, audibly pissed off.

Poor man. He'd been *so* close. I still tasted him.

I was lying there, thinking of him. Of how he'd tasted and felt. How much I'd loved his reactions, his snarled, desperate, blissed-out words. The feel of... of *control*.

A body flopped into the bunk, and I smelled Lexie—perfume and old alcohol, and...sex. "Hi."

I twisted to see my sister, her hair absolutely wild. Eye makeup smeared—it looked like she'd been crying. But her eyes were bright and happy— wild with crazed joy, if anything.

"Hi," I responded.

She snatched the blanket up and peeked underneath. "You fucked him!"

I yanked it back. "I did not!" I grinned, then. "Well, sort of. Almost."

She frowned. "Almost? How do you *almost* fuck?"

"It's complicated." I bit my lip, stifling a huge grin. "His beard stubble? Scratchy and soft against my thighs, just like you said it would be. I'm still a little tender, actually."

She squealed, wriggled close, excitement so extreme and bubbly she couldn't contain it. "He went down on you?"

I couldn't help my own excitement from bubbling over into girly squeals of hilarity and excitement. "Three times!"

She was wearing an old black faded Johnny Cash T-shirt with the sleeves cut off—huge on her, and obviously Myles's, and obviously was not wearing a scrap of anything else under it. "Tell me everything. Every. Single. Detail."

EIGHT

Crow

GODDAMN TORTURE, IS WHAT IT WAS. ABSOLUTE AGONY. Damned cock would not go down, not all the way. I've heard of blue balls before, and I've felt the tense ache of needing to get my rocks off in a bad way, but this? This was pure hell. My poor balls fuckin' *throbbed*, and not in a sexy way. In an "every move was raw brutal agony because they're so hypersensitive and tender" sort of way. My cock stayed semirigid in my jeans, and no matter how I focused on other shit, I just could fucking not make it go all the way down.

Even thoughts of Sister Maria didn't help.

Mainly because Charlie's image was superimposed over everything I looked at.

The bus had blown a front tire, which was bad news especially since we were stuck on the side of the highway in the middle of nowhere, probably several hours from Denver. We could have hobbled along if it had been a back tire, but a front tire was bad, bad news. It meant hours of delay as we waited for a maintenance team to arrive and repair it, because a giant RV like that required specialized tools and training to repair.

Which meant, if we wanted to make our show in Denver, we had to transfer whatever personal shit we needed off the bus, wait for the limos our manager Barnett had called in, and book it for Denver, and hope to fuck the rest of the crew and equipment made it there without further issue.

What time was it? Daylight, but not past noon. My phone was on the bus, and I didn't wear a watch. But growing up with only the sun to tell time most days, I knew it had to be somewhere between midmorning and near noon.

During the transition of stuff and deciding what to do, Charlie had come out of the bus with Lexie in tow, and they were giggling and chatting and damn if they didn't look alike, and sexy as hell. Lexie was wearing one of Myles's workout cutoff shirts and, if I wasn't mistaken, not a lot else. Confident in her skin, that one. Charlie was back in her clothes, black leggings and black V-neck T-shirt, and an open button down over it, unbuttoned. No bra. Perky tits pressed hard against the tight fabric, especially when she stretched languorously in the sunshine, arms overhead, shirt hem lifting to show her belly button.

Now why the *fuck* did my heart go pitter-patter at that fuckin' belly button? Who the hell has a belly button fetish? Not me. Yet the way she stretched, arching her spine inward, thrusting her breasts skyward, arms windmilling to meet palm-to-palm overhead, face turned to the sun...shirt lifting until the bottom swell of her breasts peeked out under the shirt and her belly button seemed to wink at me...Fuck, fuck. My heart thundered at the sight of her. I wanted to lick and kiss every inch of her skin, rub my beard all over her until her skin was pink.

Paint her with my sweat.

Mark her tits with my cum.

Bury myself in her mouth.

Pick her up and set her on my cock and fuck her till she screamed, till she passed out, and then wake her up with the smallest quietest tenderest kisses I could manage, and make love her to slowly and endlessly and softly.

"Gonna club her over the head and drag her to your cave, my man?" Myles muttered.

I came awake, out of my erotic reverie. Shook my head. Glanced at my best friend. "Huh?"

He chuckled. "I asked if you were gonna club her over the head and drag her to your cave." Another glance, this one at the front of my jeans. "And, by the looks of that poor zipper...put, like, eight babies inside her."

"That's not how babies work, you idiot," I grumbled, retorting on autopilot.

"Oh, so you *are* planning on doing the caveman thing?"

He was still in his leather pants—or in them again—but shirtless and barefoot and wearing mirrored Oakleys, his short brown hair wildly mussed, as if certain fingers had yanked on it a whole lot last night. He was wearing the arrowhead necklace my mammy had made him that summer when we were kids and he was kicking it with me and River Dog and Mammy. Layered over that was a braided hemp necklace faded from having never been taken off, along with a woven plain black leather necklace also faded and worn. He had a small silver St. Christopher medallion on a silver chain, and a black-and-blue bandana folded and tied around his throat. He was every inch a rock star, the stupid beautiful fuck.

"No, I'm not clubbing her over the head," I said, chuckling.

He eyed me. "She as sweet and innocent as she seems?"

I laughed. "Wouldn't you like to know?"

He rubbed the back of his neck. "Nah, that one's all you." His eyes followed Lexie as she played Hackey Sack with Zan who was, at his core, just a happy little granola stoner. And, yeah, wearing nothing but a cut-off T-shirt, Lexie athletically and vigorously playing Hackey Sack was…quite a sight. "Brother, that girl is…" He shook his head, a rough breath gusting out of him. "Didn't figure there was a woman on the planet could keep up with me, but Lexie? Shit, man. She can damn near outdrink me, out-curse me, and out-fuck me. I've tangled with some wildcats in my day, as you know. But Lexie is…" He blew a disbelieving raspberry, head shaking again. "That girl is a motherfuckin' *hurricane*, man."

I laughed. "Sounds like you got a tiger by the tail."

He stretched, scratching his chest. "No kidding. Literally—she's all teeth and tits and claws, man." He showed me his back—scratches raked down his spine and bite marks adorned his shoulders.

I shook my head, laughing. "Damn, dude."

He eyed me, then Charlie, then me again. "What?"

I frowned. "What, what?"

He indicated Charlie with a jerk of his chin. "You're looking at her weird. Like, intense. Like if you take your eyes off her, she might vanish into a puff of smoke."

I sighed. "She's just...she's complex, man." I shook my head, not taking my eyes off Charlie as she laughed, leaning against the side of the bus, watching her sister play like a schoolgirl. "Not at all what she seems. I mean, she is, in some ways, but a whole hell of a lot more."

He nodded. "Lex too. I was figuring this would be like what it usually is. Drop her off at the next stop and get her a plane ride back home, see ya, had fun. But dude, she's...different. For as wild as she is in the sack, she's...fuckin' smart, man." He rubbed his scalp again. "You know how I grew up, shit, you were with me for most of it. Neither of us got a lot of real schooling, you know? I ain't dumb, you ain't dumb, but those girls, man? They're fuckin', like, next level smart. Educated, articulate, and..."

"Sophisticated."

He stabbed a finger in the air at me. "That's the word. Lexie has this outward persona, this, like, thin layer of acting like a foul-mouthed wild child who doesn't give a shit, does what she wants. It's not fake; it's all her, all real. But there's a whole hell of a lot more."

I eyed him skeptically. "Wait, you did more than just bone?"

He made a baffled, shocked face, scrubbing his cheeks with both hands as if to wake up. "Would you believe we spent more time just talking than we did anything else? Legit, you are the only other person I've ever talked to that much all at once, ever."

I gaped at him. "What? You *never* want to talk to your conquests, Myles."

He frowned. "No woman is a conquest, Crow. I ain't like that. They're people. I respect them. I may only be interested in having sex, and casual sex at that, but that don't mean I think of the women I'm with as…as…as bags of meat, or fuckin' *conquests*."

I frowned harder. "Shit, man, I was joking, mostly."

"I know. Sorry. But Lexie especially ain't a conquest. She's not like that. Not for me."

I ran my hand through my hair. "Well…shit. Okay."

He pushed a pebble around the asphalt with his big toe. "What?"

"Just…I think you *like* her."

"No shit, man." He glanced at her. "The fuck am I supposed to do?"

I shrugged. "Hell if I know."

He swallowed hard. "Remember back when we first started touring? That old church van, just me and an amp and some guitars? You setting up, running sound, lights, doing everything but play the guitar and sing for me?"

I nodded. "Some good times, brother. Of course I remember. Why?"

"You remember when we ran out of money and got stuck in Des Moines?"

I nodded again. "Yeah, sure. You started hanging out with that group of scary-ass carnies."

He sighed, a long nasal out-breath. "Yeah. Well, I never told you, but I got hooked on coke, hanging out with them."

I glanced at him sideways. "Think I didn't know? Why do you think I never went with you?"

He nodded. Eyed the ground. "Figures you knew."

"You are about the only family I've ever had, Myles. Everyone else is dead." I clapped him on the shoulder. "What's this got to do with liking Lexie?"

He pawed his hair aggressively, making it stand up on end—and even that made him look even more like the wild rock star. "I tried, and I knew from the first fuckin' hit that I was in deep, deep trouble. It was so good, and so, so bad. It scared me absolutely stupid. Like, I just knew in my fuckin' soul that this shit would kill me real goddamn fast, because I liked it way, way too much. I couldn't quit, though. Not after the first hit. Had to have that feeling again."

I growled. "Scariest couple weeks of my life, in some ways, watching you go through that and knowing I couldn't do shit to stop you." I bumped him with my shoulder. "We left Des Moines and I'm pretty fuckin' sure you haven't touched that shit since."

He nodded. "Me and the carnies, we were sitting around in this half-assembled tilt-a-whirl, drinking Everclear and bumping lines."

I winced. "Jesus, dude."

"I don't know what happened. That shit doesn't make you hallucinate, but I swear, I saw myself die. I was laying in this half-built tilt-a-whirl, staring up at the sky, watching it spin and I saw myself laying on the floor of a hotel room, dying, coked out. I fuckin' *saw* that shit, real as you're next to me right now." A long pause. "I got up, staggered back to our van, and vowed I'd never touch anything harder than booze as long as I live."

"Again, what's the connection, man?"

He stared at Lexie, unblinking, his gaze on her exactly the way he'd said mine was—intense, as if she'd vanish if he blinked. "Lexie makes me feel like that. Scared, because I feel so fuckin'...*high* when I'm with her. Like I could lasso the moon and haul it down for her. But it's...it's got the feel of an addiction. Like..." He turned to me, and I knew the only reason he was saying this out loud was because I knew him better than anyone alive ever could, because we'd saved each other's lives and seen each other at the absolute worst, and best. "Like, if I'm not careful, I'm gonna end up fuckin' *needing* that chick in my life like I need to breathe, and I am scared abso-fuckin-lutely spitless by it. And all this from, what, less'n twelve hours of sex and talking? What the hell, man? How does this happen?"

"Didn't think anything like that was possible, but it is, I guess." I said this quietly, because his words were resonating in me. Hard.

"You too?"

I nodded. "Different, but yeah. That shit is going on under the surface, for me. Like, I feel it, but it's too hard to let it out."

"Well, my emotions run on the surface. You keep yours way down deep."

I nodded. Stretched, kicked. "Don't know what to do with it, honestly."

He laughed. "What can we do? Roll with it, and see where it goes."

I eyed the back of the bus—my bike was on a trailer behind the bus, tied off and covered. "I think I need to ride."

He nodded. "Figured you would." A glance at Charlie. "Alone?"

I shrugged. "Not if I can help it. Not sure if she'll go for riding a bike, though. We'll see."

Charlie and Lexie were in the lounge of the bus, watching Jupiter make a stupid amount of scrambled eggs and bacon. By stupid amount, I meant two dozen eggs and at least three pounds of bacon.

Jupiter: six-five, former professional bodybuilder, with a blond mohawk pulled back into a ponytail, and ice-blue eyes. His body resembled a G.I. Joe action figure turned real—he wasn't on the show circuit anymore, but staying huge and lean was a way of life for him, so he was only a little less perfectly built than he would be if he were to go back on the circuit.

He glanced at me as I slid into the booth next to Charlie. "Yo, Crow. What up, bro?"

I sighed. "You always have to rhyme everything with my name, Jupe?"

He snickered. "Can't help it. Must be a poet, just don't know it."

"The 'roids must've gone to your head."

He flipped me off with both hands, one of which was holding a spatula, the other a pair of tongs. "Fuck you. You know damn well I was natty."

I just laughed. "Yeah, yeah." I glanced at Charlie. "He feeding you, too, or just his own fat ass?"

Charlie arched an eyebrow. "Fat ass? I don't think he has a single molecule of unnecessary fat on his whole body. I've got more body fat in one thigh than he has everywhere on his body."

Jupiter blew a raspberry. "I'm at eleven percent right now. That's a lot, for me. I used to cut down to five percent or under when I was showing." He eyed her as he flipped bacon. "Don't take this the wrong way cuz I know you're with my boy Crow, but what you are is soft in all the right places, and not a single thing more, so cut that shit about fat thighs."

She blushed, shifted in the booth. "Uh, thanks."

"You know what they say, right, Charlie?" Lexie asked, her tone mischievous.

I sighed. "No, Lex, what do they say?"

"Thick thighs save lives."

She snorted. "Nice." I arched an eyebrow at her. "So you *are* saying I have thick thighs."

"Yep, and that it's a good thing." She glanced at me. "Right, Crow?"

I smirked at Charlie. "Um. I mean. I'm partial to thick thighs, so yeah, I agree."

Charlie just blushed, bless her.

Jupiter shut off the heat, pulled out plates, and divvied up the food onto three plates, then eyed me. "Some for you?"

I nodded. "Sure. Thanks."

We ate in companionable silence, and eventually I broached the subject on my mind. "So, the limos won't be here for another hour, and the repair guys for an hour after that. I'm gettin' antsy." I met Charlie's eyes. "How you feel about riding with me?"

She tilted her head. "Ride with you where, on what?"

"On my bike."

Her eyes widened. "On a motorcycle?"

I nodded. "Yep. We'd just head on to Denver."

She swallowed hard. "I, um. Isn't it dangerous?"

I smiled. "I mean, it can be. But I ain't reckless. Been riding since I could fit onto a dirt bike. You'll be safe as houses with me, darlin'."

Jupiter shoveled eggs into his mouth. "Don't let him fool you. He has literally lived most of his life on the back of a motorcycle. Personally I'd trust my old grammy on a bike with him, and I love my grammy somethin' fierce."

I grinned at him. "Why, thanks, Jupe. Means a lot comin' from you."

She eyed Lexie, who just shrugged, but it was a grinning shrug. "You do you, boo," Lexie said. "But if it were me, I'd be all over that shit like white on rice."

I could see she was trying to contain her excitement. "Then, yes." Her eyes actually, literally fuckin' sparkled. "Do I need anything?"

"Purse. I've got an extra leather and helmet you can wear."

She eyed me. "I need a leather jacket?"

I nodded. "Yep. Preferably tight jeans or leather pants, but since you ain't got your luggage, your leggings'll do."

"Won't your jacket be enormous on me?"

"Not mine," I said, and hoped to leave it at that.

She nodded. "I see."

Jupiter eyed her—his no-neck bodybuilder physique hid a smart, observant personality. "Brand had a groupie on board a few months ago. She left it behind."

He was covering for me. She'd come on board with Brand, but had gotten one look at me and hopped trains, so to speak. Between the groupies that Myles, Jupiter, and Zan had brought aboard, Brand hadn't been sore about it, as there'd been plenty to choose from. That had been one of the very few times I'd dipped my toe into those waters.

Charlie was eying me. "You don't have to be embarrassed about it, Crow. You're a single man living on a rock star tour bus." She smiled. "Groupies are part of the gig. Doesn't bother me."

Jupiter, again. Nosy butthead. "Ahh, Crow don't play like the rest of us. Once in a while he'll...unwind, a little. But the groupies are mostly for the rest of us. He keeps to himself. That was one of the only times he's done that since I've known him."

"Don't need to explain shit for me, Jupe," I said, a little tightly. "But thanks."

"And let me guess, Myles gets the lion's share of them?" Lexie asked.

Jupiter didn't answer right away. "Um."

Lexie laughed. "Awww, the big meathead is speechless. How cute."

Jupiter snickered. "I mean, he *is* Myles North. Plus, look at the fucker. Prettiest male I've ever seen, and you *know* I'm the most rabidly hetero male on the planet."

Lexie patted his arm. "Well, I plan on taking him off the market. For a while, at least." She grinned. "That won't cramp your style, will it?"

He lifted his arm and gave his best IFBB bicep flex—which admittedly was impressive. "Don't think that'll be an issue, sweetheart."

She narrowed her eyes at him. "Do *not* call me sweetheart."

Charlie snickered. "Yeah, you really don't want to do that."

He eyed Charlie, then Lexie. "My bad?"

I glanced at Charlie. "Bike is ready to go. Want to get out of here and leave these two to their posing?"

"Who's posing, bird boy?" Lexie snapped.

"You are, firecracker," I shot back.

Charlie elbowed me. "You don't want to cross wits with her. Trust me on this."

I laughed. "I'll take your word for it."

Jupiter went back to shoveling food into his mouth. "Yeah, same. No offense meant."

Charlie grabbed her purse while I dug the spare leather jacket out of the storage cubby. It was a real biker jacket, with tassels and zippers and buckles, and it fit Charlie like it had been made for her. Seeing this girl in a biker leather was...

Well, it wasn't doing anything helpful for my blue balls, let's put it that way.

I pulled the extra half helmet out of a different storage locker, gathered my phone, wallet, and other accoutrements, and led Charlie outside to where I had the bike on its kickstand behind the bus. She eyed my bike. A lot like my dad's, and I'd bought in honor of him. A 1947 Indian Chief, all original, in near mint condition, with a comfy seat for two.

She took a deep breath. "Okay. I'm a little nervous."

I popped the helmet on her head; she'd re-braided her hair into a dizzying complex triple braid, so the thick glossy mass of black hung down over her shoulder and rested just above her breast.

Clipping the helmet under her chin, I brushed her cheek with my thumb. "It's all good. I'll climb on first, you climb on behind me. Snuggle in close, and don't be shy about hangin' on tight, okay? Squeeze as hard as you want, won't bother me none. I'll go slow until you feel okay. Promise you, after the first rush, you'll be having fun."

I swung on, inserted the key and twisted it, pulled back the kickstand and balanced. Grinned at Charlie, popping my own Kaiser-style helmet on. "Climb aboard, darlin'."

She put her hands on my shoulders, hesitated. "Promise it's safe?"

"Eyes on me, babe." She met my gaze, and I held it, giving her my open soul through my eyes. "I swear on River Dog's immortal soul that you will be safe with me, always."

She saw something that made her shiver, and nodded. "Okay."

And then she threw a leg over behind me, slid on, the angle of the seat helping her press up against me. I drew a deep breath and held it, focusing on not popping a hard-on at the feel of her plump firm breasts against my back, the V of her thighs wedged against my hips. And then her hands latched around my waist, low, and that fight was near impossible.

I balanced with my feet and adjusted her hands a little higher, near my diaphragm. "Little too close for comfort while I'm ridin', babe."

She rested her chin on my shoulder, and her breath tickled my ear. "Oops." She slid her hands down where they'd been, and lower. "That, you mean? It's too close? Making you uncomfortable?"

I chuckled. "Oooh, you saucy little minx. You know I've been hard as a fuckin' rock all damn morning? Now you're teasing me?"

She sighed. Moved her hands back where I'd put them. "Sorry." Another sigh. "I'm sorry about this morning. I swear, I didn't mean to—"

"Hey, wasn't blaming you. Shit happens, I know you weren't tryin' to do nothin' like that. I just meant I gotta ride right now, and if I'm thinkin' about how fuckin' bad I want your hands on my cock, riding will be impossible."

"Just my hands?" She breathed.

I growled, my cock throbbing at the sultry promise in her voice. "No, Charlie. Not just your hands." I drew a deep breath, letting it out slowly. "Been daydreaming about the ways I want to get nasty with you, and I'm trying like hell to not do any of 'em right here, right now."

"You've been daydreaming about me?" Surprised, aroused.

Fuck, this conversation was *not* helping. "Yeah, babe. Want you so bad it hurts. Literally, the pain I'm in ain't even funny."

She lifted up, peered over my shoulder down at my groin—which was bulging painfully as my cock tried to unfold but was stuck bent in half. "You're in pain?" The worry, the concern...god, it was too sweet, too much. She was soft and tender, and ready to do anything to make me all better.

"Darlin', I was literally seconds from blowing my load when that flat popped. A few more seconds and..." I groaned. "Having to stop, and leave you naked in my bunk, and spend the rest of the day around everyone else when all I fuckin' want to do is bury my dick into your sweet, hot little mouth? Fuckin' hell, Charlie. I'm so swollen, so achy and fucking throbbing all over it's a wonder I don't just explode. Can barely think straight, honestly. Ridin' this bike with you pressed all soft and sexy up against me, whispering that seductive shit? Fuck, babe. You don't know what you're doin' to me."

Her arms squeezed around me. "I want to fix it," she whispered. "Where can we go?"

I laughed, a dark, amused, aroused growl. "Babe, not sure you know what you're askin'."

She clenched her thighs around me, pressed against me, ran her hands over my bare chest, down, close, close, then back up. "Crow, you've made me want things I didn't know I was capable of wanting. I'm not sure I know what I'm asking for either, all I know is…" her voice lowered to a breathy hot whisper against the shell of my ear, "I'm horny as hell, and the single thing I want most in life right now is to make you come as hard as you made me come last night…and this morning."

I sucked in a deep breath, clenched my handlebars until my knuckles pulsed with pain, forcing myself to not snag this woman off the bike, carry her into the grass on the side of the road and have my filthy, depraved way with her right there. Instead, I hung my head, steadied my breathing.

"Charlie, give me a chance to put some miles between us and that bus, and I'll find a place we can be something like alone, and I'll give you all the time in the world to do anything and everything you can think of, and then some."

"How many miles?" She breathed.

I laughed. "A few. I plan on makin' you scream almighty goddam loud."

I kicked the starter, and on the third kick the motor caught with a snarl. I gave it throttle, and the bike purred, and Charlie pressed her nose to my back. "It vibrates," she said in my ear. "Like, whoa."

"Yeah, you'll get used to it."

She wriggled against me. "NO, I mean…I *like* it."

I chuckled, patted her thigh. "Then just you wait till I open her up a bit." I put it in gear, let out the clutch and nudged the throttle, easing off gently for Charlie's sake. "Ready?"

She squeezed tight, nodded against me. "No. Yes. Yes." Clinging, terrified.

I just laughed. "Relax and enjoy the ride, honey."

I pulled away, feet skimming until I was balanced, and then propped my feet up. Checked over my shoulder, pulled off the shoulder and onto the rural highway. Slowly added speed, feeling Charlie still tense.

"Open your eyes," I yelled over my shoulder.

She shook her head, but then I felt her slowly relax, a breath of wonder. "Ohhh...oh wow." This was more felt than heard, this expression of wonder. She sat up a little straighter, still clinging to my midsection with a death grip, but she was looking around now.

The rural highway sped past us, cows and fields, trees, billboards, the yellow and white lines keeping us company.

As the miles sped past, she relaxed her grip a little, her seat loosening until she was comfortable on the bike. Breathing easy, and I could just feel the ear-to-ear grin she was wearing.

Being on the road on my old Chief eased my tension, gave me something to do besides stew on my boiling need to mark Charlie as *mine*. That was a whole separate worry, the need to mark her, the sense

of ownership. Not in a chauvinistic way, just in a terri-
torial, possessive way. This woman is *mine*.

But she wasn't.

She was going to Alaska.

I was on tour with Myles, and we still had…I
counted and realized we were almost at the end.
Denver, Albuquerque…a couple others which eluded
me, El Paso, and then the last stop, our sort-of home
base city, Dallas.

What then?

Myles hadn't decided. He had a notebook full of
lyrics; I had a head full of melodies. We might take
time off and record, he'd said. But we may just take
time off. We'd been touring nonstop for several years
now, only pausing in Nashville long enough to lay
down an album every year or so.

Now, with his thing with Lexie, it may be break
time for real.

Which, shit, meant I could possibly explore
things with Charlie.

If that was what I wanted. If that was what *she*
wanted.

If that was possible.

Was it?

Did I?

Did she?

God, I had no clue.

I just knew I wanted to fornicate with the woman in the worst way. Maybe that's all it would be, some good old-fashioned sex.

I tried to believe that, but couldn't.

Still, I'd been alone for so long—alone in the romantic sense, I meant; Myles and I had been touring and writing and playing together in one capacity or another since we were eighteen. Ten years. It was all I knew.

But shit, and hellfire. Charlie was sparking something hot and deep inside me. Something that made me hunger for...

I couldn't put my heart there. Couldn't.

I had no permanent home.

Not anywhere.

And I barely knew the woman, after all.

And there was shit she sure as hell didn't know about me.

Deal breaker, make her run for the hills kinda shit.

I'd tell her, though. Let her run. But, no matter what, I would tell her.

First, though, I needed just one more taste of her sweetness. Needed to know what her softness was like. What all that thick black hair felt like draped all over my chest as she rode me to completion. What it would be like to have a woman as good and kind and sweet and real and smart as Charlie Goode, even if just for a little while.

I was under no illusions about the kind of man I was. I had a past that a woman of such refined sweetness and light like her wasn't meant to touch. It would be like a mechanic's grease-stained hand pawing a pristine white wedding dress.

Like sin darkening the perfection of an angel.

I could dally with her, but I couldn't be with her, not really.

I could taste her, though. Just once more.

NINE

Charlie

WHAT—A—DAY.

He'd been right: after the initial terrifying rush of air and speed and the road humming
inches from my feet, and nothing around us...I was
able to relax and just enjoy it. And god, I enjoyed it.

The rumble of the engine growling between my
legs, the clear blue sky overhead, the warm air against
my face, the wind in my hair, Crow's broad back a
pillow for my cheek, his muscled torso a firm wall to
cling to, warm skin under my hands as his leather vest
flapped. It was intimate and wild; a sense of freedom
I never knew was even possible.

My heart just...sang. My soul rose, brightened.

No matter what else happened, these hours on the bike behind Crow were a gift I'd never forget. He'd given me so many gifts already.

He'd made me feel safe, protected. Taken care of.

Listened to.

Appreciated.

Desired.

Needed.

Sexy, beautiful.

Powerful.

This morning, with him in my hands, watching him lose control under my mouth and my touch, I'd known power. He'd given it to me, surrendered it willingly. I understood it, then, the allure of that particular act. It can be used to dominate and degrade, yes, but so can many things. Done the way we'd done it, it was him surrendering to me. Honestly, it had been beautiful.

And, oh god, so unbearably erotic. His size, all for me. His body under my hands, his gasps, his stomach tensing, curling in, his thighs bunching powerfully, his head thrown back and then craned to watch me take him to the heights of pleasure.

And now this gift: freedom. Exhilarating, primal freedom.

I wanted to finish what we'd started, but there was just one problem: I was ravenously hungry. My stomach was growling loud enough to be heard over the roar and rumble of the bike. I kept one arm around his waist and with the other, I curled my hand up under his armpit, clinging to his shoulder to draw myself closer to his ear.

"Crow!"

He turned his head to the side, nodded. "Yeah?"

"I'm hungry!"

He nodded. "I'll find something."

We were in Colorado, by now, well into it. We rumbled another twenty minutes down the freeway before we found an exit that was marked as having food. He seemed to hesitate, and then the roar quieted and we leaned to angle off the freeway. The exit wound around, and I felt Crow lean into the turn, and the angle and the speed and the gravity were suddenly very real and very scary.

"Lean with me!" he shouted. "Look over my left shoulder!"

I tried to do so, to move with him, mirroring his body movement, but my heart was thundering, pounding, palms sweating against his chest, which I had a death grip on. Then we were stopped, idling at the red light.

"Okay?" He tossed over his shoulder. "Shoulda warned you about the turn earlier. Freaky for a first timer."

I nodded, slowing my breathing. "It was scary, but I'm okay. I hope I didn't throw you off at all."

"Nah, been doing it long enough. Just gotta remember to trust me, and just lean with me. Look over my inside shoulder and lean a little bit, and it'll be fine."

I nodded and looked around. "The sign said there was food at this exit, but…I'm not so sure."

There wasn't much, just a rural highway extending left and right, late afternoon sun golden-red on the trees, and a few billboards, a gas station, small and desolate and aging. Not much to see in either direction except trees.

The light turned green, but he hesitated. "Sign said left in a couple miles. Could be a dump, but you never know. Wanna try?"

"I'm really, really hungry. Plus, my legs ache, and have to pee. So yeah?"

He nodded. "Okay. Here we go."

Off we went, and this time I leaned with him like he'd instructed, and it wasn't as scary the second time. Slower, now, at a sedate highway pace, fifty or so. Slow enough to enjoy the scenery, the wind, and the lowering sun. In a couple miles, a building appeared in a clearing.

It was small and squat, no windows, lit with red and green and blue neon signs advertising beer and liquor and food. We pulled into the parking lot, which was fairly packed, surprisingly. There was an even mix of motorcycles and jacked-up pickup trucks—it was clearly an establishment that catered to…a certain sort.

My heart clapped erratically, but my bladder was suddenly screaming, and my legs were screaming, and my back hurt, and I was vibrating all over, and my stomach was yawning with rumbling hunger.

Crow had stopped in a parking spot, but hadn't shut the bike off or put the kickstand down. He twisted to glance at me over his shoulder. "Kind of a rough place, babe. Wouldn't bother me none, but a sweet little filly like you…might be a little sordid for your taste."

That put my back up a little. "Can you protect me from any unsavory elements?"

He chuckled. "Babe, anywhere we go, *I* am the unsavory element."

"Is that a yes?" Sweet little filly, my ass.

"Yeah, babe," he growled. "Walk you through hell itself, and the devil won't lay a finger on you."

That warmed me, more than a little. Because damn, I believed him.

"Then let's go, before I piddle in my sweet little filly underpants."

He chuckled, eyeing me. "That irritated you, did it?"

I swung off the bike, and my legs wobbled—his hand caught me. "A little," I said, finding my land-legs, so to speak. "I understand calling me darling and sweetheart and things like that are just how you talk, but calling me a sweet little filly is…condescending, at best."

"I apologize." No excuses, no justifications, just the apology. How extraordinary.

I took his hand and smiled. "It's okay. Just be glad you didn't say that to Lex. She'd skin you alive for a comment like that."

He snickered. "Wonder how Myles is making out with her, then, because he's worse about that kinda shit than I am."

She made a face. "Eek, not well, I'd imagine. She doesn't like being called smarmy pet names. At *all*."

He turned off the bike, put down the kickstand, unclipped his helmet and slung it off the handlebar. I unclipped mine and handed it to him. He took his time swinging off the bike, stretching, cracking his back side to side, flexing his legs.

I danced. "Not to be a problem, but I really, *really* have to pee."

He snickered. "Come on, then."

He took my hand and I power walked to the entrance. He opened the door and ushered me in, and I was blasted by smoke and noise and laughter and music and beer smell and man sweat and leather. It was dingy, low ceilinged, dimly lit. The air was fogged with smoke, despite the statewide nonsmoking ban which was common in most states, nowadays. Music thudded from speakers—"Boot Scootin' Boogie," Brooks and Dunn. The crowd was a raucous, rowdy, carousing wall of broad shoulders, leather and denim MC cuts, camouflage, beards, and hard eyes; the barroom full of laughing, yelling, swearing men was seamed through liberally with bottle blond and red hair, massive cleavage whether natural, pushed up by a bra, or surgically enhanced, along with tall boots and short shorts, and more than one lower back tattoo.

Yeah, no way I'd have gone in here on my own.

As it was, I suddenly wondered if maybe I could hold my pee a little longer.

Nope.

My eyes were turning yellow, as my dad used to say. I spied the ladies' room and made a beeline for it, pushing my way through the tumult, and probably not making any friends with the elbows I was throwing. I made it to a stall, sat down, and was nearly thrown off my pee game by the graffiti on the stall walls. Heinous, evil shit. Like, seriously, who even thinks that stuff, never mind writes it on public property?

Finished, I washed up and exited the bathroom,

stopping just outside the door to scan the crowd for Crow. I found him at the farthest end of the bar, bellied up to it with one boot up on the rail, big hard fist curled around a bottle of domestic beer, eyes roving the crowd, assessing. He saw me, lifted his chin, and jerked his head to indicate that I should join him. Well, duh. Like I'm going to join the crowd of booty-scootin' boogiers? Nope.

I had to cross through the crowd, but this time I used about...oh, 85 percent less elbow. I still drew a number of dirty looks, mostly from the women if I appeared to be nearing too close to their man.

The men looked at me as I passed, mind you, but their looks were...well...equally dirty, but in a whole different sense of the word.

A giant of a man—six and a half feet tall easily and every bit as broad in a circumferential way, head shaved and tattooed with the likeness of a grinning skull that had a bright yellow serpent slithering between the eye sockets and gaping, grinning mouth— stepped in front of me, halting my progress.

"Hey now, sweet tits, where you goin' in such a hurry?"

Want to make me see red? That's how.

"Hey now, frog butt, why don't you get the fuck out of my way?"

He snorted, amused. "Frog butt?" He looked

around, a gesture meant to indicate his ownership of the bar. "You in the wrong place to be talkin' smack like that, missy."

"Only smack that's happening is my hand across your face." I glowered at him, hoping like hell my backup was on the way to enforce my ballsy shit-talking.

He guffawed. "You just try that, sweet tits."

One thing to know about all of us Goode girls is that Mom taught us to not ever, ever take shit from men. A man gets in your face, you get back in his. He talks shit, you talk shit right back. Give as good as you get, and then give more. Most men are actually just cowards, and if you get in their dumb faces and make it clear you aren't taking their crap, they'll back down.

Some...won't.

This guy wasn't.

Mom prepped us for this, too.

I put my face in the big guy's face, gave him my most evil, cut-you-to-pieces stare. "Call me sweet tits again, thunder dick."

He bent to tower over me, trying to intimidate me with the extra foot of height and the well over a hundred pounds of weight he had on me. Here's the thing. Doesn't matter how big they are, their nuts all still smash the same.

Therefore: I kneed him in the big fat sac. Once. Twice. Reached up, grabbed him by the neck and leaned close, and put all my weight and momentum into a third upward scythe of my knee into his balls.

He propped himself forward, cupping his wounded...well, brain, such as it was. The only brain a lunk like him ever used, anyway. Now, leaning over, he was in the perfect position for me to give him my hardest open-handed slap. Not a girly, how-dare-you slap, either. A martial artist trained open-handed palm strike to the ear and jaw.

With a windup, and a twist of my body to add power, and follow-through, aiming my strike for the *other* side of his dumb ugly head.

The big bitch went down.

And the bar was silent.

Crow was...right where he'd been. One foot hooked over to prop his toe on the ground, elbow on the bar looking equal parts tickled pink by my little display of badassery, and ready to pick me up and carry me outside and fuck me silly up against the wall.

I stepped over the moaning lump of empty bravado and sat myself primly in the chair beside Crow, who made an elaborate show of stepping into me.

He leaned over me, palmed the back of my neck, and slashed his mouth against mine. "That was hot as fuck, Charlie," he murmured, and then kissed me hard enough that I saw stars and forgot to breathe for a few seconds.

Adrenaline was pounding through me, making me shake, making me daring and bold. I reached up and scraped my fingers into his hair and pulled him down to me, gripping his leather cut in my other hand and kissing him back, adding tongue to taste the crisp malt beer on his tongue, kissing him until he growled in his chest and yanked away.

"Fuckin' hell, woman, you *want* me to drag you into the bathroom and drill you up against the stall wall?"

"*Drill* me?" I arched an eyebrow at him.

"Way I'm feelin', darlin', that first time won't be slow and pretty." The primal promise in his voice made my sex clamp, heat rushing wet through me until I felt it literally, actually soak my underwear. "So yeah. You keep kissin' me like that, woman, and you're gonna find out what it means to get drilled, hard and fast."

"That's crude and demeaning," I murmured. "And strangely arousing."

He rumbled a laugh. "You handled that big asshole like you've done that before."

"Mom sent all of us girls to self-defense classes for women. We all went together, every Saturday morning at eleven, from the time I was twelve and Poppy was six. I went all through high school, until I graduated. And yeah, I've had to do that before. Men are pigs."

He frowned. "Not all of us."

I smiled at him. "No, not all of you. You're one of the good ones, Crow."

His frown didn't dissipate. "Wouldn't go as far as that, but thanks for the sentiment."

"Why didn't you step in, out of curiosity?" I asked.

He shrugged. "I was gonna, but then you got in his face and I wondered how you'd handle it. You were god almighty feisty that night we met, and had you been sober I don't think those fuckers would have wanted to tangle with you. So, yeah. I wanted to see what sober Charlie would do when threatened." His eyes met mine, hard and serious. "I was only a few steps away. I'd have stepped in before he laid a hand on you."

"So what you're saying is, you trusted me to handle myself, and only planned on stepping in if it became more than I could deal with?"

He nodded. "About sums it up, yeah. You ain't no helpless little thing, Charlie. I called you a sweet little filly, and that pissed you off and I get it, but don't for a fuckin' second think I underestimate you." His eyes, those deep turbulent dark brown eyes were hot and serious, and not at all tame.

"That means more to me than you can imagine, Crow," I said.

"You're a hell of a woman, Charlotte Goode."

My eyes stung. My heart squeezed. Had anyone, ever, thought as highly of me as he seemed to? Had anyone ever in my life shown such admiration for and belief in the woman and person I was?

Mom, perhaps, but that was her job. Not that I valued it less for the fact that she was my mom, by no means. But it was her job to prop me up and believe in me, and she had. It was getting that from…well… from a man that I craved.

My dad had been great at being playful and affectionate when we were kids, rarely raised his voice, called us beautiful. But as he grew older and we grew older, and as whatever it was eating him up inside gnawed away at his soul, he'd withdrawn from us all. That affection and playfulness and love had slowly been taken away. And when he'd died unexpectedly, it was gone forever. But, in truth it had been gone well before that.

I'd been searching for that validation for a long, long time.

And suddenly, in the wild nomad that was Crow, I'd found it.

And it scared me half to actual death. More than that, actually.

I couldn't hold his gaze for long. I was too afraid of falling into those eyes. Too afraid of falling any farther into…anything.

I dropped my eyes and scratched a fingernail on the sticky bar top. "I'm hungry."

He nodded, accepting my change in subject. "Well, I hope you like a cheeseburger and fries, because that's about all they got, and that's what I ordered us."

"Sounds perfect," I said. "I could eat a shoe, about now."

The bartender came by and set a beer in front of me, but didn't leave right away. His eyes cut to me, and then Crow. "Watch your backs."

Crow showed no surprise at the unexpected, low-voiced warning. "He's got buddies, I imagine."

"Mean ones. The Yak doesn't take kindly to strangers at all, much less those who make a fool of him in his own territory." The bartender was tall, thickly built, with long blond hair and beard, resembling Fat Thor from that last Avengers movie.

I snorted. "The Yak?"

"His name is Yakowski, or something along those lines. But his build? Folks just call him the Yak."

"Well, he makes me wanna yack."

The bartender laughed. "Beers are on the house, because I've wanted to see someone take that dickhead down to size for years. The fact that it was a gorgeous woman is just fuckin' gravy on the roast, man."

"Thank you," I said. "You didn't have to do that."

He shrugged. "Just...do me a favor. Eat, have some drinks, and skedaddle. Don't want to see you get hurt."

"Thanks for the warning, but I can handle whatever comes our way." Crow said this with no sense of boasting, just calm confidence.

Having seen him in action, I knew it was no idle brag.

"Been around enough to know you ain't lyin', just lookin' at you, man. But Yak has a lot of friends, and he ain't the biggest or the meanest of 'em. So just watch it."

He went back to the other end of the bar to take an order, and Crow and I drank our beer in silence.

"You worried, Charlie?" Crow asked.

I shook my head. "I remember very well how you handled those guys at the concert. I just don't want to be the cause of any more trouble. Especially not for you."

He rolled a shoulder. "Eh. Been in trouble my whole life. Shit, I've *been* the trouble. A little bar fight with some big drunk bikers? I'll be right at home."

I frowned at that. "I guess I'm a little confused at the timeline of your life."

He laughed. "Me, too." A sip of beer, and then our food came, and we dug in; he started talking around a mouthful. "So, when my parents died when I was eleven. That time period is a blur, so I don't remember exactly. Maybe that's weird, I don't know. You'd think I'd know the exact day, you know? But I don't. I wasn't with them at the time. River Dog and Mammy were down in Mexico somewhere, off the grid as they always were. Mom, Dad, Uncle Snake, and a big portion of the MC was gone, and I was left alone at the compound with Crutchy and his old lady, Delilah, and a few other kids. All's I remember is I was doing schoolwork. Delilah had been a grade school teacher before hitting the road with Crutchy, and she was, I guess you'd call it homeschooling me, along with the others. Then, we heard the bikes. You always know when the crew is back, you know? But there weren't enough bikes. Tran, Boots, Brady, Slovac…Yank, and…Queer." He scrubbed the back of his neck. "They're the only ones who came back, out of the twenty who had left that morning."

"Queer? Really?" I half laughed at this, around bites of burger. Which was, surprisingly, very good.

He snickered. "It was a joke. He was as straight as anyone else, but he was just weird as fuck. So Tran used to say he was just queer, in the old, original sense of the word, like weird. Teasin' him. And, as shit like that goes, it stuck."

I shook my head. "You boys have the weirdest nicknames." I cocked an eyebrow at him. "Except you."

He laughed. "Angling for the full name again, huh?"

"I'm curious. Can you blame me?"

He laughed, shrugged. "Nah. Guess not." Sobered. "So yeah. Mom, Dad, Uncle Snake, everyone I knew best and loved most was dead. I was never close to the guys who did come back except Tran—they weren't my parents' part of the crew. You don't care about those old inter-crew politics. Point is, I was eleven and suddenly an orphan. No one knew where River Dog and Mammy were. Dad may have, because he seemed to always just *know* where they'd be, probably because they'd been making the circuit from Mexico to California through the four corners into Texas and back down again since Dad was a kid."

"How did they make a living, just out of curiosity?"

"Who? My parents, or my grandparents?"

I shrugged. "Both, I guess."

He sighed. "Full of tricky questions tonight, ain't'cha? Mom and Dad got their living from the club. Which, to be honest, operated largely in gray areas of the law, or on the other side of it. That's how the shootout happened that killed 'em all—a deal gone wrong. The risk you run, livin' that way, I guess." He shrugged. "What exactly my parents did for the club, I've never known. Didn't know as a kid—and I knew better than to ask—and then I didn't wanna know later. River Dog and Mammy? They were artisans. Mammy made jewelry, small fine leather goods, stuff like that. Not cheap roadside shit, either. She sold it to museum gift shops and the fancy tourist stores in places like Sedona. Expensive shit, real quality artistry. May have seen my antler-handle knife—she made it. River Dog was a luthier."

I frowned. "I've heard the term, but can't remember what it is."

"He made guitars." His voice was quiet. Distant. "Best guitars you'll ever hear. Taught me to play, taught me to make 'em, too, but I haven't tried my hand at that in years."

I blinked. "You can *make* a guitar?"

He nodded. "Yeah. I've got a storage unit in Dallas full of River Dog's old tools, and some of his guitars, their truck and Airstream." A long pause. "Including the one he was working on when he passed. Been thinkin' I'd finish it, one of these days, if I ever get the hankering to quit being a nomad."

"Wow." I shook my head. "You are a complicated man, Crow."

He made a face somewhere between a frown of puzzlement and a shy, complimented grin. "What? Why?"

"You look the way you do, you're a hard-as-nails

ass-kicking biker. You're sweet, you're sexy, you're incredible in bed. You can play the guitar, *and* you can make them?"

He grinned. "I've written the music for most of Myles's songs. May as well add that to the list. He writes the words, I write the music, we hang out with a bottle of whiskey and smash the two together, and he's got a song."

I rolled my eyes. "Is there anything you can't do?"

"Resist you."

Shit, shit, shit, shit, shit. Direct hit.

"Smooth," I said, swallowing only with major difficulty, and sounding like it.

He touched my cheekbone. "Ain't a line, and I wish to fuck I was kidding."

"You wish you could resist me?"

He nodded, and I saw no humor in him. "Helpless to resist feelings ain't a fun place to be, you know?"

"Feelings?" I tried to joke us out of the conversation. "Lust doesn't count as catching feelings."

"Lust is way the hell up there, not gonna lie, babe. I wanna do some real nasty, dirty, sinful shit with you, and I want it in the worst way. Want things that I'm not sure you've even dared fantasize about."

I swallowed hard. "Like what?"

He just smirked. "Not gonna sidetrack me with

that this time, Charlie. Yeah, babe, I got a whole hell of a lot of lust for your sweet-ass body. But I'm catchin' some serious and seriously scary feelings for *you*."

"Don't say that," I whispered.

"Why not? You scared?"

I nodded. "Yeah, I am."

"Me too."

"You're a nomad. You live a rock star life. Your life is totally incompatible with everything I thought I've ever wanted in my life: stability, a family, a good job doing something I like. Sure, it's vanilla and boring, but it's what I want."

"Well, there ain't a single goddamn thing about me that's vanilla, so I don't know where that leaves us."

"Me neither," I whispered. "Because I'm catching feelings, too, and that's why I'm scared stupid by it all, because you represent everything that's…literally just the complete opposite of who I am. Yet I still want you."

"You do?" A flat statement and a question at the same time, both sounding a little surprised. "Want *me*, or feel lust for me?"

"Both." I whispered it, admitting it to myself as well as him. "A *lot* of both.

We lapsed into silence, then, and it wasn't tense

or uncomfortable, but it was clear we both had deep thoughts circulating in our brains.

Crow tossed a stack of cash on the bar, and didn't wait for change. "Come on." He took my hand.

"Where are we going?"

"I gotta piss, and I ain't leavin' you alone in this crowd. Too pure, too beautiful. You draw trouble like honey draws flies." He winked at me. "Don't worry. I'm in control. I won't deflower your fucked-in-a-bathroom virginity just yet."

"Awww," I said, staring boldly at him, heart hammering, core clenching, thighs shaking. "I've never been *drilled* before, much less in a public bathroom. Sounds kinda…*fun*."

We reached the bathroom and he yanked me in behind him. Two men were at the sinks, washing their hands; Crow seemed to swell, his presence and his persona and his energy just…darkening. Threat poured out of him.

"Out." His voice was the icy hiss of a razor blade sliding across a whetstone.

The two men—both gargantuan and tattooed and decked out in leather cuts and ragged jeans and chain wallets and pocket knives and shit-kicker boots—took one look at Crow, at each other, and left without a word, their hands still wet.

Scary.

And then he turned, whirling on me. Palms pressed up against the door. One hand slid down and turned the lock. The *snick* of the lock hitting home sounded awfully final.

His eyes were nearly black, radiating primal, feral hunger. That aura of hyper-threatening dominance was now turned on me, and in my case, he wasn't threatening violence, but something…similar.

Potentially violent, in a delicious, erotic sort of way.

Oh god. I didn't want rough sex.

Did I?

Wait, wait. *Did* I? I hadn't thought so…until this moment.

Shit, shit. Did I really, truly want the kind of raw, demanding, violent *fucking* Crow's eyes were promising me?

Until now, sex for me had never been anything but sweet, and gentle.

And half-assed, if I'm honest.

Pathetic, in comparison to the way Crow had made me feel so far.

"Do *not* tempt me, Charlotte." That low sharp rasp was still there, but this time it was guttural with heat, rather than icy with menace. "Self-control ain't a strong suit of mine, babe. Look at me the wrong way, say the wrong thing right now, and I can't promise I'll be able to hold back anymore."

I held myself tall, staring boldly up into his eyes. "Is that a threat, *Crow*?" I ran my hands up his bare chest. "I'd use your full name, but I don't know it."

A long, hard silence. He chewed on the inside of his cheek. Sighed. "Corvus Crow. No middle name."

I bit my lip, blinking. "Corvus." I racked my brain. "Isn't that the—"

"Latin name for crow." He hooked a single index finger in the front of my leggings.

I giggled. "Ah. Now I see. So your name, literally, is Crow Crow."

"Yeah. Fuckin' stupid. Parents were stoned when they named me, and that ain't a joke."

"I'll stick with Crow," I said.

"Good plan." He tugged down. Bared the very top of my sex, an inch or so, but no more. "Tell me no, Charlie. Tell me you're too good for this shit."

"What shit am I too good for, Crow?" I didn't dare blink, didn't dare look away from him.

I had my fingers clawed into his chest, adrenaline racing through me.

He tugged again, but the leggings were stuck on the swell of my ass—his hands scoured around, palming my buttocks and sliding down, taking the leggings with his rough, fiery touch. "This dirty-ass bathroom." A pause. "Me."

"Crow…" I breathed.

"You're too good for this kinda thing, Charlie."
He sank to his knees in front of me, bringing my leggings down around my ankles. Stared up at me. "Too good to let me do this to you in a fuckin' dirty-ass dive bar bathroom."

"What if—" I gasped as he kissed up the inside of my thigh. "What if I…holy shit, Crow. What if I'm tired of always being *too good* for everything?"

"You say that now, when it's feelin' good, babe. But will you still feel that way when we gotta walk outta this bathroom together, everyone in that bar knowing what we were doing in here? What I *did* to you, in here?"

A thought occurred to me, then. "On the bus—Myles, your whole band, they were all on the bus too."

"Yeah."

"I wasn't quiet."

"Nope."

"So they all knew. Jupiter knew. He sat across from me and talked to me like…oh shit. Like nothing had happened. And he's your *friend*." I let my legs fall open as he kissed from my knee to my groin, switched to the other thigh and started over, each kiss taking him closer to my sex, and I felt each kiss in my core, in my stomach, in my thighs, in my bones. "You think I'm so pure, so good."

"You are."

"I'm *not* so good, Crow. And I don't *want* to be good all the time anymore." I pulled his face against me. "I'm okay being…not so good."

He resisted. Gazed up at me. "Tell me no." He sounded like he was pleading with me, in a weird way.

Like, if I let him do this, he'd be totally unable to resist me. To stop himself from taking all of me. As if that scared him, and he wanted me to stop him, so he wouldn't fall any further into…

Whatever this terrifying thing was.

I shook my head. "Crow, I…" I thrust my hips against his face, begging for what he could make me feel.

He growled. "Dammit, woman." He slid his tongue up my seam. Hot, wet, slithery, incredible. "Told you I can't resist you. Been trying. Had a fuckin' hard-on from hell all goddamn day, lookin' at you, wanting you, needing you. Wanting to bury my cock so deep inside you you'll…you'll fuckin' taste me from the inside. Trying to be good, for you. To give you the experience you deserve."

"What is it you think I deserve, Crow?" I played with his hair, scraping fingernails against his scalp, feathering them through his hair, over the upper shells of his ears.

He murmured a wordless sound in his throat, as

if my fingers in his hair was the best thing since...
well, since my mouth on his cock, this morning. "Shit,
woman, you deserve a palace. Roses. Champagne.
A limo to a five-star hotel. Room service. Candles,
fuckin' Mozart or whatever. Beethoven, some soft
romantic classical bullshit. A big white bed, and me
takin' hours to show you what it's like to be fuckin'
worshipped like the goddess you are. That's what you
deserve."

"That sounds nice."

"Yeah, so—"

"I'm *here*." I palmed his cheeks. Wiggled my foot
out of my shoe and then yanked my leg out of my
legging and slung my naked thigh over his shoulder.
"I'm *here*, Crow. With you. In this bathroom, in this
dirty fucking dive bar. I'm here, with you, and I want
this."

He peered up at me. "Why?"

"Hell if I know, but I do. And I'm not going anywhere." I knotted my fingers in his hair. "Not until
you make me scream."

"Fuckin' hell, woman," he snarled, exasperated.
"You're crazy."

"Yeah, I realize that."

He licked me again, this time pausing at the very
top of my sex to nudge my clit with his tongue. Then
he circled it slowly, until I gasped. "You understand

there's no fuckin' chance of this being over till I'm inside you, right?"

I whimpered. "Yes." I watched him press his tongue to me, stiffen it and slide it into me. "Please?"

"Please what?"

"You. Inside me. Please." I was, suddenly, incapable of coherency. "Now."

He slithered his tongue over me, in me, through me, and when I began to flex my hips and gasp, he added a finger. And then two. And then three, in a triangle, inside me, slicking them inside me where I wanted *him*.

It was quick—I was always quick to the first one, especially when he spent more than enough time building me up, backing me away and then driving me to the edge again. I ground myself against him, thigh around his neck and shoulder, writhing against him—or trying to, awkwardly, with one foot on the floor.

He withdrew his fingers from me, hooked his arms under my knees, and without warning lifted me, sitting on his shoulders, and stood up. Slammed me up against the door—I braced my hands on the low ceiling and screamed, thrusting against him wildly now as he devoured me to the edge and beyond, not stopping when I climaxed, but going past it. Tasting me and thrashing me with his tongue until I was shaking and pushing against his mouth and up against the ceiling and screaming through gritted teeth, coming and coming and coming so hard I saw stars flash in front of my tight-shut eyes.

And then, when I was quivering and boneless, he let my thighs slide off his shoulders, caught me, and settled me on the floor. My legs gave out, so I held onto him—catching at his belt.

"How convenient," I murmured, my knees shaking even as my core begged for more…or no more, I wasn't sure which.

I unbuckled him, unzipped, unbuttoned. Different underwear. Different black jeans, for that matter, but same leather biker cut. Yanked his underwear away from his body and down, past his surging, straining cock. Shoved them down. Fondled him in my fists, both of them plunging down to circle and twist at his base.

"Fuck, fuck Charlie—slow down. Do that much more and this'll be over before it starts. On a hair fuckin' trigger right now, babe."

"I don't care, Crow. I just need you."

He reached down to his sagging jeans. Fished two fingers into his right hip pocket and produced a condom. "Shoved this in there before we left, hoping for…well, the plan was a hotel bed, but here we are."

I took it from him. "Here we are."

He was concentrating, focused hard as I caressed his length with one hand and stuck the condom wrapper in my teeth with the other. Ripped it open, withdrew the ring of latex. Rolled it onto him.

He palmed my ass, cradling it. "You can still tell me no, Charlie."

I clutched his hardness in one hand and his neck in the other, pulled him in for a kiss. "Not going to. Don't want to." Another kiss. "Can't. I need this too bad, baby."

His eyes met mine, darkening, deepening. "Baby."

"That okay?"

The sharp line at the bridge of his nose sharpened. "Never been called baby."

My heart did something funny, at that. "Baby." I scratched the stubble on his cheek. "Quit stalling and *drill* me."

He snarled. Began to lift me, two hands on my ass. "Wait. One thing, first."

I started to question him, but he was too fast. He pushed the leather jacket off my shoulders and let it fall to the floor, ripped my shirt up and off so fast my breasts ached from the sudden bounce. Bare, now, my nipples went harder yet.

"That's better," he growled. "Need to see those big juicy tits bounce when I fuck you, babe."

And then he lifted me, pulled my legs around his waist. I reached between us and fit him into me. Then clung to his neck.

He pushed, a gentle flex of his hips. "Ready, Charlie?"

I shook my head. "No way I'm ready for this." I let go of his neck a little, pushing my ass downward, to take him. "Don't let that stop you."

And ohhhhh god, oh god. I was *not* ready. Not for the aching burn of taking him, all of his many thick inches. I groaned raggedly as he filled me, shuddering all over with a kind of pain that was delicious and beautiful and raw all at once, the burn of stretching around an unbelievably, improbably huge cock. Which just filled me and filled me, and kept filling me. Until I was glutted on him, overwhelmed, crying with confused bliss at the sensation—so much *more* than I had imagined it possible to feel, and so much *better*.

I clung to him. Shuddered. Pressed my lips to his ear. I wanted to scream, but I was too breathless at the feel of him. "*Crow*."

He groaned, equally as raggedly as I had. "Fuck, ohhhh fuck, Charlie. Fuck, you're so *tight*." He adjusted his grip on my ass, lifting me, pressing me up against the door. "Hurting you?"

"No," I breathed. And then he pulled back, and I cried out. "Yes, but it's good."

"Tell me if I gotta stop."

"Slow, just...go slow. Till I get used to you." I had to bite his neck to keep from sobbing—we'd just started and I didn't want to sob yet. "Holy shit, holy shit, holy shit, Crow, you're so fucking *huge*."

He laughed. "Not gonna lie, I *really* like how you say that."

I wanted to laugh, tried, but it came out as a half moan, half laugh. "Like you...oh god—like you don't know your cock is enormous, Crow." I planted my forehead against his, gasping. "It's how you use it that...oh my fucking *god*—that's killing me."

He was doing something slow and hard, somehow managing to move slowly and carefully but still forcefully. And then a little faster.

And then slower.

And then the pain of accepting him was gone, and all I had within me was raw ravenous burning *need*.

I raked my hands down his chest. Nipped his ear. "Crow?"

He pushed in, then when he was seated deep, throbbing within me, he leaned backward to gaze into my eyes. "Yeah? You okay?"

So worried for me. So sweet.

"Now."

He frowned. "Now?"

"You. Me. More—*now*. *More*, now, please."

I couldn't formulate sentences. Had to show him.

I lifted, pulling on his shoulders to rise up, my thighs clamped around his waist. I kept my eyes on his, mine wide and frantic for more, his deep dark brown and primal and raw with aggressive sexuality.

When I couldn't rise anymore without losing him inside me, I sank down.

Hard. Felt him fill me with a slap of bodies meeting, and the sensation of taking all of him so suddenly split me apart with delirious ecstasy, and I screamed.

"Awww *fuck*, Charlie…" he snarled. "Tryin' to hold back so I don't I nail you to the fuckin' wall."

I dug my fingers into his chest, let him see the need in me, rose and sank again, and again, faster, harder, using all my body, all my power, to show him. I clamped down with my inner muscles as I took him all the way, squeezed around him as hard as I could.

He let out a growl, then. Something I'd never heard—a release of desperation. Giving in, utterly abandoning himself to his deepest need.

"Hold the fuck on, Charlie-girl," he whispered, a ragged sound.

I clung to his neck and clenched my thighs around his hard wedge of a waist, and he once again adjusted his grip on my ass cheeks, this time so he could pull them apart and get deeper. Hunched over me, he took a mouthful of my breast and sucked, nipped, tongued my nipple, and then...

He showed me what I've been missing my whole life.

Raw masculine abandon.

Testosterone-fueled sexual aggression.

Mastery over my body.

He pounded into me, his powerful glute muscles driving him up into me, slamming me into the door, driving up onto his toes to get as deep and as hard as he could. I screamed in surprised bliss, crashing against the door and writhing, trying to match him, but all I could do, I realized, was hang on and take what he had to give me. The door slammed against the frame, hard, loud, banging as he fucked me.

Pulling out slowly, he paused. And then he fucked me hard, so I slammed back against the door again, harder than the last time, yet I felt only him, only us, not the crash of my head and back against the door. Again, and again, he drove into me, each time harder and faster than the last. His face was buried between my breasts, and his breath on them was frantic, ragged, moaning. Each stroke of his cock into me hit something inside me, touched some nerve, sent me flying higher and higher and higher, made me cry out louder and louder, more and more frantic, desperate.

I felt myself reaching another edge, felt it like a tsunami within me. "Crow—"

He tilted his gaze up to mine.

"I—oh, god, Crow, baby, oh god, oh *god*—" I crushed his face in my hands and tried to kiss him through the pounding merge of our bodies, "don't stop, just like this—oh yes, god yes, now, Crow, look at me, look at me, I'm coming Crow, look at me while I come—"

He snarled and groaned, and thrust into me as I came apart, breaking into sobs all over him as he drove me to an orgasm I could not even begin to cope with, too much of everything to process the wild rush of mind-bending purity.

I felt us moving.

Felt him lower me.

Pull out.

I opened my eyes. "Wha—? Crow?"

I was facing a mirror, dirty, spotted. A sink, chipped porcelain, pitted chrome handles. He was behind me, huge and powerful, a dark avenging angel bent on my destruction. He reached between my thighs and touched me, found my slit. Fit himself to my opening, and slid in. Drove in, possessing me utterly as he filled me.

My legs didn't work; I didn't need them to—I was held up by him, by his hands around my hips and his cock inside me.

He gathered my complicated braid in his hands. Yanked the elastic band free and made quick work of shaking the braid loose. My hair cascaded in a thick glossy waterfall of black down my shoulders, my back, down to the top of my ass.

"God*damn*, Charlie. You have a *lot* of fuckin' hair." He gathered it in his fists, bunched and wrapped it around one hand.

"Never cut it. Not more than an inch or two to trim it," I murmured.

"Like it loose like this."

"In the way, most of the time. Pain in the ass."

He wasn't moving—not to fuck me, at least. His hand, the one not gripping my hair, was caressing my body, shoulders, back, spine, sides. Down to my ass, patting one cheek, then the other.

Back to my shoulders, pressed his palm between my shoulder blades, a gentle pressure. "Bend over, sweetheart."

I slid my feet wide apart and bent forward, hands on the sink, gripping the sides. I looked at him in the mirror—like this, I could see us. Both of us. Me, my tits swaying and my hair loose and crazy around my face and back and shoulders, caught up in his hands to pile it on my head and still spilling everywhere. Him, huge and sun-bronzed, hard-muscled, lean, heavy stubble on his angular jaw, eyes burning, hair messy.

My ass spread out, round, his hips sharp angles behind my curves, framing my spread-out ass.

I looked…sultry. Erotic. My cheeks were flushed. Spine curved and sinuous, generous heart-shape of my ass and pale skin in contrast to his darker flesh. My breasts hung heavy under me, swaying, nipples hard. I had never seen anything so erotic in my life. I felt a level of sensuality I had never felt before and I wanted more.

"Touch your pussy, Charlie. Want you to come again before I do." His words reverberated, low and growled.

BAM-BAM-BAM. A fist on the door. "Gotta piss, man."

"Fuck off." Crow's voice was a bark of command.

Nothing else from the other side of the door.

"Where was I?" He ran his empty hand down my spine, to my ass. "Oh yeah."

I braced one hand on the sink. Slid the other between my thighs, found my clit. Touched it, circled it. A single touch, one soft swipe of fingertip around the turgid little nub, and I was flying, core squeezing, fluttering, gut flipping and tightening, thighs shaking. "Crow…"

He pulled back, eyes meeting mine in the mirror. Slow, gentle. Letting me get reacquainted with him. "Charlie."

I felt my fingers working faster, now, moving of their own accord, and my hips followed suit, flexing, tipping, swiveling. He began matching my rhythm, pushing into me faster and faster as I built myself up to climax.

I watched myself in the mirror—watched my mouth drop open, eyes go wide. Watched my tits sway back and forth as I melted into his thrusts, met him with my own. Watched my ass smash back into his hips, watched the way my ass jiggled as I met his body.

God, I was sexy.

Him, fucking me—that was sexy.

He was sexy.

But I was...I was a goddess. Made for sex. I was made for Crow, for him fucking me.

I let a loud cry slice out of me, let my groan become a scream as intensity built, as my hips pivoted and my ass pushed backward into Crow. He grunted, feeling me tense, feeling me use my inner muscles to clench around him as my climax built to a crescendo.

"Charlie, fuck—I feel you comin', baby."

"I'm coming, Crow, I'm coming again."

"I feel it. Feel you squeezing me."

I clenched hard again. "Like this?" I lost the ability to control it, then, as the climax took over, and I felt myself just spasming, squeezing. "Ohh fuck!"

"Come for me, Charlie!" he snarled. "Love the way you come all over my cock, baby girl."

I lost all thread of control then, and just let go. I screamed, tears running down my cheeks, slamming back against him, shaking all over.

And then he was roaring, and his hand in my hair tightened, yanked. Hard, a twinge of pain, but just enough to make the orgasm I was still lost in all the more powerful.

Especially when he stopped matching my rhythm and gave me his own. "My turn."

I met his eyes, and felt my whole body shiver, felt goose bumps all over my body at the look on his face. "Oh fuck...yes please."

He laughed, a low rumble of amusement. And then he powered into me.

My tits bounced hard enough to ache. And that made something I thought was overtaxed within me spark all over again.

He didn't pull back slowly or gently this time. Oh no. A quick backward movement, and then he yanked my hair again to pull me backward, and his huge throbbing cock drilled into me, and at the moment he filled me totally, and his hard hips met my ass with a loud slap, his empty hand cracked across my ass cheek, stinging it, making me shriek—

And making that spark conflagrate into a wildfire

of another—yes, *another* imminent orgasm. How many could I have? Jesus, so many.

Backward, and this time I was ready. Or I thought I was.

I wasn't ready.

He fucked me, yanking my hair, and spanking my other cheek, and now both stung, warm. Again—thrust-yank-spank.

Faster, now. He spanked my ass with each thrust, hard, alternating, until my ass was throbbing with the hot sting, and that only built the fire of my orgasm, and this one threatened—promised—to be the most intense, body-ripping, soul-melting one yet. Building slowly, in exponential degrees, the shaking and quaking and the heat and the tightness and the wild insane mind-scrambling nerve-shredding desperate ecstasy more than I thought a human body was capable of feeling.

And I was watching him do it to me.

Watching my body respond. Watching my tits bounce and sway under me, watching his hand rise, pause at the top, and swing down to slap across my ass, watching my ass ripple with the impact, watching myself lurch forward, eyes wide and mouth open, skin going flushed crimson all over with sweaty exertion.

He fucked me, hard.

Again and again. Hard, harder, harder.

He was snarling, growling nonstop, each thrust a grunt, a shout. As if he was chasing own orgasm, as if despite his words of barely there control over his imminent orgasm he was pursuing something relentless and evasive. As if it was buried inside me, and he had to fuck his way to it, and if he didn't reach it, he would die.

Desperation. Never had I seen such raw, unmasked vulnerability and desperation in a man, or heard it in a man's voice.

He let go of my hair, and both hands gripped into my ass cheeks, pulled them apart, yanked me backward by my hips, to leverage himself inside me harder, deeper.

I screamed again, louder, him filling me to the point of an aching overfullness, so I was ripped open by him from the inside out, and it was the most incredible feeling in the world.

I was his.

Utterly.

Yet, I knew, *knew* in my soul that he was equally mine. It was written on his face. Painted on his features, scribed in the weathered lifelines of his face.

"Charlie!" A savage growl of my name, knifing into my heart. He needed to come. Needed it, so bad.

"Come for me, Crow!" I cried. "Please, baby, let me feel you come inside me."

He yanked me backward, fingers in my hips leaving bruises on my pale skin, and we watched us, eyes meeting in the mirror, the slap of our skin and the gasps of our breathing in unison, and the cries and grunts a music unlike any other, the soundtrack to this orchestral orgy of mutual abandonment each to the other.

"Fuck me, Crow," I whispered, too far gone to speak any louder. "Fuck me harder, baby."

And he did.

Oh god, he did.

And then, with a rabid, feral, guttural roar, he pounded into me, shuddering all over, pushing deep, and I felt it, then. Felt him release. Felt his cock slide deeper as he pushed into me, harder, deeper, felt his balls tap against my sex, felt his stomach against me, his thighs against mine. Instead of pulling out, he just tried to go deeper, and he throbbed inside me.

"Charlie—" his voice dropped to a whisper. "Oh fuck—oh god, *Charlie*."

And then he finally pulled almost all the way out and slammed deep again, falling over me, chest to my spine, gasping, and now his thrusts were quick and relentless and he righted himself and gave over to hard fast thrusts, arching backward and yanking me, growling, still coming, his thrusts without rhythm, without timing, without technique, just raw wild primal fucking.

And that—*that* was when I came. Truly, wrenchingly came.

I couldn't even scream.

He yanked free of me, and I knew what he was doing without having to be told. I whirled, leaped, and he caught me, slid back home, and I screamed around my teeth clenched into his shoulder, leaving what was sure to be nasty teeth-mark bruises, and he was fucking me so beautifully, just holding me, and I was clinging to him, wrapped around him, skin to skin, body to body, melted and melded to him.

Finally, we could stand no more. He sank to his knees, sitting on his heels so I was sitting on his thighs. I collapsed against him, but had to kiss him. Kissed his shoulder, his neck, where I'd bitten him—twice—felt ridges on his back where my fingernails had left marks, smoothed them with my hands, kissed his jaw, his cheekbone, his forehead, his temples, and then his mouth.

His mouth, endlessly.

Lost myself in kissing him, breathless with my orgasm, which was still shaking me, wracking me, a slow deep rolling tide of wave after wave orgasmic bliss wracking me and wracking me and wracking me, with him still buried inside me as I sat on him, kissing him, tongue sliding and tangling with his and tasting his mouth and scouring his lips and kissing him until we were breathless.

He finally broke apart, gazed at me in wonder. "Charlie…"

I feathered my hands in his hair. "No words, Crow…there are…there's just no words for that."

He shook his head, but it was an agreement. "No. No words."

"I don't know if I can walk, Crow."

He laughed, resting his head against my breasts. "Me either." There was an impatient fist against the door. "We gotta scram, baby."

I palmed his cheek. "Call me baby again, Crow."

"You're mine, Charlie-girl. You're my baby. All mine."

I shivered, this time from the impact of his words, and the way he had just changed my life.

Direct hit.

"Yours," I whispered against his throat, tasting his pulse. "All yours."

TEN

Crow

SHAKEN TO MY VERY CORE, I WORKED WITH TREMBLING hands to help Charlie get dressed, and then made quick work of my own clothing. Both of us dressed, Charlie stood in front of the mirror, her fingers nimbly, swiftly braiding her hair. Once braided, she twisted it into a bun low on her neck, then turned and faced me.

I reached out, taking her hand. "Ready?"

She shook her head. Lifted her shoulders up and back, took a deep breath, let it out in a short, sharp huff. "Nope. Let's go."

I laughed. Unlocked the door, and tugged it open. There was a semicircle of ugly stares, crossed arms, and pissed-off body language.

"About done?" someone snarled.

I kept a neutral expression. "Yep. Sorry for the inconvenience."

The speaker, an older guy with a graying beard and ponytail, continued to glare. "Had to piss in the ladies' room."

"Did you grow tits?" Charlie asked.

He turned purple. "No, I did not grow *tits.*"

I restrained a snort and kept my face blank. She was baiting an already nasty crowd, but shit, she was feeling good. I let her speak her mind. I could handle just about anything that came our way. Despite feeling a little weak in the knees from what we'd just done, I also felt like I was on a mountaintop, surging with possessive adrenaline.

"Dick still there?" Charlie asked.

He stepped toward her. "Sure is. Wanna see?"

I growled at him, and he paled, backed away. "Don't think so," I murmured, putting a snap of authority and threat into it. "We're leaving."

The speaker stepped aside. He had a new grin on his face, one that I didn't like. "Be my guest. Please."

My hackles rose at the amusement on his face. Something told me there was a surprise waiting for us outside. I felt my body tensing, muscles tightening, coiling.

My breath came short.

Head went airy, light, my sense of time shrinking—each moment stretching out.

"Charlie." I spoke low, held her close, my arm around her waist, tucking her against my side. "Just gotta warn you, babe. Gonna be trouble outside."

She hissed. "How do you know?"

I shook my head, shrugged. "Just know. I can feel it. That fella back there was awful amused when I said we were leaving. Pair that with the warning the bartender gave us and it doesn't add up to anything good."

"So what do we do? We can't stay here." She sounded nervous, scared.

"Babe." I touched my lips to her ear. "Remember how we met?"

She nodded. "I'll never forget it."

"So, don't worry. I got you. We're cool."

"What if there are a lot of them?"

"Wouldn't be the first time." We reached the door, and I paused to look her in the eyes. "Couple things, one, *do—not—help*. Stay outta the way. Don't call the cops. Don't panic. Two—don't be scared. Especially not of me. No matter what you see me do, you do not have a thing to worry about. I'll always treat you like the queen you are, okay? Three—I'm probably gonna take some hits. I'll be fine. By now you know I ain't lived the cushiest life, yeah? I can take a hell of a beating, so don't worry about me."

I held her gaze, and she nodded shakily.

"I'm still scared, Crow."

I smiled. "Darlin', you're with me. I *got* you."

She nodded, lifting her chin. "Okay. I trust you."

I just hoped that would remain true when this shit show was over—I had a feeling. A bad feeling. One other time I had this feeling, and that ended up being the worst, darkest day of my life. One with lasting consequences.

I opened the door. Shook myself, loosening my muscles, letting my breathing go slow, even, deep. Senses on alert. Scanned the lot as I opened the door, saw trucks now parked around my bike. Men waiting. Glanced to either side before I left the building—all clear. They were waiting at my bike.

If they'd touched my bike, this was gonna get fucking ugly.

The bartender was behind us. "Don't go out there, man."

I relaxed my shoulders. "Gotta. Ain't gonna hide in the damn bar."

"Your funeral, man."

"Nope, it'll be theirs." I glanced at him. At Charlie. "You strapped?" I asked the bartender.

He nodded, wary. "Yeah, but—"

I gestured at the ring of trucks and bikes around my Indian. "I can handle them, but not if I gotta worry about her."

He lifted his chin. Reached behind his back and pulled out a Ruger snubnose revolver. "Won't interfere, but nobody touches your old lady."

I met his eyes. "I'll make sure the AzTex are aware of it."

He nodded—even up here, the name of my MC drew recognition and respect. We were a one-percenter MC, and if you don't know what that means, best I don't tell you. I may not have the patch on my cut because I ain't proud of how I earned it, and don't want to advertise it, but I do have the one-percent tattoo hidden in my right sleeve.

Charlie grabbed my arm. "I'm your old lady?"

I grinned at her. "If you wanna be."

She glanced over my shoulder, her smile fading. "I don't like this, Crow."

"Me either."

The bartender's eyes whipped to mine. "Crow?"

I nodded. "That's me."

"You're patched in with the AzTex? Any relation to Coyote Crow?"

"My dad."

He scrubbed his hair with one hand. "Coyote

saved my ass, years back. Used to live in Flagstaff. Had my back against a wall, some meatheads making trouble. Coyote waded in, just because he felt like ten on one wasn't fair odds."

I nodded. "Sounds like Dad." Extended my hand to him. "Crow."

He shook my hand with a firm but easy grip. "Leif Bjornsson." He said it *Leyf BYORN-son*.

"Thanks, Leif," I said.

"Sure thing. Anything for Coyote's family."

I reached out, brushed my thumb against Charlie's cheek. "Be back soon."

"You'd better be."

I straightened my back, tilted my chin up, and left Crow the lover and nice guy back there with Charlie. I moved toward them, slow, limbs feeling liquid. I counted—eight? Maybe ten guys.

I waded through the ring of trucks, and stood in the middle, next to my bike, arms at my sides.

"Gonna take that cut off you and send you home in bag, wrapped in it," a deep voice said. Yak.

"Can you read?" I snarled. "You know the name. You sure you wanna do this?"

He prowled out from between a truck and a big tricked-out Harley. "Your little bitch disrespected me."

"My old lady showed you she wasn't anyone to fuck with. You got what you deserved." I pivoted in a slow circle. Eight, nine…ten. Eleven. Felt a flutter of nerves. "You don't want to do this."

"Yeah, we do." Yak smirked. "She's gonna watch us turn you into hamburger, and then I'm gonna have a whole hell of a lotta fun teaching that sweet little pussy a long, hard lesson."

Good thing for me I know how to hold my temper. He wanted me to charge him. I was seeing red, but I knew how to wait.

"You're gonna regret those words." I forced myself to sound cool, unconcerned.

I was, though—concerned, I mean. Eleven was a lot.

And they looked mean.

I had a collapsible baton in my saddlebags, and normally I prided myself on being able to handle myself without needing a weapon, but with eleven on one, it seemed like a prudent time to even the odds a little.

I was leaning on the saddle and slipped my hand into the saddlebag, moving by feel. Found it, withdrew it. Six inches long collapsed, with a single flick of my wrist, it would extend to twenty-five inches of heat-treated steel, with a lead weight at the tip, for counterbalance…and bone snapping.

I held it in one hand, collapsed and faced Yak. "Gonna take me all at once, or one by one?"

He just grinned, ugly, evil. "Got yourself a little toy, do you? Fine. Let's do this."

He stepped toward me. Reared up to his full height, swelling his chest to look even bigger. He had a nasty grin on his fat ugly face, like he was about to have fun.

Joke's on him. I don't play games.

"Last warning, Yak-face. You and your buddies fuck off while you can still walk on your own two feet." I restrained the urge to charge, and to bury my fist in his nose. "I ain't gonna be nice about this."

He just laughed, shook his head like I'd said something absurd. "You see the numbers here?"

"Yeah. And you better hope you have enough friends that some you won't all need the hospital."

He was done talking, apparently. The grin wiped away, he took a long lunging step toward me, a big meaty fist swinging. I ducked under the telegraphed punch, swung the butt end of my baton, still collapsed, into his ribcage on the right side. Then I pivoted and drove my knee into his left side, near his liver and kidney.

Then all hell broke loose.

Two more came at me from my right, and I hopped sideways from left foot to right, slicing a side kick out straight, nailing one in the stomach. I kept the momentum going and used it to pivot around into a scything roundhouse kick to the second, landing it in his ribcage, under the arm he thought he was going to be punching with. Then I had no time to think—it was just me, and all of them.

I snapped my baton out, jabbed it into a gut, swung it around and felt a kneecap explode, heard a scream. Busted a skull open. Broke ribs. Used my feet and knees, and my off-hand for follow-up strikes—this was no game; they were going down, and hard.

I felt a fist hit my ribs, near my kidney, pain lancing through me, and the pain sent me into a tailspin. Most fights were one-sided—me taking them out, fast and hard, ending it as swiftly as possible. Seldom does my temper enter the fray—I can't afford to let it.

When it does rise, like now, it's...vicious.

Seeing red is when someone pisses you off, insults your old lady or you or your friends. When that happens it's not my temper you see, it's my honor being crossed. And while not smart, given what I'm capable of, it never turns lethal.

But this?

The thrust of a fist in my side, another to my liver, a third to my jaw...

The pain awakened some instinct inside me, bringing a dark and violent thing to life.

Now, I saw black.

The edges of my vision darkened, went hazy.

My vision narrowed and I saw everything in absolute clarity, as it happened, all around me. My opponents were moving in slow motion. I saw a fist angling for my nose, turned my face aside to take it on my cheekbone. Another burst of pain.

A fist to my lips, splitting them against my teeth.

Blood fountained from my nose.

I heard and felt myself roar, and then I was done taking hits. The baton was a blur, and bones crunched and shattered, cartilage dissolved. My feet moved in lightning footwork, knocking out knees sideways, slamming into ribs. My off-hand went hammer-fist into livers. Knees scythed.

I took hits. Plenty of them. I was a mass of pain, blood pouring from my nose and lips. I had a bruised rib for sure, a split cheek, and other places that just *hurt*.

But now it was just me and Yak. He'd made it to his feet, and was assessing the pile of moaning, crying bodies around him. I stood, bleeding, savage rage on my face. Watching him, baton in hand.

He was holding his ribs. "Come on, fucker," he said as he reached into his pocket.

"You pull a knife, you'll be leaving on a stretcher with your friends."

He pulled it anyway. Big, long, fuck-off black,

folding blade, at least four inches of blade, if not more. Drop point, assisted open. Serrated.

"Come on, man. You're done. It's over. You think you're getting anywhere near me with that?"

"I'll cut you to pieces, bitch," he growled. "Your little stick won't help you."

Little stick my ass. Tran, the current president of the AzTex is Filipino, and an expert in Filipino stick fighting. Which he taught me.

I hated this part.

The part where this injured, hopelessly out-matched idiot decides to push his luck. I was in pain, angry, and not in control. If he came at me with the knife, I couldn't guarantee he'd live to walk away.

He held it like he knew what he was doing, but little good that would do him.

Hold back, I told myself.

I repeated that injunction as I waited for Yak as he circled, knife waving, tip circling. Hand out, light on his feet for a big guy.

Hold back.

But when someone comes at you with a knife, there is no holding back. He swung, and I danced backward, the tip missing my belly by a whisker. Danced back again, and again. Then he did something stupid. Tried to fake me out with a feint.

I faked like I was going to counter his strike, and

he turned the feint into a real strike, which brought him off-balance.

I used my free hand to snag his wrist, twisted, turning his elbow and wrist the wrong way, and I brought my baton down, hard. His elbow turned inside out.

He dropped the knife and went to one knee, growling through gritted teeth.

I backed away, hoping it was over.

He lurched up, the knife in his off-hand. He moved faster than I'd have believed him capable of, and I only just barely managed to twist aside, so the knife sliced along my ribcage, opening my skin deep, but not penetrating the way it could have.

He was way off-balance, having put everything he had into that charge. I was forced into a spin, my own twist taking me around a full three hundred and sixty degrees to land outside of his range; my baton swinging, hard. It was a black blur, my foot stomping to plant a blow to his head.

I hit his temple with the baton.

He collapsed, instantly.

It was over—with Yak down, the fight was over.

I staggered to my bike. Braced my hand on it, tossed the baton to the ground and pressed a hand to my bleeding ribcage.

I saw Charlie tear herself away from the

bartender. "Stay over there, Charlie," I called. "Don't need to see this."

She ignored me. Stepping over bodies, blanching at the sight of limbs bent the wrong way, blood everywhere, she prepared to take her shirt off, grabbing it by the hem.

I snagged her wrist with my good hand. "Much as I'd appreciate a gander at your big ol' titties again, Charlie, this ain't the time."

"For your wound, you idiot."

I pointed at the saddlebag. "In there. Got a spare T-shirt. Use that, not your own."

She fished it out and pressed it to my wound, holding it tight. She pulled it away to peer at the damage. "You need stitches."

"Nah, fuck that."

She was shaking all over. "Crow, you're very badly cut."

"Stitches mean questions."

Leif was on the phone as he stood in front of the door, barricading it to keep onlookers inside.

"What are you going to do, then, just bleed everywhere?"

I moved around to the other side of the bike, dug in my other saddlebag, and found the roll of duct tape I keep there. I folded the T-shirt into a thick rectangle and pressed my hand against it, and had Charlie wrap the duct tape around my middle, tight and bracing.

"There. Good as new," I said when she was done. I faked a breezy grin and tone I didn't feel—that shit hurt like a motherfucker, but I wasn't about to show that to her, though. "Come on, babe. Let's ride."

I popped my helmet on my head, clipped it. Plopped hers onto her head, clipped it on. Collapsed my baton, tossed it into the saddlebag, and swung on. Dug my key out of my pocket and started the bike.

She was staring at me, and then she turned to look at the pile of limbs and bodies. "Crow…"

"We gotta go, babe."

"What about them?"

"He's got it," I said, gesturing at the bartender.

"What about the authorities? Shouldn't we wait to make a statement?"

I shook my head. "Not how shit like this works, babe. Not in this world. Not for me."

She swung on, hesitantly. I could tell she was scared. Shaken by what I'd done. By the whole scene. She glanced at Yak, who wasn't moving. At all.

"Is he…?"

I twisted the throttle more aggressively than I needed to. "Don't know, don't care," I shouted over the roar of the engine and the screech of the tires. "Not my fuckin' problem."

Not sure she heard that last part, drowned out as it was by the noise and the wind. She held on tight, and I put the hammer down, hauling ass back to the freeway and hitting it at about Mach one. She was shaking, her fingers digging into my chest.

"C-Crow?" Barely able to get a breath out. "Please. S-slow down."

I glanced at the speedometer and realized I was doing ninety-five, and this was her first time on a bike. I slacked off on the accelerator. I had to make a call anyway.

I slowed, pulled off onto the shoulder, leaving the engine idling and propped us up with both feet as I tugged my helmet off and pulled my phone out of my jeans. I dialed Tran's number—which, a long time ago, I'd hoped to never have to call again.

It rang, once, twice, three times. "Crow."

"Hey, Tran." I swallowed hard. "How ya doin', bud?"

He snorted. "Only reason you'd call me is because you're in some shit. So cut the crap and tell me what you need."

"I fuckin'…I messed up, man."

"Again?"

"There was eleven of 'em, and my old lady was watching."

"You got an old lady?"

"It's recent. And she ain't from the life, you know?"

"Shit. She saw it?"

"Yeah." I growled. Then I paused as I waited for a bunch of traffic to pass. "It was bad, man. Eleven of 'em."

"You okay?"

"Yeah, I'm fine. Fucker creased my ribs, but nothing some duct tape won't fix."

"This wasn't just fists, then."

"Had my baton, just because there was so fuckin' many of 'em. I tried to keep it from going that way, man. I did."

I heard him sigh. "I know it." A pause. "Where?"

I pulled the phone away, put it on speaker, and digitally shared my location with him. "Little dive bar off the freeway. Not sure what it's even called."

"Denver area, though."

"Outside it, yeah."

"Myles got a show there, huh?"

"Yeah."

"All right, well, I know some folks. I'll make some calls, get this taken care of so it don't blow back on you. With a previous manslaughter on your record, you can't afford to get made for this."

"No shit, Prez."

Fuck, it was still on speaker. Fuck, fuck, fuck. No

NOT SO GOODE 295

point in turning it off now that was out of the bag. I felt Charlie stiffen behind me. But I had to finish talking to Tran. God, this was bad. End of the road for Charlie and me, that kinda bad.

I was silent too long, apparently. "You're awful quiet, Crow." Tran was wicked smart. "She didn't know, did she?"

"Not yet, no."

"And she's on the back of the bike, listening, ain't she?"

"Yep."

"An' if she ain't from the life, that shit is probably not gonna fly over too great, is it?"

"Probably not."

"Name?"

"Charlie Goode."

Tran raised his voice. "Listen to me, Charlie Goode. Crow is a good man. One of the best I've ever met. Don't let this shake you. He does what he gotta do, but it ain't all of him, okay? So try not to hold this against him."

Charlie nodded.

"Tran can't hear a nod, babe," I murmured.

"Yes, I hear you," she said. "Thank you."

"She's freakin'," Tran said.

"It was a mess, and this is a shock," I said.

"Go. Deal with it." A pause. "Word of advice from your ol' Prez, Crow-bro?

Crow-bro. Haven't been called that in a while. "Sure."

"Take it off speaker."

I did. "All right."

"She's gonna run, brother, and you just gotta let her go. If she ain't from this life, she won't get it. She'll need time to process it. And you can't force it. Don't mean you gotta let her go forever, but you gotta give her time."

"That what happened with you and Mahalia?"

"Sorta. She wasn't from the life, but she wasn't soft, either." A moment of silence. "How soft is she?"

I laughed. "She's from Connecticut. She's got a double major from Harvard."

"Yale," Charlie corrected from behind me.

"Yale, my bad. This is the first time she's been on a bike, and she was raised not to curse."

He laughed again, whistling. "You snagged yourself a real nice piece of silky soft, didn't'cha?"

"Yes, sir, I did." I sighed. "Hopefully that's not past tense."

"All right. I gotta make those calls. Just be cool, okay?"

"Okay. Thank you, Tran."

"You're family. You may be out, but you're still Coyote's boy, and you still earned your patch and your tattoo. You got no worries, my man."

We hung up, and I pocketed the phone, sat in silence for a moment, the bike rumbling between my thighs.

I didn't try to look at her, couldn't. "So."

She had her hands on my shoulders. Wrapped them around to hold on to my chest. "How far to Denver?"

"An hour or so."

"Just...go. I need to think."

"Okay." I hesitated. "Remember the second thing I told you back there, yeah?" I paused. "Don't be scared of me, no matter what you see me do."

She didn't answer.

I put the bike in gear and pulled away, heart thumping.

Knew we shoulda toughed it out instead of stopping. But then, I also knew that record of mine was gonna make trouble. A sweet, soft, smart, sexy, safe woman like Charlie Goode, and a hard-ass orphan biker with manslaughter on his rap sheet, and nowhere to call home...I didn't stand a chance.

We reached Denver late, well after sunset, found the venue, and pulled up near the tour bus. I shut the engine off, put the kickstand down, and swung off. Charlie already had her helmet off and was sliding off.

"Charlie."

She shook her head. "I need some time, Crow. I'm sorry."

"Knew this would fuckin' happen."

She stopped, spun around on a dime. "You killed a man, Crow."

"There were fuckin' *eleven* of them. He had a fuckin' knife, Charlie, and he wasn't plannin' on fuckin' ticklin' me with it."

She gulped. "I know that, but—"

"You'd rather I let him stab me? You think you're shaken up now? If I'd gotten stabbed in that fuckin' rathole, and you were there on your own with a pile of fucked-up bodies and no way to get anywhere? *That* would have really messed up your day, sweetheart."

"I know, I know. I just…" A helpless shrug as she ran out of words. "I don't know anything right now, Crow. I know you wouldn't hurt me, it's not that. I'm just…" She trailed off, shaking her head, swallowing hard.

I glanced to the left, where the bus was. We had an audience: Myles, Lexie, Jupiter, and a cluster of road crew—they all must have only recently gotten here, since they hadn't scattered for free time yet; the show wasn't till tomorrow, so everyone got tonight and part of tomorrow off, until set up and sound check.

"Ya'll enjoying the show?" I snarled. "Fuck off."

The crew vanished, but Myles, Lexie, and Jupiter remained.

Myles caught me in a hug. "You okay, bro? You look like you took a walloping."

I shook my head, pushed him off me. "I'm fuckin' fine."

Lexie stared at me, at Charlie. "What the hell happened?"

"There was a fight." Charlie was whispering. "It was my fault."

"The fuck it was," I growled. "It was that asshole, Yak."

Lexie snorted. "Yak?"

"You'd be proud of your sister, Lexie," I said. "The dude was shit-talking her, called her sweet tits. She slapped him so hard his mama probably felt it, and then kneed him in the balls, not once, but three times. Took down a six-foot-six dude who weighed more than both of us combined."

"Wish I'd been there to see it."

"That part was pretty awesome," Charlie agreed.

"What came after was pretty awesome too," I murmured, low enough only she could hear me.

She blushed. "Stop," she hissed.

I laughed. "Not what you were sayin' then, baby."

She stiffened, and I knew then that I'd lost her. "Crow—"

I remembered Tran's words. "Charlie, what was I supposed to do? That wasn't a situation I could walk away from. They had my bike surrounded."

"He's *dead*, Crow."

"Better him than me," I snapped. "And it was him or me. You were there, darlin'. You know that."

"I just don't know if I can do that life, Crow. I'm okay being a little on the wild side." She was facing me, suddenly forgetting our audience or her embarrassment, gesturing angrily. "Sex in a public bathroom? Sure. It was the most fun I've ever had, and the best sex I've ever had, by several orders of magnitude. I'd do it again. In fact, I kind of want to. But brawls and knife fights? Watching you get beaten up by almost a dozen men? Watching you...just *destroy* them like they're little children? Some of those men will never walk without a limp again, will never be the same. One of them has permanent brain damage, I guarantee you. And Yak is *dead*. Good riddance to bad rubbish, sure. He was bad man, and he would have killed you and raped me. Again, I get that. I do. But that's way far beyond being a little on the wild side."

"Charlie—"

"And you have a record? Manslaughter? When were you going to tell me that?" She paused. "Did you go to jail?"

I sighed. Paced away. Stuffed my fists in my jeans

pockets. Braced a shoulder against the side of the bus, leaning against it. I felt her behind me. Waiting.

"Two years at Florence. Maximum security prison in Arizona." I rubbed my scalp, felt the bottom drop out of my stomach. "Manslaughter."

"So this is the second time."

I nodded. "The first time…" I sighed. "Don't really wanna tell that story. Not sure I can."

Myles spoke up, "Charlie, listen to me, please. Crow is more than my best friend. He's more my family than anyone blood ever could be. Don't make him tell that story. It was…bad. And not his fault."

She was silent a while. "Myles—you tell it then."

I looked at her.

"Sure," I growled. "What the fuck ever. But on the bus, not out here."

Myles groaned. "Shit, I don't wanna relive that either." He met her eyes. "Not gonna change anything, Charlie. He's still the man you know."

"One who's killed two people."

Oh, sweetheart. If only you knew. The one-percent tattoo on my arm isn't about the manslaughter charge. That's a tattoo I had to earn the hard way.

Well, in for a penny, in for a pound. Might as well scare her all the way gone.

I stomped up onto the bus, yanked a bottle of Johnnie Blue from the cabinet, and cracked it open. I swigged long and hard, till it burned, and then some more. Plopped down on a couch, popped open my guitar case and gingerly drew out my guitar—the one River Dog and I had made together.

I began plucking strings, fingering a melody, something I've had floating around my skull for days, now.

Myles, Lexie, and Charlie followed up onto the bus, and I knew Jupiter was going to park his ass outside the door and stand guard.

I paused in my playing, took another drink. I'd need it to get through this.

Charlie didn't sit by me—she sat next to Lexie, facing me, eyes sad and scared and confused. Watching me play.

"Did River Dog make that guitar?" she asked.

I nodded. "Me and him. The last thing we did together before he died." I traced the grains in the wood. "This is Brazilian Rosewood. Super rare, super exotic. Him and Mammy traveled to Brazil and bartered services for enough wood to make one guitar."

"I know nothing about guitars, but it's beautiful."

I laughed. "He wasn't famous. But in custom guitar circles, he was well-known. Getting your hands on a River Dog Custom is the holy grail for high-end collectors." I patted the guitar. "This one? I mean, to me it's invaluable because of the memory, the sentimental value. But to someone else? Shit, this thing could go for…thirty grand, easily, probably closer to forty."

She blinked. "Wow. I had no idea."

"He'll never make any more, obviously, and their quality is second to none."

Myles laughed. "I've known Crow my whole life, and was half raised by River Dog, and *I* don't have one of his guitars."

"Oh."

Gesturing to Crow, Myles said, "I been after his ass for years to try his hand at making one, but he won't." He sounded easy breezy, but his eyes were shuttered. "You want a drink, Charlie?"

She shook her head. "No. I want the story."

"Why?" Myles asked.

"I need to know."

"You won't sleep for a week, I'm warnin' you." He stared her down, gave her a rare glimpse at serious Myles. "And it won't change anything. He is who he is. It's history."

I took another pull. "Just tell her, Myles."

"Everything?" He sounded skeptical.

"Everything."

"You had enough?" he said to me, gesturing at the bottle.

"Hell no." I handed him the bottle. "I'll share, though."

He accepted the bottle and took a swig, handed it back. "All right, well, here we go. I'm guessin' he's given you the broad outlines of his life. Dad and Uncle founded AzTex MC. Those two were matches and dynamite, Coyote and Na'ura. Your mom was a badass bitch, man."

Lexie bristled. "Myles."

I cut her off. "That would have been the greatest compliment you could have given my mother. Don't go taking offense on her account. She's dead anyway."

Myles chuckled. "One time, we were, what? Eight? Nine? She'd brought you and me and Tania to a pizza place. Had her leather on with the club patches an' everything, but since she had us, she was driving a truck. No clue where she got it. But anyway, she had us, the three of us, loud and wild youngsters all crazy on Cokes and gummy bears. And these four college douchebags started talking shit about us for being out of control brats or some shit. Na'ura didn't like that."

I had to laugh. What a memory. "Mom gave those assholes a thrashing I guarantee you they never forgot."

"With a pizza tray. One of those metal ones they serve pizza on, you know? She whupped 'em up one side and down the other, till the manager begged her to stop. Those little bitches ran off crying. The manager probably would've tried to kick us out, if not press charges, but he'd seen Mom's colors and knew better than to fuck with the old lady of an AzTex patch."

Charlie offered a small smile. "She sounds amazing."

"She was," I said.

Myles sighed. "I really don't want to talk about this, Charlie. I had to do Skype sessions with a therapist for weeks to get past this shit. I do *not* want to unbox it all."

She let out a ragged, hoarse sigh. "I'm sorry. I just…after what happened, I need to know."

Myles looked at me again. "Crow. Your story, man."

I shook my head. "Not telling it. Can't. But I'm fine with her knowing. She's already scared of me, so I may as well put it all out there for her. I just…I can't. Sorry, brother."

Myles sighed. Hung his head. "Fine. But I'm gonna need another hit of that." He drank from my bottle, rested it on his knee, and drank again. "Shit. Okay. Fine. Here you go."

And he began talking.

ELEVEN

Charlie

I WATCHED CROW SINK INTO HIMSELF. HIS EYES WITHDREW, his presence just…receded. Shrank. Darkened. Iced over. His fingers moved on the guitar with a speed and fluidity that spoke of remarkable skill, even though he was only picking at it absentmindedly. He was miles away, years away.

"Right." Myles sighed again. "So. Tania. We grew up like siblings—well, Crow and her did. I was the tag-along little brother, sorta. Didn't grow up in the club, but when Dad was touring, I basically lived with Coyote and Na'ura and Crow, so I looked at Tania as a sister."

"She was Yank's daughter, not his old lady," Crow clarified without fixing his eyes on anything.

"All the old ladies basically took care of all the kids, as needed. It was very insular. If you needed someone to watch your kids, one of the ladies from the club would do it. And usually, it was Na'ura. The kids loved her, and she loved kids."

"Takin' too fuckin' long," Crow snarled, surly and pissed off. "Quit stalling and tell her what the fuck happened. She don't need the fuckin' Lifetime movie version."

The amount of F-bombs he dropped was always directly correlated to his mood, I was discovering. The more aggressive his mood, the more he said "fuck."

Myles nodded. "Anyway, Crow and Tania were basically an arranged marriage. Yank was a founding member, and Coyote was president of the MC."

"Yank was a top dog, but he didn't want no real job, like treasurer or some shit," Crow put in. "But he was Dad's right-hand man. A good dude."

"So. Him and Tania. Raised like siblings, but by the time ya'll were, what, thirteen? You were...well, together, sort of."

Crow nodded. "Thirteen. First kiss, first everything with her."

"Right. So, then the deal goes bad, Coyote and Na'ura, and more than half the fuckin' club gets iced. Somehow, Yank managed to get out alive. One of the few."

Crow snorted. "Nobody says iced, moron."

"Fine. They were killed. He probably told you this, too. Nobody could find his grandparents, so he lived with Sister Maria in Mexico for like, eight, ten months?"

"A year."

"Yeah. During that time my mom disappeared, Grampa died, Gramma went into the home, and Dad was on tour over in Louisiana. I lived with Tran till River Dog and Mammy showed up, looking for Crow." He was distant himself, remembering. "Shit. Anyway. They took you in, took me in, and we rode in their Airstream with 'em for…how long was it? Two years?"

Crow nodded again. "About that. River Dog died on my sixteenth birthday."

Myles scratched his jaw. "Tryin' to keep it short. Anyway. Um…yeah. You started running with the AzTex, then. Earning your patch. You had it early, I know that."

"Tran was prez after Dad and Snake both died, and he was like a second dad to me. He knew I needed that patch, and he made sure I got it."

I glanced over at Crow and could see he was far, far away. Not looking at me, not looking at anything.

"You earned it. And them being a one-percenter MC, I don't even want to know what you did to get it."

"Even if I could talk about that, I wouldn't. Can't. Not allowed to. And wouldn't, anyway. Nobody's business but mine and the Devil's." That deep, rough voice. So hard, so cold. Yet part of me wanted to soothe it.

"What's a one-percenter MC?" Lexi asked.

"An outlaw club," Crow answered. "Means ninety-nine percent of MCs are decent law-abiding folks who like to ride motorcycles and shit. Rough characters, maybe, but mostly just decent folks. The one percent, like us, are not. It means the club has defined itself as being outside the law."

"Oh. So…criminals," I breathed.

Crow laughed, and it wasn't a nice sound. "Yes, Charlie. *Criminals.*" His voice was scathing, sarcastic.

"Patching into a one-percenter club is not an easy or simple thing to do," Myles said. "It's like hazing, but worse, from what I understand. I wanted to join, but Crow wouldn't hear of it. Neither would Tran, for that matter. Said I was destined for different things."

Crow spoke again, "Well, he was right, yeah?"

Myles sighed. "Yeah, but still. Back then, I just wanted to be in the club."

"You just thought you did. I was born into it. It's different."

"Just gotta get this timeline right—been a few years, hard to remember it all straight. So—your mom and dad and a good half of the club died when you were thirteen, you lived with Sister Maria in Mexico for a year while your grandparents were off-grid down on the Yucatán, and then we lived with River Dog and Mammy for two years—making you and Tania…sixteen?" He nodded. "Sounds right. Anyway, you and Tania were a thing, when you returned to the El Paso compound after River Dog died. You and her were inseparable. In *luuuuurrrrvvvvv.*" He drawled the word, making a joke of it.

Crow's scowl turned on Myles. "Don't mock, motherfucker."

Myles sighed. "Sorry. Just tryin' to lighten the mood a bit."

"It's an old ugly story. Lighten the mood later. Get to the fuckin' point so we can be done with exhuming the memory of my dead fuckin' fiancé." I'd never heard anyone, ever, sound so bitter, so morose, so unhappy. The darkness in his eyes was vicious, subsuming, swallowing, boiling.

Maybe this telling of truths had been a mistake.

But I'd…I'd watched him kill someone. Watched him singlehandedly decimate eleven tough men. He'd taken a beating without flinching, taken a nasty cut to the ribs and patched it up with a T-shirt and duct tape. Speaking of which—

"I should look at your ribs, Crow," I said.

He shook his head. Swigged from the bottle of Johnnie Walker. "Nah. I'm fine. It's a cut. Had worse. Forget about it."

"It needs stitches," I said.

"I ain't getting no goddamn stitches, woman, so fuckin' forget it," he snarled. "I don't do hospitals. I don't do doctors. It'll heal. If it don't, who the fuck is gonna care? I won't bleed to death from that little cut."

"It's not little," I pressed. "It's six inches long and very deep."

He stared me down, eyes colder than anything I'd ever seen. From him or anyone. "I said I'm *fine*. Quit pushing, Charlotte."

I bit back emotions. "I'm just concerned, Crow."

"Don't be. I'm just a killer, right? So why fuckin' bother?"

"That's not—Crow, I'm not—"

He turned away from me, a clear dismissal. He took another long pull, and I realized he'd already had nearly a quarter of the bottle, yet showed no signs of inebriation.

"Just fucking tell her the story, Myles." His voice was clear, steady, sober, and angry.

Myles shook his head. "Eighteen years old, you and Tania both. You were a fully patched-in member by then, and Tran's right-hand man. Involved in everything. Don't know how you managed it all, but you were everywhere, all at once. Acting as guitar tech, manager, and stage crew for me, living with Tania, and working for Tran and the club, all at once. Not sure when you slept."

"Didn't. Couple hours a night, three or four usually. Never needed much sleep. More than six hours a night and I get cranky from too much. Four is about my peak. Been that way since I was a kid. Drove Mom and Dad nuts. They'd put me to bed at nine, and I'd be up for the day by one in the morning. Then they let me stay up till midnight, but I'd be up for the day by three or four a.m."

"Makes sense. You'd run a show for me at some bar in East Texas, and then you'd haul off on your bike to do some sort of club business in Arizona or New Mexico or somewhere else in Texas. You were on that bike for hours a day." Myles waved a hand. "Anyway. You, Tania, Yank, and Boots and their girls were all out partying one weekend. I joined you later in the night with a girl I was seeing at the time."

"Seeing? You were screwing her. And three other women that I knew of," Crow put in. "Let's not paint too rosy a picture."

Myles shrugged. "Sure, fine. Jessica was a friend with benefits." A glance at Lexie to assess her reaction.

She just grinned at him. "I had four friends with benefits on rotation, once, during my sophomore year at U-Conn."

Myles was relieved, visibly. "How'd you rotate them without pissing anyone off?"

She smirked. "I didn't. I just texted whoever I felt like fucking at the time, based on which dick seemed to fit my mood. They knew the score, and if they wanted this poon, they played by my rules." Lexie laughed, running a hand through her messy hair. "I wasn't about to play games. It was sex, plain and simple. No place for feelings, especially not jealousy. Start acting possessive, or try to tell me what I can do or with whom, you get ghosted real fast."

Myles chuckled. "Hard ball, huh?"

"I mean, I have a very healthy respect for my pussy. I know what I have to offer, and if you don't wanna play by my rules, you don't get my poon."

I huffed. "Lexie, you are *so* vulgar. You're worse than most guys I know."

Myles grinned at Lexie. "Well, all I'm gonna say is, where do I sign up for a slot in your rotation?"

Lexie didn't grin back. "You're Myles North. There is no rotation." Her gaze was heated in a way that made me deeply uncomfortable—it was too personal, too private. "You're not sharing me as long as I'm not sharing you."

Myles was equally intense. "You seen any groupies lately, Lexie?"

"No."

"Then there you go."

"ANYWAY," Crow groused. "On with it. Enough of the sex eyes."

Myles grabbed the bottle of whisky. Swigged. "It was three in the morning at this honky tonk in, like, McShitsville, Texas. Middle of nowhere. Not even a fuckin' cow for ten miles. How the place stayed open, I could never figure out, but you guys loved that bar."

"It was a front, dumbass," Crow muttered. "We moved product through the back. I was there as an enforcer. Boots handled the product, Yank was the money man."

"What product?" Myles asked, looking genuinely surprised.

"Dope. Coke mainly. Small amounts of meth, some acid, and lots and lots of pot. We ran some prostitutes through there, too." He glanced at me, and then Lexie. "We only worked with women who'd chosen to be there. We weren't slavers, and we took down any rivals who did deal in any women who were underage or there unwillingly." A shrug. "That was Tran's rule. His ma had been kidnapped by traffickers, of which he was a product, back in

Manila. So he had a real hard-on for making sure the girls were there of their own choice, and over eighteen."

"How decent of him," Lexie droned, her voice sarcastic.

Crow just shrugged. "I didn't like that end of it, personally, but I was just a kid. I did what I was told. It's how shit works, babe, whether you like it or not."

Myles rolled a hand. "So, to continue. That bar, which I now understand, was a business front. It was just a club for guys and their women, and a few regulars I don't think were affiliated with the club. Some hard-looking dudes rolled in, unexpectedly. A rival gang, maybe?"

Crow nodded. "The Scorpions. A small-time local club hoping to seize some territory and influence by pulling one over on us. They'd been warned not to fuck with us, but they didn't listen."

"There was, what, ten, twelve of them that night?"

"At least, that's how many had come inside. There were more of them outside. Inside, it was just me, Boots, Yank, and Tommy, the guy who ran the bar. He wasn't a patched member, but he was loyal to the club, since we made sure he got a nice fat cut of the profits. So there were, like, four of us, and twenty of them."

"With innocent women around," Myles added. His expression darkened. "I wasn't there when the shit went down since Jess and I had left to...um, you know...but as I understand it they walked in, spread out, and started shooting."

"Jesus," Lexie breathed.

I couldn't speak.

"Thing about the AzTex is, we didn't do guns if we could help it. You start shooting, shit gets real fuckin' complicated real fuckin' fast. We preferred to deal with shit the old-fashioned way—fists and feet, bats and chains, knives, knuckle dusters, saps. Keeps things civilized, Dad used to say."

"A knife or a bat is more civilized than a gun?" I asked. "How is that?"

Crow didn't look at me. Kept his eyes on his guitar, and his fingers flew on the strings, playing a complicated series of pinging tones. "Anyone can pop off a shot. Takes no guts, no balls, no skill. Literally, a kid can do it. Takes dedication and a big sac to walk up to someone and slug 'em till they don't get up. You gotta be real about what you're doing. Keeps a motherfucker honest, feeling their face under your fist."

I shuddered at the ice in his voice, and in his eyes. "I see," I whispered. "Do you carry a gun?"

He shook his head. "Nope. Mom and Dad were shot. That turned me off guns for life. I've never so much as held a gun in my life, and I never will. Made that vow the day I saw Mom and Dad's bodies in that morgue."

I blinked hard. "You saw their bodies?"

He nodded. "I was the only next of kin—I just had them and Uncle Snake, since River Dog and Mammy were off-grid. I had to ID 'em."

"God, I'm so sorry," I murmured.

His eyes finally met mine. He heard the genuine sorrow in my voice, the compassion. "Yeah."

"Well, Boots and Yank didn't have your compunction about guns," Myles said. "They returned fire, and they didn't miss. Not the way the other guys did."

"Fuckin Scorpion assholes thought it would be like a movie," Crow growled. "Thought they could roll in with cheap Uzis and spray the room like they're fuckin' Rambo or some shit. Don't work that way. Couldn't hit the broad side of a goddamn barn."

"Well, they missed. Boots and Yank didn't. Took about sixty seconds for Boots and Yank to drop all of those fuckers." A long, long silence. "When I say they missed, I mean they missed Crow, Boots, Yank, and Tommy. They hit Tania."

"Oh god," I whispered.

Myles sighed. "Don't start the 'oh gods' just yet. That was just the beginning." Another pause. "Tania didn't die right away."

Crow was silent for a long time. "She was pregnant."

"Oh Jesus," Lexie gasped. "No. No way."

Crow nodded. "Four months. Hadn't been planned, but we were excited. We had support from the club, Mama Mahalia, Mama Yank."

I felt my eyes start to well up. "Crow."

He shook his head. "Took a round to the chest and another to the stomach. Went septic, lung collapsed, lost the baby…they couldn't do shit. I sat in the waiting room at the hospital for three fuckin' days. Wouldn't let me see her, 'cause we weren't married and I wasn't actual family. Got violent about seein' her, until they called the cops. If I wanted to see her, I had to quiet my ass down, so I quieted my ass down. I was just some tattooed Indian thug to those racist fucking backwoods fuckin' rednecks." A pause. "Didn't get to see her. She died. I sat in that fuckin' waiting room for three days, not eating, not sleeping, unable to see the woman I loved, the mother of my unborn child. And she fuckin' died."

"Crow, my god. I'm so, *so* sorry." I couldn't help crying.

He reached across and brushed my cheek with his thumb, a glimmering hint of the soft, kind Crow I'd known only hours ago reappearing, however briefly. "That was ten years ago. It still hurts, but I'm as over as I'll ever be. No point in you cryin' over it."

"Well…too bad. Because I'm going to. You shouldn't have had to go through that."

"But I did."

Myles was gazing into the middle distance, lost in the memory. "Crow eventually showed up at the club compound looking…fucking *haggard*. And angrier than any human being I'd ever seen in my life. He grabbed a pair of knuckle dusters and tore off on his bike. Looking for the president of that club, the Scorpions."

Crow laughed. "He knew he'd fucked up—hadn't been there for the hit, the pussy. He ghosted. Ran to Seattle or some shit. Never found him."

"Crow looked for three days. Not sleeping, hadn't eaten, drinking like a fish. Ended up in a bar outside Tucson, hammered off his ass and full of hate." He sighed. "He'd been up for almost a week at that point. Skin and bones, surviving on liquor and hatred."

"Don't remember much of that week. I remember the hospital waiting room. Remember the doctor, accompanied by six security guards, telling me Tania had died and so had the baby. Remember it took all six guards and two tasers to get me off him. I remember combing most of Texas, New Mexico, and Arizona, going to every biker bar I knew of between Tucson and El Paso. You said it was three days—it was longer than that. She died on a Thursday, and I regained consciousness, in handcuffs, in the back of an ambulance the following Wednesday.

"All I remember after the doctor and the tasers is being on my bike, on the highway, going ninety or a hundred, reckless, not giving a shit if I wrecked. Bar after bar, every little place I'd ever been. I would drink at every bar, shot after shot after shot. Probably should've died of alcohol poisoning—not sure how I didn't. Barely ate, maybe a burger once or twice. I think I fell asleep standing up at a urinal in a rest stop bathroom."

A pause.

Crow continued. "Don't remember how it started, or who I killed. Nothing. I was blackout. Conscious and operating, but I don't remember jack shit about it. As far as I know, some asshole picked a fight with me and I snapped. Him and his buddies beat the shit out of me, but not before I smashed the poor fucker's head in. They fuckin'…they nearly killed me. I remember wishing they had. Spent a week in the hospital under armed guard. Then I got transferred to county lockup and got arraigned, tried for manslaughter, convicted, even though I didn't remember shit. I'd done it, so I was still liable whether I remembered it or not. The club hired a good defense attorney, and got me a reduced sentence seeing as my blood alcohol level was inhumanly high, and

I'd just lost my girlfriend and a baby. Mitigating circumstances or some shit. Even so, I still got two years at a maximum-security pen, because of how violent the fight was. I mean, it was ugly as fuck, apparently."

"You said you don't remember it?" I asked.

He took a swig of liquor. Swallowed, hissed. Refused to look at me. "Want the truth? I wish I could forget. It's like watching a movie. I had absolutely no control. His face is nothing but a blur. Some big asshole, and six of his big asshole friends. Seems like the guy's face was familiar, but shit, I don't fuckin' know. The memory I have is vague and just flashes and fragments. Some assholes talking shit, calling me little Indian boy. Just picking a fight. I don't know. I just know I remember seeing...black. Black rage. Berserk, uncontrollable rage. Like all the hate and evil and pain in all of hell was inside me, and...that dumb asshole triggered it."

"He wasn't himself. There was no Crow in him left." Myles stared at his friend. "I saw him in the hospital, and he was just...gone. Someone else. Nothing. His eyes were dead and unfocused. He wanted to die."

"Tried. But they made sure I couldn't." Crow bit the words out.

I swallowed. Ached. "Crow..."

"Those two years in the pen saved me," Crow said. "My cellmate saved me. Not gonna say much about my time in the pen, but it was boredom and exercise, reading, working in the shop. Talking to my cellmate. He got me to the point that I understood I was responsible for what I had done, that the life I'd chosen was how I'd gotten where I was. He'd found Jesus, my cellmate. Tried to convert me, but I couldn't get there. Got to the point that I understood my culpability in all the shit that had gone down. Mark, my cellmate, told me the day I got let out that I had a chance to start over. Make different choices."

Myles moved to sit beside Crow. They shared the bottle, passing it between them, swig after swig in an old, easy pattern. They finished the bottle. "You got out, and Tran sent Yank to get you. You told Yank you wanted him to bring you to me." A look between them, speaking of years of brotherhood. "You showed up at my apartment at two in the afternoon, in the same bloodstained clothes they'd arrested you in. Told me you couldn't go back to the club. Wanted to go on the road with me."

"You made it seem like I was doing *you* a favor," Crow said.

"You were!" Myles said, laughing. "I'd done precisely dick in the two years you were locked up. Local shows in the Texas, Oklahoma, New Mexico, Arizona bar circuit. Same as my dad, same as Gramps. I was drinking my proceeds, had no music, was stuck doing covers and the same dozen or songs you and I had written together before you got locked up."

"That was your grind, man," Crow said. "Your ten thousand hours. Learning to tour, to play, to perform. You weren't doing dick, you were learning."

"But I got nowhere without you. You showed up that day, and we wrote, what, fifty songs together in the next two months? We wrote about everything. You poured your soul into those songs. All the shit you'd been through.

"You took over managing me, got me bigger gigs, better pay. Kept me from drinking all the profits so we had some money to put into better gear, and a van to travel in. Then we played in that bar, opened for that act that later blew up. Got seen by some exec, recorded a demo, and off we went."

Crow eyed me. "So. There you go. I was a criminal, an enforcer for an outlaw motorcycle gang. Lost my girlfriend and baby in a shooting, killed a guy in a drunken bar brawl, spent two years in a federal maximum-security penitentiary for manslaughter." He waited. "Now you know. You want to know more? Might as well know everything. The years I worked for Tran as an enforcer, I was a monster. I was angry about Mom and Dad. Started to feel invincible. I beat people to a pulp for crossing the club.

Did evil shit for the club. Pulled the trigger for the club more than once."

"I thought you said you'd never held a gun?" I asked.

He shrugged. "Yeah, well, I lied. I don't carry a gun, haven't since I got out of jail. I hate guns now and I did then too, but when Tran gave me an order, I followed it. Tran's a good guy, but don't get in the way of his business, and don't cross him. He's my second dad, but I had to stay clear of him when I got out of the pen. I knew I'd end up right back where I'd been—enforcing, going down that violent path. I wanted something different. I wanted to live, and if I went back to the club, even though Tran had cleaned up the club, gotten rid of the nastier drugs like meth and quit running the prostitution circles, it was still an outlaw club, still ran pot in serious amounts, as well as really top-tier pure Columbian blow. I wanted none of it."

I was confused. "I thought once you joined a gang like that you couldn't leave."

He laughed. "Call it a gang in front of Tran and he'd be pissed. It's a *club*. Different." He sighed. "It's not simple, no. You're in for life. Especially when you're deep in the elements that put it outside the law, like I was. But I'm Coyote's boy, and Dad had saved Tran's ass more than once and most significantly, the day of the big shootout, and he'd half raised me himself. So Tran let me go my own way on what we say is an 'out good' basis, meaning I'm not part of daily operations, but I'm still a full patch member of the club in good standing. I wear the cut, ride a bike, and if I need anything, I call the club. I'm still a proud member of the AzTex. I just don't live the life. Can't. If any those guys ever showed up needing me, I'd be there for them no matter what, but they know I've got a good life, teching for Myles, so they don't involve me."

I locked eyes with him. "Which is why you called Tran, after what happened."

He nodded. "Tran knows people everywhere. Has connections in the Denver PD specifically. But more than that, he's the president of my club. One of the few men I truly trust, outside of Myles."

"And you're out of the life, as you say, but you're never really, truly ever going to fully leave the club." I had to get my mind around this.

He shrugged. "I was born into the club. My father and uncle founded it. My mom was part of it. I lived my entire life, with the exception of a few months here and there, in the club, on the compound near El Paso. It was my whole world. The guys are my family, but I've just chosen a different path." He held my gaze. "This is who I am, Charlie.

I have a violent past. Blood on my hands. I can't change that. When I'm faced with trouble, I'm not gonna back down. I use my fists to solve shit when I have to. I ain't ever gonna be some tame-ass bank clerk. I don't even have a high school diploma, much less some fancy-ass college degree."

He held out his arms, guitar in one hand, a now-empty bottle of Johnnie in the other; his face was bruised, he still had the T-shirt duct taped to his ribs, the white shirt now red with blood; his knuckles were bloody, and blood was crusted on his nose, mouth, jaw, and chest.

"This is me, babe," he said. "Take me or leave me, but I ain't ever gonna be anything but what you see."

My heart ached. He'd seen so much pain, so much turmoil. He was kind. He was gentle with me.

The sex had been...out of this world.

His kisses were a drug.

His touch was addictive.

But...he'd killed men with his bare hands. He was frighteningly capable of extreme violence.

And I just...I wasn't sure I could get past that.

What did I want for my life? To live on a tour bus with him? Never have a home? How could I remake my career if I was on the road with him? I couldn't. I wanted him, the man he was. I wanted the man he was when it was just him and me, alone, in bed, talking.

But I wasn't sure I was ready for the man he was out in the world—handling problems with his fists and asking questions later.

His past was past, but there would always be the specter of Yak in my mind, on the ground. Motionless. Blood seeping from his nose and a deep bloody dent in his temple, eyes open and glassy. I would never forget the men on the ground, moaning, grown men crying in agony, limbs and skulls and bones destroyed.

I couldn't unsee all that.

I swallowed. My eyes watered. "Crow, I…"

He nodded. "Yeah. I know. I saw it the moment you looked at me when that fight was over." He set the empty bottle aside, stood up—wobbled a little, and it was oddly reassuring to know he was mortal enough to feel a whole bottle of whiskey. His eyes were lucid, searing. "An angel like you don't belong in the life of a man like me, Charlie."

"It's not that, Crow. I just…"

He took his guitar, holding it by the neck, and moved to the exit of the bus. "Rip the Band-Aid off fast, Charlie. Just go."

And with that he was gone.

I looked at Lexie. "I need to get to Ketchikan," I said. "I…I can't be here anymore. Let's go."

Myles didn't say anything, but his eyes widened as he turned to Lexie.

She swallowed. Hard. "Um. Charlie...I—I'm staying. With Myles."

I felt a fist to my gut. "Lex, come on. You just met him."

"I didn't say I was marrying him, but I'm having fun. I like him. We're good together."

"Lex, I—what about the road trip?"

She winced. "I'm not ready for Alaska yet, Charlie."

"What are you going to do, Alexandra?" I heard myself snapping, taking it out on her, unfairly, but I couldn't seem to stop myself. "Drink and fuck with a rock star until he gets bored of you?" I glanced at Myles. "No offense, Myles, really."

He lifted an eyebrow, irritation on his face. "I mean, I do take offense to that, Charlie. I'm not like that, with anyone, and I never have been. Plus, I genuinely like Lexie, a lot. And we do more than just drink and fuck. Not to fucking mention, what business is it of yours what we do together?"

"Lex, we had a plan. What about college? What about what happened? What is your plan?"

"Charlie, don't." She stood up and faced me, nose to nose. "This is what I want. I'm sorry that doesn't fit into your plans for my life, but I don't answer to you."

"Maybe you should."

"Because your judgment is working out *so well* for you," she snapped.

"Girls, come on—" Myles said.

"Shut up, Myles," Lexie and I snapped in unison.

I stared at Lexie. "After what happened back East, I think you'd—"

"You don't *know* what happened back East, Charlotte!"

"Because you wouldn't tell me!" I shouted. I glanced, saw Crow leaning in the doorway of the bus, watching. I ignored him.

"You want to know? Fine, I'll tell you. Today must be the day we unburden ourselves of terrible secrets." She stood tall, eyes proud, pain and anger on her face. "I got pregnant with Marcus's baby. I took about a dozen tests, including a blood test at a hospital. I told him, and he...he—" Her face crumpled momentarily. "At first he didn't believe me. When I showed him the results of the blood test, he accused me of doing it on purpose. To trap him into being with me. I left, and he showed up at my dorm. I wouldn't see him. So then when I decided we had to talk, I went to his house. He...we...we ended up screwing again, what we both sort of knew was going to be the last time, and that was when his wife showed up. Caught us in the act."

"Oh god, Lexie," I breathed.

"His kids were there. They saw us too. Saw me fucking their daddy." She blinked hard. "Want to know the real kicker, which I didn't know until later? His wife was the school dean's niece. She went to him. Got me kicked out of school. Revoked my scholarship. The dean himself called every other dean he knew and blacklisted me." A sob. "And Marcus...told his wife I'd seduced him. Some brain-dead story that made it all my fault."

"What an asshole," I muttered.

"That asshole gave me three grand, told me I knew what to do, and that he never wanted to see me again." She picked up the empty bottle of Johnnie, stared at it as if wishing it were full. "I took the money, and I did exactly what he expected me to do."

I covered my mouth. "Alexandra, no."

"Alexandra, yes." She chewed on her lip. "What was I going to do, Charlotte? Run back to Mommy, knocked up at twenty-one by my university professor? I don't think so." Her eyes cut to mine. "So yeah, Charlotte, I had an abortion."

I felt gutted. "Alone?"

"Yes, alone. Went in alone, went through it alone, came out and went home, alone. It was only later I went a little crazy and called you. When I realized I had to leave school, and that I had nowhere to go. I packed up the bulk of my shit and sent it to Alaska, to

Mom. It's already there. What's in your car is every-thing I have with me." She blinked back tears. "Well, it's in Myles's room, now. My stuff, I mean."

I couldn't hold back tears. "Why didn't you call me earlier?"

"And have you talk me out of it? I have plans for my life, Charlotte, and they don't include kids at twenty-one, when I haven't accomplished any of my life goals."

"What are your life goals, Lex?"

"I don't even know anymore!" She turned away, stared out the tinted privacy glass window. "You know what I wanted to be when I grew up, my whole child-hood?" She didn't wait for an answer. "A musician."

I rocked back on my heels. "What?"

"You were busy with school and all your over-achiever extracurricular activities, so you never saw, but you know where I was? In my room, alone, with my guitar and my ukulele, writing songs. I have a folder with hundreds of songs. CD recordings of my-self. Videos of myself taken on Mom's old phone, saved to a cloud drive." She paused. "Then, when I was a junior, Dad sat me down and...and told me I was—that I wasn't talented enough to make it as a musician, and that I should set my sights on a more realistic goal."

I shook my head. "He didn't."

"He fucking did." She was shaking. "That... it killed me. Destroyed me. I cried for days. I mean, he was my *dad*. I thought he...if he said that, it must be true. I didn't know any better. He didn't believe in me. Shut my dreams down. So that's when I figured I'd just..." She shrugged. "Go to school. I'd planned on moving to Nashville and working my way up as a singer-songwriter, but when Dad said that to me, I just...I lost myself. Got accepted to U-Conn, and found something like a passion for life in feminist lit and all that."

"Lex, I—"

"The point is, here, on this bus, this tour, Myles, the whole thing? It's a chance to start over. To really find myself. College is gone, done. Never going back. I'll never get a degree, which means those years are wasted." She fixed her eyes on mine. "So what do I have, now? My guitar and my ukulele, and a man who thinks I'm pretty all right, as a person. Who doesn't judge me for my stupid decisions. Is it love? Fuck if I know. I don't think he does either. Maybe it'll burn out. I don't know. I just know I'm not going to Alaska...yet." She held my gaze, shook her head. "You go. I'm staying here."

Tears burned in my eyes. On my cheeks. In my mouth. "Lex, I—"

"We have different paths from here, Char-Char.

That's *okay*. You came and got me when I needed you, and I'm thankful. I love you. I don't expect you to understand. But this is where I'm going, for right now. See this through, whatever it looks like."

I hugged her. "Okay, okay." I clung tight. "You should have called me sooner."

"You'd have talked me out of it. Maybe it's wrong, I don't know, but it was what was right for me. I couldn't have that man's baby. Wouldn't. It was all a mistake, I know that, but I wasn't about to pay that price. I'll probably burn in hell for it, but it's done, and I had to do it alone."

"Just...don't get into the same situation with Myles," I murmured.

"I won't. We're careful." A squeeze. "Plus, he's different."

"Lex—"

"We're good right now, Charlie," she said. "Shut up so you don't ruin it."

I laughed. "Fine. Just be smart."

She pulled away. "For the record, I think you walking away right now is a mistake."

I frowned. "Now it's your turn to shut up before you ruin things."

She held out her hands. "All I'm saying. He's a good man. And he's good for you." She hugged me, kissed my cheek. "But you do you, boo."

"I will, Lex. I will."

She nodded. "And that's your right, as a person. Just like this is mine."

I groaned. "I'm going. You have your stuff?"

"I brought it all on earlier." She hugged me again. "You sure you're okay?"

I nodded. Shook my head. Shrugged. "I don't know. I just…I need to be in Alaska. I need to think."

"Be safe, okay?" She shoved me away. "Go. Say hi to Mom and Cass for me."

"I will. What should I tell them?"

"That I'm doing my own thing, and I'll be along…whenever." She sighed. "Tell them whatever you want. The truth, even."

I shook my head. "No, that's your story to tell, not mine."

"You can't lie for me, Charlie. You're incapable of that."

"I know. But I don't have to say anything, either. I can just say what happened and what you're doing is your business."

She smiled. "Perfect. Love you, Char. Thank you."

"Love you too. Be good."

She snorted. "Nah. That's boring."

I laughed, and left the bus. I had to push past Crow, who refused to move out the way. My car was waiting, idling, brought around for me, probably at the behest of Crow.

"Thanks," I murmured.

"Alaska, now, huh?" He stood with his fists in his pockets, gazing steadily at me, his expression carefully blank.

"Crow, I..."

He held up a hand. "Don't explain. I don't need it. I get it."

"You're amazing." I swallowed. "What we did was...amazing."

"Takes more than that though." He sighed. "I know it. I knew it, all along. I'm grateful for getting to spend time with you. It was my honor and my privilege."

My eyes stung. "Crow, dammit."

"Just sayin' the truth."

"I like you. I just—"

He touched my lips with one finger. "I said don't, Charlie. I don't need an explanation." He opened my car door, ushered me in. "Drive till you get tired. Get a hotel, sleep until you wake up. Don't think about me. Don't miss me. You're probably makin' the right decision. I ain't right for a woman like you." He closed my door, and I lowered the window, he leaned in. "But I can sure as fuck appreciate my privilege at getting what I got with you. I won't forget it."

I swallowed. I couldn't get past his violent past at this moment, but...I also couldn't help wondering if maybe I *was* making a mistake. "Goodbye, Crow."

He waved. "Bye, Charlie-girl."

I drove away, and I didn't look in the rearview mirror. Not even when I felt tears on my lip.

I was making the right choice. There was no future here.

There just wasn't.

There couldn't be.

Could there?

TWELVE

Crow

WATCHING THAT WOMAN DRIVE AWAY RIPPED MY heart out.

Wasn't much point in telling her I'd fallen in love with her. Wouldn't be fair to tie a woman like Charlotte Goode to the kind of life I could give her.

When had I fallen in love with her? Somewhere in between her kicking Yak in the nuts and feeling her come all over my cock in that nasty-ass bathroom.

I'd wanted better for her, but she'd taken to the experience with…gusto. I mean, god, the woman was a tiger, once she got going. I still had her claw marks on me, and bite-shaped bruises on my arms. I relished each one.

I missed the shit out of her.

The Denver show was a success. So were the back-to-back shows in the Twin Cities. Lexie and Myles were inseparable...and trouble. Wherever the crew was, partying, there they were. Laughing, drinking, the life of every moment. I envied them. They made it look so easy.

Shit, though, I knew there were things he wasn't telling her. He wasn't without his own demons he wrestled with in the small hours. Clearly neither was she. But that was their gig, not mine. I tuned and cared for the guitars, drank way too much whiskey, and played my guitar. I missed Charlie, but refused to call her—yeah, I had her number, and I'd programmed mine into her phone. Not that I was expecting a call.

Denver, Minneapolis-St. Paul, Milwaukee, Salt Lake City, Vegas, Albuquerque, Tucson...the shows went on, and the more time Myles spent with Lex, the more explosive his sets became. The woman had lit something inside him, I had to admit. I heard them playing together in his room, her on that little ukulele, singing in a voice that wasn't technically pure or sweet, but was somehow mesmerizing in a husky, Adele sort of way. She was good, and her dad had been an idiot, God rest him.

Days, a week. Two weeks.

Three.

A month after Charlie left the tour hit El Paso, and then shit went sideways.

Tran showed up at the show.

He pulled me aside when it was over.

Tall, wiry, lean, hard, tattooed from head to toe, black hair in a graying ponytail, wearing a denim cut over a black T-shirt and blue jeans, chewing on a plug, his hard-bitten eyes assessing me.

"You look like shit, boy." Rough, dark voice. Same as ever.

I hugged him, slapping his back. "Thanks, old man. Good to see you, too."

He laughed. Shoved me off. "Where's that girl of yours?"

"Alaska," I bit out. "You called it."

"How long she been gone?"

"Not long enough," I said, without meaning to. "Too long."

He drilled a stare into me. Seeing me as only a wily old fox like him could. "You love her."

"Shit, man. What the hell is love, anyway?"

He snorted. "Quit the bullshit, son. That maudlin philosophical horse dick ain't gonna impress me."

I growled. "What can I do, Tran? She saw what I did, heard what you said, and got the story. It was too much. She was soft, and good, and everything that's sweet and light in the world, but with a hidden wild side."

He laughed, cracking me across the back of the head. "You love her, ya dumb fuck. Go get her ass."

"And offer her what? More bar fights? Another manslaughter charge?"

"That's taken care of. That Yak character was wanted in three states for rape, kidnapping, sexual assault, and human trafficking. You did the world a favor, and I persuaded certain powers that be to see that. It's gone. No worries."

I sighed. "It's...the whole life, Tran."

"You ain't in the life anymore, kid."

"But I'm always a patch, and I ain't ever gonna be some tie-wearing Harvard type." I winced. "Yale, I mean. She'd correct me."

"She wants you to be that?"

"Well, no. That was her ex. He was a piece of shit, didn't appreciate her. Cheated on her."

"And she asked you to be somethin' you're not?"

I growled. "No, but she still left. Said she *just couldn't*. Whatever that means. Figured it just meant a man with a past like mine is no good for a woman like her."

"I may be not much but a crusty old road dog, but it sounds to me like she's just scared of loving you. You're a hell of a lot of man to figure out, not sure you're aware of it." He roughly cupped the back of my neck and shook me. "You're scared of her."

I snarled at him. "I ain't scared of shit."

"Then go see her, son. Better yet, quit this job you're wasting your talents on, empty out that storage locker, and haul your shit up to Alaska. You know damn good and well that if you took a mind, you'd be every bit as good of a luthier as your gramps was. You got the gift. I still got that piece you made me, and it sounds sweet as honey to this day. You are wasting your fucking life away as a guitar tech, Corvus. Quit bein' a goddamn pussy and go get the life you want."

Corvus. He was the only person, ever, to call me that, and he only used it when I was being stupid. It stung. Cut worse than the scar on my ribs had.

"That was a phase, man," I muttered. "I ain't touched wood since I got locked up."

"Because you still think you ain't worth enough to put down roots." He rubbed his stubbled jaw, fingernails skritching. "Shoulda never patched you in, like I did with Myles. You got talent beyond being some enforcer in an outlaw MC. Worst mistake I ever made."

"Bullshit, Tran. I was born into it."

"Don't mean it's all you are. Music is in your blood. Na'ura had talent, but she wanted what Coyote had— freedom. Doing what he wanted. Living dangerous.

She grew up sheltered, protected, guarded, and she resented it. But she coulda been something, just like you could." He jabbed a finger into my chest, eyes boring into me. "Do us both a favor, Crow."

"What's that?"

"Take off the cut. Fold it up. Put it in a box, and forget it. That's past. Quit hangin' on to it. You have my permission, Crow. You're not just out good, you're out for good. I'll always answer your call, no matter what, no matter when. But if you don't quit clinging to this goddamn fool notion that you don't get to have more than this—?" He gestured at the tour around us, the bus, the semi full of equipment, the bustle. "You'll never be anything *but* this. If it was all you were capable of, I'd get it. But you know that ain't true, and shit, I know Myles knows it, I've talked to him about it. He don't need you. He keeps you on because you're his brother. But he'd be happy to see the back of you, if it meant you were doing something worthy of the talents you got."

I felt him, then—Myles. Turned, saw him leaning against a semitruck tire a few feet away, listening. Lexie was leaning against him, hand on his chest, dressed in ripped tight jeans and a white sports bra and nothing else, not even shoes.

He left Lexie, and came over to me and grabbed my shoulders. He shook me. "Crow. Listen to him."

I shook my head. "She left me. It ain't meant to be. This is my life."

Myles shoved me, hard. "You know damn well she was just scared. You let her go because you're just as scared. You found something you want, and the minute she wavered, you caved. You talk a big talk about being a fighter, solving shit with your fists. And you know, there's not a soul on this planet I'd rather have at my side in a fight, or with a guitar, on the road. But you're a fuckin' coward and a pussy, Crow." He was pissed—*pissed*. "You been wasting away doing this shit for *years*, man. This ain't your dream, it's *mine*."

Hurt blazed through me. "Fuck you, Myles."

He grabbed me, and refused to let go. "You are my brother. I'd be stuck doing dive bars without you. I don't know what I'll do you without you." He lifted his chin, and I saw that look in his eye, the one that said he was fixing to tackle a tiger. "You're fired, Crow."

I reeled back on my heels. "What?"

He glanced at Alyn, the kid I'd been training to be a backup tech. "You're my new tech. Crow is moving on. Got it?"

Alyn's eyes widened. "Um. Yeah. Yes. Yes, sir!"

"You can do it, yeah?"

He nodded eagerly. "Yes, sir! I know all the songs. I know how to take care of all the guitars. I can tune by ear in the dark, one handed."

I felt Tran grab me by the shoulders as I lunged at Myles. "The fuck are you on about? That kid ain't ready."

"You trained him. You told me just last month you thought he could take over once in a while."

"Yeah, once in a while! Not full time!"

"Trial by fire. US tour's over in a few days anyway. He'll have time to brush up before the overseas leg starts."

I knew what he was doing, but it still gutted me to pieces. "You can't fire me, Myles."

He stepped into me, snagged me by the neck, butted his forehead against mine. "I can, and I am. Only way you'll figure out what the fuck to do with yourself." He held me, and refused to let go. "Make me a guitar. Write me songs, record on them your phone and send 'em over. Go get your girl."

"She's not my girl."

"She wants to be. She should be." He shook me. "Your *girl*. Your *woman*. Not your old lady. That ain't you no more, brother. Go *be* someone, goddammit."

I hadn't cried since Mom and Dad died, and only then alone in bed, stifling it into a pillow. Now, I felt the tears sting. "Fuck."

He laughed. "Got you, finally." He shook me again, released me. Shoved me. "Go, motherfucker. I mean it. I know you still got River Dog's truck and

Airstream, all his luthier tools. Go get it, and drive up to Alaska. Put it all out there for Charlie, *all* of it. All of *you*. She may say no. She may break your heart worse'n it is now. But you'll regret it your whole fuckin' life if you don't at least try."

"Me and him, the people you're closest to in the whole fuckin' world," Tran said, "we're both sayin' the same damn thing. Think we're both wrong?"

I pivoted away, hands in my hair, staring at the sky, orange-red with that wide Texas sunset. "No. You're not both wrong." I trembled, knowing what I had to do, knowing it was right, and scared as fuck of it.

"If she says no…" I started.

"She won't," Lexie cut in. "Trust me."

"How do you know?" I rasped.

She showed me her phone.

The last text from Charlie: *I miss him so much.*

"It was the *life* she wasn't sure about, Crow, not *you*."

"I ain't ever known nothing but the road," I said. "I don't know nothin' else."

"Just love her," Lexie said. "You can figure out the rest."

I stared at Myles. I'd been with him for years, now. Day in, day out. Life on the road, from nobody cover artist to worldwide phenomenon. "Myles…"

He gripped my shoulders, spun me around, and shoved me toward my bike. "Yeah, yeah, yeah. I'll miss you, I love your dumb ass, you'll miss me, you love my dumb ass. I get it. Just go, already."

I didn't need shit on that bus, except my guitar case. I zipped my guitar into the backpack-style case, slung it over my shoulder, and yanked my helmet on.

I kicked my bike to life, pointed it toward the storage facility which was, in a perhaps not so strange twist of fate, only a few miles from the concert venue. El Paso—on the border with Mexico—was only a short distance away, and was where River Dog lived a good portion of his life, where he'd learned the art of guitar making, where he'd taught it to me.

I hadn't been to this facility in years—I pay a guy to come out twice a month and check on things, keep the tools clean, start the truck, maintain the RV. There's security, it's temperature controlled—the stock of wood River Dog piled up is expensive, and rare—more so, now, in these days when forests are vanishing and wood supply is low, so keeping the wood preserved is vital.

Fortunately, Myles pays me a mint, plus I'm credited as a songwriter on most of his stuff, so I get royalties from all that. Meaning, I'm set, financially, for life. I spend nearly nothing, living on the bus as I do, and I put all my income into a fund which one of Myles's money management dudes takes care of—investing in smart, safe, reliable avenues. Diversification of assets, he says. What it all means, I don't fuckin' know. He tries to explain it to me once a year, and I tell him I don't really give a shit, as long as I got money when I need it, and he ain't skimming. If I catch him skimming, I told him, he'll wish I'd just make him vanish. I know some old Apache warrior torture techniques, and if I find him stealing, I'll use 'em, I told him. So, after he cleaned up his pee-stained pants, he set about making damn sure to take *real* good care of my money.

I guess I got real estate in New York of some kind, stock in companies which have never done shit but turn a tidy profit, and some other investments. I really don't give a shit. Money is useful for getting shit done, for keeping me fed, for putting booze in my belly when I wanna forget. It ain't ever been a motivator for me. Myles neither, really. He likes the trappings of fame, the fans, the attention, but really, he's in it for the music. It's in his blood.

Now, sitting outside the storage unit, bike off, feet on the ground, helmet tipped back on my head, I'm wondering what the fuck I'm doing.

This is scary.

I wasn't scared back in my enforcer days. I had zero fear of anyone, of dying, of pain. It didn't matter to me. I could walk into a den of angry bikers and take 'em all on, and not feel a damn thing.

Now? The prospect of climbing behind the wheel of that old truck and heading north to tell a woman I barely know that I fell in love with her, and want to be with her? Terrified. Shaking in my damn boots.

I ain't no goddamn coward. But, fuck you for this, Myles.

I swing off my Indian, dig my keys out of my saddlebags, and unlock the unit. Roll up the door. Flick on the lights. And there it is—River Dog and Mammy's set up.

1955 Dodge Power Wagon in fire-engine red, bought at an auction in Mexico City for a steal, restored, modified, and maintained by handy ol' River Dog himself. The mods were aging, now, since he'd done the job back in the eighties, but the old man knew how to take care of things, so it ran like a top. Plenty of low-end power, comfy plump leather bench, four on the floor transmission running a burly crate V-8, and the stock AM/FM radio because River Dog preferred windows down and radio off, just the silence and old Mammy's voice chattering on as she liked to do.

Behind it, a vintage Airstream—classic streamlined silver body, gleaming windows, updated interior. A few years ago, I'd had an idea I'd like to follow the tour in this setup, so I'd had the interior stripped and refitted with current stuff, still keeping the vintage look but more useable and comfortable.

He kept his lutherie tools in several locked toolboxes and storage bins inside the trailer, with a custom airtight storage cubby under the couch for keeping the rarest wood—the rest was kept under a tarp in the bed of his truck. I went with the same setup, but I'd planned on hauling my bike with me in the truck, so I'd partitioned off the sides of the bed with built-in covered bins, an expensive but tidy solution.

I stood, staring, trying to summon the courage to really do this.

It was real, now. Myles had fired me. I mean, he'd support me no matter what, I knew, but this was just his way of forcing me out of the nest, so to speak.

Hands shaking, nerves firing, I lowered the bed of the truck and slid out the ramp, hauled the bike up and into the bed, tied it down to the custom tie-down points I'd had installed. I had a tarp rolled up in the cab in case of bad weather, and maintenance tools and spare parts in a toolbox in the bed, because you don't own a vintage bike and not expect to have to fix it now and then.

The bike stowed, I peeked into the trailer—diner-style checkered table with red leather booth benches, chrome trim everywhere, stainless steel fridge, matching induction stovetop range and microwave. Vinyl flooring made to look and feel like dark cherry hardwood—all but indestructible and easy to clean. Red leather couch, butcher-block countertops to match the floors, white cabinets, and a deep, porcelain farmhouse sink. The look was somewhere between fifties cottage and an old country farmhouse.

One bed, a king size, fitted into the rear, under a huge window. Storage underneath for clothes, bookshelves overhead. A bathroom big enough for me to stand up in, and room enough that I didn't knock elbows against the wall washing my hands or taking a shower.

Clean, maintained, and ready to go.

The truck interior was spare, but comfortable. Crank windows, of course. Updated A/C and heater, but with the stock vintage controls. I stuck the key into the ignition, floored the clutch, and she rumbled to life with a snarl.

I pulled out of the unit, heart slamming in my chest. I parked and went back to make sure nothing was missing or left behind, shut off the lights, closed the door, and drove away—stopping at the office to make the first decision which would seal my future...I closed my account, handed in my keys, and let the unit go.

I'd had a little work done to the truck interior—installing a USB charging port so I could keep my phone powered, and play music if I wanted.

I plugged my phone in, set Ketchikan, Alaska as my destination, and headed north.

For the first time in my life, I chose my destination just because I wanted to.

THIRTEEN

Charlie

THE DISASTER THAT IS MY LIFE CONTINUED UNABATED.

I got a speeding ticket outside Seattle. Dropped my phone in the toilet in the bathroom of a rest stop an hour later, forgot the replacement on the table of a diner in Vancouver—which was an hour out of my way to begin with, meaning I had to go back for it, requiring an extra almost three hours of unneeded drive time. My car's GPS got confused in a low-signal area, redirected me down a rutted two-track from one highway to another, where I got a flat tire.

No phone to call a tow truck.

Slipping in mud from a recent rain, I thanked

the spirit of my father for having taught me how to change a tire.

Running on a mini-spare on a two track at ten miles per hour, it took me three hours to reach any kind of civilization which had a shop that could fix my flat tire and dented wheel. I had to stay in a flea-bag motel—which is where I was at the moment, and I wasn't sure where that was, exactly, except some-where in Canada—eating nasty fast food, watching Wheel of Fortune on a TV older than me while I got things back on track.

Unable to fall asleep, my mind wandered to the one place I'd been trying far too hard to forget: Crow.

His hands.

His mouth.

That cock.

I squirmed in the bed, remembering.

I blushed, remembering what I'd let him do—what *I'd* done. What I'd begged him to do, which was fuck me up against the door of a dive bar bathroom, and then fuck me bent over a sink.

I had that image burned into my skull: me in the mirror, bent over the sink, tits swaying as he pounded into me, his body lean and hard and dark and strong, his eyes wild and primal, his hands clawed into the round curve of my ass cheeks as he fucked, fucked, fucked me into blithering oblivion.

To say it was the best, hottest, most erotic, most intensely orgasmic sexual experience of my life would be an understatement on the order of saying the sun is a little warm.

I squirmed in the uncomfortable motel bed, wriggling, uncomfortable, aching in my core, throbbing between my thighs. Remembering how I'd ached with him inside me, and how deliciously sore I'd been afterward. How badly I'd wanted him again, even as things fell apart.

His mouth...god, his mouth on me was something I *craved*. I'd never felt like that until I met him, never knew what I'd been missing, and now I woke up in the middle of the night craving his stubbled jaw scraping up the tender silk of my inner thighs, his soft wet slithery strong tongue driving into my clit and making me come apart again and again, each time harder than the last.

I gave in and let my fingers slip under the waist of my underwear, picturing him—Crow, tall and strong behind me, the feel of his cock driving into me, splitting me apart in the best possible way...his mouth on my sex, tongue flying and circling. His cock in my mouth—I wanted to finish that. Finish him that way, what we'd had interrupted.

Each thought, each image was more arousing than the last, until I was aching with need and my clit was throbbing and I was arched off the bed as my fingers blurred over my sex, flicking back and forth faster and faster, until I let go with a gasp—

"*Crow!*" I heard myself screech, breathless and soft.

God, I was screaming his name as I brought myself to release.

I was so drained by the time I came down from the wild high of my orgasm that I couldn't move, just lay there in the hard, squeaky bed, my hand still inside my underwear, panting, eyes tearing up as my whole body ached, brain to toes, soul to heart.

Had I made a mistake? Had I done the right thing? I still didn't know.

I saw, again, the body of Yak.

The pile of near-corpses he'd created.

I mean, we'd met that same way—him saving me from six men, whom he'd sent to the hospital.

Could I tolerate such violence in my life? I didn't think so. Mom had raised me to be calm, to solve problems with our words and our logic and our will, not through yelling and screaming and violence. Hitting someone was a last resort, only if our very life and physical safety was on the line.

Crow was from a different life.

I fell asleep wrestling with myself, fraught with need and doubts in equal measure. I was as scared of

him and the life he represented as I was deeply desperate to be with him, to be in his arms.

In his life.

Once my car was fixed and run through a car wash
to rid it of the mud, I cruised along the Canadian
highway northward, until I ran out of road in Prince
Rupert. I took a ferry, then, for something like seven
hours. Despite the spectacular scenery, the hours
were long and boring. I strolled the deck, had something to eat, slept, and read on my Kindle.

The only books I had in my Kindle were ro-
mances, and each of them left me desperately missing
and wanting Crow even more.

Even as I ran as far away from him as I could get,
short of moving to freaking Siberia or something.

Every time I thought of him I refused to sec-
ond-guess my decision.

This was for the best.

I couldn't tame him, and it wouldn't be fair to try.
And I wasn't cut out for the kind of life he lived—not
by a long shot. Maybe I wasn't tough enough, or ad-
venturous enough.

All I knew was that I couldn't live a life on the
back of his bike, or on a bunk in his tour bus. I needed

a home. I needed a career. I needed stability. Some adventure now and then was fine, and I now knew I needed more spontaneity and adventure in my life.

But bar fights which resulted in people dying was way too much.

No. I'd made a tough decision, but it was the right decision.

This was best.

I would miss him. Of course I would. I would ache for him. I would probably be celibate for the rest of my life, because there was just no possible way anyone could ever top how he'd made me feel. The thought of being touched by anyone else made my skin crawl with something like revulsion.

Crow had marked me as his, and now, without him, I was lonely, aching, and morose.

But what else could I do?

I pulled up into Mom's condo complex parking lot, parked the car, shut it off, and thunked my head against the steering wheel. I was utterly exhausted, completely spent both mentally and physically.

It had taken me almost a week to get from Denver to Ketchikan, what with all the disasters and detours and the occasional side trip to an outlet mall where I spent money I didn't really have on purses and shoes I didn't really need, but which filled, at least temporarily, the yearning ache inside me.

A tap on my window. "Charlie?" Mom's voice, concerned. "Is that you?"

I swallowed. I peered out at her—it was after ten at night. "Hi, Mom."

"You—you're here."

I nodded blearily, raggedly. "Yep. Here I am."

"Are you—are you okay?"

Mom. I needed my mom. I pushed at my door, and she opened it, grabbed me by the arm and pulled me up. I collapsed gratefully into my mother's arms.

"Momma."

She didn't miss a beat. Shushed, soothed, stroked my hair. "You're here now. I'm here. Momma's got you."

I hated the burn of tears in my eyes, hated that I had no words to relate what I'd been through. But I was glad as hell to be with my mom again

"Liv, I, uh—I'll go. Let you take care of your girl." A deep, bear-like growl, with a southern drawl.

I opened my eyes and saw a simply enormous human being—Jupiter, but in thirty years. Six-six easily, built like someone had turned a grizzly bear into a human. Muscled like a bodybuilder, with a graying goatee and close-cropped hair, black T-shirt stretched around impossible muscles.

Mom shook her head. "No, Lucas, it's all right."

"That's him?" I muttered.

She held me away. "Charlotte, this Lucas. He's my—well, we're not sure what to call it. Boyfriend seems childish and trite, but neither of us are super keen to get married any time soon. So he's just my person." She turned with me to Lucas, who was physically terrifying, but his eyes were kind and deep and warm. "Lucas, this my eldest daughter, Charlotte."

I extended my hand. "Call me Charlie."

"Pleased as punch to meet you, darlin'." He winced. "Sorry, habit. Pleased to meet you, Charlie."

"It's Lexie you want to be careful around with that, not me. Doesn't bother me." I suppressed a sigh—it didn't bother me at all, not after Crow.

Mom glanced into my car. "I was under the impression you and Lex were together."

I rubbed my face. "Long, long, long story, Mom. And I'm too exhausted to tell it now, for one thing and, for another, most of it is Lexie's story to tell, not mine."

"Is she okay?"

I shrugged. "I have no idea. Seemed like it. But with her, it's hard to tell."

"Are *you* okay?" She palmed my cheeks and gazed into my eyes. I knew then I had no chance of lying.

I shook my head. "No, I'm not."

"What can I do?"

I sucked in a deep breath, held it, letting it out slowly. "I'm starving. I'm exhausted. I need to eat some kind of real food, I need to sleep for about eighteen hours, and I need to…honestly, to not have to talk about what happened until I'm ready."

Mom guided me to her front door. "I've got you, honey. I won't ask any questions, and I'll just expect you tell me what's going on in your own time."

We went inside her condo, which was a modern design masterpiece in light and dark colors and clean lines. She went to a linen closet and pulled out sheets, a pillow, and a blanket.

"Lucas, can you make her something to eat while I make up the spare room?"

"Sure thing, sweets." Inside the condo, he was even bigger, improbably massive in height and muscle, yet his eyes were inviting and trustworthy and genuine. "What'cha want, Charlie? I ain't fancy, but I can rustle up some grub to fill you."

"Something quick and filling. An omelet?"

He nodded, turned to the fridge and began pulling out fixings. "You like it how your mom and Cass both do? Spinach and cream cheese, mostly egg whites?"

I felt my eyes widen. "You know how Cassie likes her omelets?"

He chuckled. "Sure do. The whole clan meets for breakfast every Sunday morning at Badd Kitty, and all of us who like to cook take turns doing the cooking."

"Clan?"

Mom laughed from extra bedroom, where she was making up the bed—she popped her head out to comment. "You have no idea what you're walking into, Char-Char. Lucas is the patriarch of a huge family. Eleven men, each of whom is married or has a significant other, some with kids, plus now Cassie and Ink."

"You have eleven sons?" I marveled.

He guffawed. "Hell naw, I got a pair of hell-raisin' triplets—Roman, Remington, and Ramsey. The other eight are my nephews, my deceased brother and sister-in-law's huge brood of boys."

"And you raised them?"

He sighed. "That there is a long story, too, Charlie."

Mom came back into the kitchen. "Short version is, no, he didn't. But the whole story of how it all came together here in Ketchikan is, indeed, a very long and complicated story."

I watched Lucas move easily and fluidly in Mom's kitchen. "Well, I'll listen while I eat. Anything to get my mind off of my own drama, and Lexie's."

"Bacon?" Lucas asked. "Only got real, none of that turkey crap."

I laughed. "You got Mom off of turkey bacon?"

He chuckled. "Took me some doin', but yeah. Managed to convince her that if she was gonna eat bacon, it might as well be real bacon and not that totally unconvincing turkey garbage. Compromise was, we only have it on the weekends, cause I'm watchin' my figure." He did a hyper-masculine impression of a woman popping a hip, which made me laugh.

I glanced at Mom, smiling. "Wow."

She knew what I meant. "He's something else, isn't he?" she whispered. "Cassie has started calling him Papa Bear."

I stared at her. "The hell you say."

She laughed, and didn't even correct my swear word. "She does. Really."

I noticed they were both dressed up a little—Mom in a tight little black dress, wedge heels, her hair longer than it had been for most of my life, loose and little messy, him in nice jeans, plain shirt, and black boots.

"Did I interrupt you guys going out?" I asked.

She and Lucas locked eyes, and I caught something pass between them. "We were just on our way back from a date," she said. "You didn't interrupt anything."

"Few minutes later and you may have," Lucas muttered, under his breath, but I heard it.

So did Mom. "LUCAS!"

He ducked his head. "Sorry." But his shoulders were shaking with suppressed laughter.

I couldn't help a snicker. "Eew. But…I'm glad for you, Mom."

She sank onto the stool next to me. "You are? It took Cassie a little bit to warm up to the idea of me in a relationship. I'm most worried about Torie and Poppy handling it."

"I'm happy for you. I really am. I was old enough that I saw how unhappy you were, there at the end before Dad passed. I'm glad you found someone who seems to make you happy."

She hugged me. "He does make me happy, Charlie. So happy."

"Did I really interrupt you guys, um…being alone together?"

My mother actually blushed. "Well, yes. But it's not like we'll never get any other time alone." A pause. A deeper blush. "Or like we don't find…um… plenty of, um…*time*."

"Quit talking saucy, you little minx, or I'll really embarrass you," Lucas grumbled.

I rested my head on my hands on the counter. "Sorry I asked. But, um, good for you two."

My mom. Getting it on, a *lot*.

I could tell, just by the way she was glowing, by the way she looked at him. By the blush. She was covering a whole host of things I probably didn't want to know about with those ellipses in her speech.

A moment later, Lucas slid a plate in front of me—a huge egg white omelet, filled with melted cream cheese and sautéed spinach, and several slices of crispy bacon.

"Damn, Lucas. You delivered on the breakfast food."

He grinned, munching on a piece of bacon. "At your service, m'lady."

I ate, and ignored the meaningful googly eyes Mom and Lucas were making at each other. It was so sweet it was saccharine, yet I couldn't mistake the undercurrent of heat sizzling between them.

Weird.

Very, very weird.

Seeing your mom in love, making sexy eyes at a man you've never met before is just…weird.

But she was radiating happiness, looked healthier than ever—as if she'd even put a little weight on, some extra softness to her build, which was good in her case as she'd always been so hyperactive, and after Dad's unexpected death she became so obsessed with health and fitness that I worried she'd get too skinny.

So I was happy for her.

Even though it made me miss Crow all the more.

I ate, wolfing down the food in record time.

And suddenly I was so tired I couldn't see straight.

"I need to sleep." I smiled tiredly at Lucas. "Thank you, Lucas. You don't know how much I needed good food. I've lived off fast food for the last week, and it's making my face break out. And my ass is probably five times bigger than it was."

"The last thing you need to worry about is the size of your ass, Charlie," Mom said. "Skip a meal or two and let Lucas cook for you, and you'll be back down to size in no time. But don't stress—worrying and obsessing over it only makes it worse."

Crow would probably say the same thing, and add something along the lines of liking my ass a little juicier.

How I knew what he'd say, I couldn't have told you.

Mom saw my mood shift. "Who hurt you, darling?"

I shook my head. "He didn't hurt me. If anything, I hurt him."

"This isn't Glen we're talking about, I assume," Mom said.

"Twinkle Mouse? No. Hell no."

Mom snickered. "Who let that nickname out of

the bag? I warned the girls not to let you hear them call him that while you were seeing him, or it would start world war three."

"Lex," I said.

Mom patted me on the shoulder. "Just rest, honey. There's time enough to tell me everything after you've slept."

I sagged against her. "He was amazing. But too wild. And I just...I think I made a mistake, Mom. What if it could have been the best thing that ever happened to me?" I felt myself word-vomiting, and couldn't stop it. "He killed a man right in front of me. In a fight. Over me. And he was in jail for something very similar. But...you wouldn't think it, when he's being the kind, amazing, crazy, wild man I..." I trailed off.

"You love." Mom finished it for me. "You felt safe with him?"

"Yes."

"Was it malicious? Or self-defense?"

"There were eleven of them, and just him. They had his motorcycle surrounded." I swallowed. "He ahh...had this baton, and he just...he was a one-man wrecking machine."

"*Eleven*?" Lucas said, whistling in amazement. "And he came out on top?"

"He took a beating. The leader of them came

after him with a knife, and he got cut on the ribs, but not, like, a mortal wound. He wouldn't get stitches, just duct taped his shirt to it, and we rode away."

"Sounds like a hell of a hard-case."

"He was the son of the founder of a motorcycle club."

"Which one? I used to be a regular at a bar back down in Oklahoma, knew quite a few of the bigger outfits."

"The AzTex."

His eyes widened. "He's ol' Coyote Crow's boy? Hell, Coyote and his crew used to swing through that bar every few months. They had a…umm…business connection over in New Orleans, I think."

"I know exactly what kind of business they were into," I said.

"Ahh." He nodded. "Coyote was a scary customer, no doubt. His brother Snake frightened me plumb silly, and I ain't ashamed to admit it."

I shook my head. "Seems like everyone knew Coyote Crow."

He nodded. "Oh, yeah. Anyone in the biker and underworld sorta circles knew him. And they were scared of him." He scratched his jaw. "Matter of fact, I think I 'member reading about what happened with Crow, back in the early aughts. That business with the bar fight."

I stopped breathing. "What did you hear?"

"He shoulda never been served to begin with. He walked into that bar pissed off his rocker, so all-fired drunk and crazy with grief that he wasn't even barely coherent. That dumbass bartender oughta been the one who went to jail, not that poor boy. Lost his folks, his uncle—half the club was his family—all in one day. That there was a hell of a thing. Like something out of a Hollywood movie. Thirty-two people dead, an entire MC nearly wiped out, but they took the other guys out totally. Pyrrhic victory, I guess. Then, later, his own fiancé, pregnant, was murdered in front of him. He just went haywire, according to the stories. Went on a drinking spree across five states, looking for the man responsible for calling the hit. Never hurt anyone, till that dick at the Arizona bar picked a fight with him."

He paused, meaningful, heavy, significant. "That fella, the one Crow killed in the fight? He was a member of the crew who'd tangled with the AzTex and killed Crow's folks, but he'd stayed behind to watch the compound. He knew who Crow was, knew what had happened, and picked that fight on purpose. Crow oughta have died, that day. Nearly did. Head was all but caved in, nose broke in four places, lost teeth, busted jaw, busted ribs, but he finished his man and then some."

I swallowed. Blinked back tears. "He doesn't remember it. Doesn't remember who the guy was."

"Not surprised, not as drunk as they say he was. Miscarriage of justice, him being convicted, if you ask me." A glance at me. "He carryin' guilt about it?"

I shrugged. "I think so."

"He shouldn't. Not a bit. His blood alcohol level, when the ambulance took him in, was somethin' like point-three-two. Shoulda been fatal. Then the beating he took? Damned incredible he survived any of it. And that fella he killed was bad, bad, *bad* news. Picked that fight a'purpose, thinkin' he'd finish the job his crew started, I guess. Revenge, maybe, seein' as the AzTex took out his whole club."

I blinked, but tears trickled down anyway. "The fight I watched him get into, he couldn't have stopped it either. Couldn't have walked away."

"I can see how you'd be scared, though," Mom said. "That's not the world we raised you in."

Lucas made a gruff sound. "A man defending himself ain't a crime. He oughta never have gone to jail. He faced down men tryin' to kill him, and he was so drunk he was beyond any kind of reason. And even that was understandable, given what had happened. You ask me, can't really hold that against him. Man like him? He'd never hurt you. He'd die first."

"But you have to remember how I raised my girls, Lucas. Violence is unfamiliar to them."

"Cushy and sweet, which is what makes you and

your girls—the ones I met so far—so attractive to men like me, like Ink, and like I figure Crow is. We like the soft and sweet. But we don't figure we deserve it." He held up his hands, huge, monstrously powerful hands, scarred and weathered. "We think hands like these'll leave stains on you."

I couldn't hold back the tears anymore. "I was scared. He's so…rough. So wild."

Lucas rested his massive paws on my hands. "Lassoing a man like Crow is no joke, darlin'. He ain't ever gonna be tame. You gotta know you want the man as he is, and want all of him, and know you ain't ever gonna make him different. You cain't. Nothin' can."

"I was too afraid to try, so I ran away."

"Well, I knew Coyote well enough to know he didn't raise no pussy. Crow might've let you run off, knowin' you needed time. But ain't no way in hell he'd let you stay gone. I'd just be countin' the days till that hard-ass son of a bitch shows up here, lookin' for you." He winked. "An' if he's any kind of man, your ass being a little bigger is only gonna fire him up, darlin'."

"Lucas, really." Mom's heart wasn't in it, though.

I blushed. "I've got a feeling you're right on that last part, at least." I sighed. "And I can only hope you're right on the first part."

FOURTEEN

Crow

SIXTY-TWO HOURS AFTER LEAVING EL PASO, I PARKED River Dog's—*my*—truck and RV near a place called Badd's Bar and Grille.

I'd texted Lexie asking her where I'd find Charlie, and she'd done some asking around of her own—her sister Cassie, I believe—and I got this place as the answer.

So I sat taking up too many spaces in the lot, watching the open door of the bar. It was busy inside. Bustling with tourists. Outside, a monster of a dude sporting a ponytail mohawk and WWE-worthy physique sat on a stool, arms crossed, idly watching the crowd.

I finally summoned the gumption to leave my truck,

and shrugged my shoulders at the unfamiliar feel of the plain black T-shirt I was wearing. Shit, I hadn't worn anything but that old cut in years.

I ambled to the door of the bar, and the monster on the stool glanced at me, assessing my age. "Have fun, and no trouble. I'll toss you on your ass so fast you'll meet your own ancestors, if you make trouble."

"Actually, I'm looking for Charlotte Goode."

He tilted his head, eyeing me. "Charlie?"

I nodded, swallowing. "Yeah, Charlie. Heard she may be here."

"Depends on what you want."

"To talk to her."

"She wanna talk to you?" He was protective, and I got it, appreciated it in fact.

"I don't know. Maybe not."

He let out short, piercing whistle. "Yo, Ink!"

A truly gargantuan man ambled out—bigger than Jupiter, broad as a barn door, covered in native-style tattoos, with a long beard and long black hair, barefoot, shirtless, wearing nothing but a pair of gym shorts. "Yeah." His voice was the deepest thing I'd ever heard.

"Charlie tell you about expecting anyone?"

The giant with the tats shook his head. "Naw. But I know she was dealing with some shit, and wasn't ready to talk about it, least not with me. She may've told Cass about it, but not me."

The bouncer eyed me. "You got the look of trouble, friend. Just being careful, cause she's family, and new to it."

I was used to looking like trouble, so I got it. "Family?"

"Of a sort, the way it is around here." He extended his hand. "Baxter Badd."

I shook his hand. "Crow."

"Just Crow?"

"Just Crow."

He nodded. "How about I call Livvie and see what she knows. I ain't gonna go giving out her daughter's location till I know you're safe."

I nodded. "I understand. I'd do the same."

He dialed a number. Waited as it rang. "Yo, Livvie, it's Bax. I got a fella named Crow at the bar, askin' to see Charlie." He waited, listened. "Oh, okay, cool. Just bein' sure. Cool. Where is she? Okay, I'll send him." He hung up, glanced at me. "She'll see you. She's at Cassie and Ink's."

I glanced at the big fella. "Well? Mind showin' me?"

Ink stared at me, assessing me. "Why're you here, man?"

"I love her. I let her go, and now I need to get her back."

He nodded. "Good enough for me." He shuffled across the road. "Come on."

"I have my truck and trailer."

He waved a paw in dismissal. "Nah. Walkin's easier. Ain't far. Plus, you ain't gonna find many spots to park your rig."

So I followed a tattooed giant named Ink several blocks across Ketchikan, through a closed and dark tattoo parlor, which he moved through as if he owned the place, to a tiny home built among the trees behind the strip of buildings.

I could see her, in the window. Talking to another girl who looked like her, but blond.

Ink led me in through a side door. "Cass, Charlie? Got a visitor. Cass, can I get you to come over to the shop…like, now?"

A second later, the blond woman—Cass, I assumed—squeezed past me and left with Ink.

I stopped in the doorway. More unsure of anything than I'd ever been, except that I loved this woman. "Hey, darlin'."

She looked up. Saw me. She had a coffee cup in her hands, and it started shaking. "Crow," she breathed. "You're here."

She set the mug down, carefully, and moved toward me. Stopped inches from me. "I…Crow, I should never have left. Not the way I did."

I cupped her chin. "You did what you had to. I get it. I just…I can't live without you."

She blinked hard. "You rode all the way here?"

I shook my head. "Nah. I got River Dog and Mammy's truck and trailer. I drove."

She palmed my chest. "You're wearing a shirt."

"Figured it was time to leave the club behind."

"Not for me."

I shook my head. "Naw. For me."

"You sold your bike?"

"Hell, no. I got it in the back of the truck."

She gazed at me. "You can't live without me?"

I shook my head. "Tried. Made it a month, and about went nuts. Myles fired me."

She was shocked. "He what?"

"Had to get me to leave somehow. That was how." I rubbed a hand through my hair. "Now I'm here, and I'm...I don't know how this works. I just know..." I swallowed hard. "I know it's nuts, but I—Charlie, I'm in love with you. I don't know how to be—anything good enough for you. I can drive a truck and wear a shirt, but I'll always be a biker, and my hands ain't ever gonna be no cleaner."

"My mom's boyfriend knew your dad. He also knew the man you killed in that fight." She held my eyes. "He was part of the club that was responsible for your parents' death. He picked the fight on purpose, knowing who you were."

"No shit." I rocked back on my heels, stunned. "No shit?"

"And the fight at the bar *was* my fault. Or at least it was because of me. There wasn't anything you could have done differently except get killed." She ran her hands through my hair. "I've been here over a month, waiting for you."

"Waiting?" I swallowed hard. "What do you mean, waiting?"

She touched my cheek, and my whole body lit on fire. "I love you, Crow. It is crazy. We spent, what, a couple days together? But it was enough to know I want you in my life. I don't want you to be...anything or anyone but you."

She stripped my shirt off. "I like you in the cut. I like you on a bike. I like being on the bike with you." She ran her hands over my chest. "I like what we did in that bathroom...a *lot*. I've missed you. I don't know that I can go on tour with you and Myles, but I'll be here waiting whenever you come back."

"Shit, woman, I don't know where to start with any of that." I let out a heavy sigh. "I can wear the cut if you like it—I ain't comfortable in no stupid shirt. But I'm done with the life. I ain't going back to the tour, either. I been recording songs for Myles at night and messaging them to him." I swallowed. "Also been trying my hand with River Dog's tools."

She looked eager, excited, hopeful. "You...you have?"

I nodded. "I'm rusty, and my initial efforts with cheap wood have been pretty rough. But with some practice, I figure I can pick up where River Dog left off." I scrubbed my jaw. "Figured maybe I could restart River Dog Custom Guitars, but as a stationary business, here in Ketchikan." I hesitated. "That was my plan."

She smiled. "I like that plan."

"You do?"

"I do." She smiled. "How do you feel about a little one-room condo facing the channel?"

"Better than the back of my Airstream, maybe."

She scratched her nails down my chest. "Maybe." Her voice dropped. "But maybe we go check out your trailer, just to be sure."

My hands came to rest on her waist. "It can't be this easy, can it?"

She shrugged. "For now, yes. Later, we'll have to cross some bridges together."

"Together, though."

"Together." She palmed my cheek. "Just…you have to know, Crow—I will never ask you to change. So don't, okay?"

"I already have, darlin'." I tugged her by the hand. "Come on. Let's go find somewhere remote to park the trailer."

We bumped into Ink and Cassie at the back of the shop, talking quietly.

As if he knew what we needed, Ink spoke up. "Take the highway north a few miles. There's some side roads you can park on. Nice and secluded."

"Thanks," I said, but my attention was on Charlie.

On the look in her eyes. The hunger, the heat.

Yeah, just a few more miles to go.

I parked the truck a few miles down a deserted one-lane dirt road that, according to the maps, didn't lead much of anywhere. Nothing but trees and scrub as far as the eye could see.

The old engine ticked, and the cab was quiet.

"Wanna see the trailer?" I said, my voice feeling too loud in the quiet cab.

"I just want you," she whispered. "Here, on the ground outside, anywhere. I just want *you*."

She was wearing a skirt, short and black and pleated, with a blousy white button-down shirt. Been looking at those legs of hers the whole drive here, wondering what she had on under that skirt.

I kept my eyes on hers. Slid my hand over the bench, onto her knee. She bit her lower lip. Let her knees fall open, a few inches. As much of an invitation as I needed.

I grazed my palm up her thigh, bringing the skirt with it. Higher, higher.

Exposed her sex—bare.

"Damn, girl."

"I haven't worn underwear in weeks, hoping each day you would show up, and...and want me. Want this."

"Want ain't the word, babe," I said, dragging a finger up her soaked slit. "Need is the word."

She slid lower on the bench, opening her thighs. Gazed at me. "I need you too, Crow. Need you more than you know." She licked her lips. "I've made myself come every night since I left you, wishing my fingers were yours." Bold as you please, god love her. "Wishing it was your mouth."

"My mouth, huh?"

There wasn't much room in the cab, but I'd been dreaming of her for too long to wait any longer. I grabbed her, twisted her onto her back. She went willingly, spreading her legs open. I pushed her skirt up. Went to my belly, awkward and too big for this little cab, brought her to my mouth. Her fingers went into my hair, and she sighed.

"Oh, thank god," she breathed, as I tasted her sweet sex. "Thank *god*."

I laughed, and flicked her clit, slid two fingers into her. "Wanting this real bad, huh?"

She just arched, flexed her hips to drive her sex into my mouth, knotting her fingers in my hair.

"You have no idea, Crow. My fingers just don't do anything near as good as your mouth. God, I'm gonna come already."

I tasted her as she came, a small shaking precursor to what I was gonna do to her.

I kept her going, through the orgasm, into the next one, and would have tongued her to as many as her body could handle, wanting her to come and to come and to come, just relishing the feel of her, the sound of her voice as she gasped and sobbed through her orgasms.

"Enough, god, enough," she gasped, pushing my face away. "I need a break."

She reached up, found the door handle and opened it, sliding backward and out of the truck. She waited for me. I followed, my jeans tight and aching.

"God, Charlie," I said, staring at her as she stood in the evening light, sun bathed golden-red. "You are so fucking gorgeous."

She looked around. Saw that we were the only ones on the little road, and likely the only ones there ever would be. She bit her lip around a shy yet seductive grin. Peeled her shirt up, revealing a lacy white bra, nearly sheer and showing her little pink nipples standing hard. Unzipped her skirt. Stepped out of it. Tossed them past me into the truck cab. Stood in just that white bra, no underwear, thighs touching, lip caught in her teeth. Yanked that bra off, tossed it past me. Stood naked in the sunlight.

Big pale breasts hanging heavy, swaying with her ragged breathing. Her sex a slit hazed by close-trimmed black fuzz. Thighs strong, thick. Hips perfect curves.

"I fuckin' need you, Charlie," I growled, reaching for her.

"You just got me."

"Not what I mean, and you fuckin' know it."

She sidled closer to me. "There's one thing I've been really fantasizing about, ever since I left."

"What's that, babe?"

She sank to her knees on the dirt road, reached for my belt buckle. "Finishing what I started, that day on the tour bus."

I groaned, knowing exactly what she meant. "Fuck, woman. I ain't had anything but my own hand since you left, and even that didn't feel right, till I talked to you. I'm on a hell of a hair trigger right now. And I need you. About to fuckin' pop, if I don't get inside you right the fuck now."

She tugged my boots off. My socks. My jeans. Tossed them all in the truck. My underwear last, and then we were both naked in the sunset light, and she was cradling my shaft in her hands. Stroking me.

"Just let me do this, Crow. I want to. I need to. I've been fantasizing about this for weeks. If you're really that close to coming already, then all the better—I can get you hard all over again and we can fuck until we pass out."

I palmed her cheek. "Don't wanna just fuck you, Charlie. Want to make love to you."

"I want it to be both. Everything. I want to find out what it is. How many different ways it can be." She twisted her fist around the head of my cock, gazing at it. "And right now, it's going to be me making you come in my mouth."

"Fuuuck," I snarled. "Careful what you wish for, darlin'."

"Oh, I think I know exactly what I'm wishing for."

She suited words to action, taking me in her mouth, and as I watched my cock sink between those plump pink lips, felt her tongue on me, felt her mouth tight and wet around me, I knew I wasn't going to last a fucking minute.

I also knew I was helpless. I wanted this.

"Fuck, Charlie," I groaned again. "Don't know what you're doing to me."

She made a wordless sound, an affirmation, and I was gone, just gone, watching her slide her mouth up, lick the tip, slide back down. Taking her time.

"I'd be…oh fuck. I'd be lying like a dog if I didn't admit I'd jerked off more than a few times, imagining you doin' this."

She smiled around me, gazing up at me as she slid her lips down around me, tongue fluttering and licking. Palm around my sac, massaging, cradling. Her other hand moved around my base, gently stroking the root, pumping me.

She let me pop out of her mouth. "I watched videos on how to do this."

I choked. "You—you what?"

"I watched porn video tutorials on how to give a really, really good blowjob."

"You…" I lost my breath and my train of thought as she sank me into her mouth. "You really didn't need lessons, babe. Did just fuckin' fine the last time."

But damn, did she put what she'd learned to good use—made me feel like I'd never felt in my life. Desperate. Brought me to the edge and stopped, did something else, until I was aching and pulsing and growling.

"Goddamn, Charlie, what the fuck are you tryin' to do to me?"

She just shrugged, a lithe, sinuous movement that made her tits do incredible things, and then kept going.

All of a sudden, she stopped playing.

Her fist started pumping faster, and her mouth moved up and down relentlessly, and I rose to the edge, lifting on my toes, rocking back on my heels, snarling. An instant, and I was there.

Riding the ragged messy edge of climax.

"Charlie—shit, shit, shit, I'm gonna—oh fuck, right now, Charlie, I'm gonna fuckin' come so goddamn hard…"

She went deeper, and I had my hands in her long thick hair, holding on to her braid, pulling, and she backed away, gasped for air, and then slid me down her throat again, pumping me hard and fast, and I was helpless to hold back now.

I exploded with a bellow, hips thrusting hard, and she used both hands on my shaft, pumping me until I lost my breath, cum detonating out of me and her mouth sucked hard around me and I heard her swallowing, gulping, gulping, and she didn't stop, kept pumping me until there was nothing left and I was shaking, shuddering, weak in the knees.

Finally, she let my softening cock flop out of her mouth and I helped her stand up.

"Jesus, Charlie," I gasped.

She grinned, wiped at the corner of her mouth. "Wow. Just…wow."

"Yeah, I'd say wow is about right."

She tugged me by the hand to the trailer, and

opened the door. She looked around as she went in. "This is so cute, Crow."

"I had it remodeled a few years ago, in case I ever wanted to use it. It was pretty dated."

"I love it." She shut the door behind me, glanced at the end of the trailer where the bed was. "I could see us living in this. I love it." She backed toward the bed, pulling me with her. "Right now, though, I only care about one thing."

"What's that?"

She sank back on to the bed. Shimmied backward, reaching for me. Pulled my face to her thighs. "This. More of this. Make me come again, Crow."

"Until you beg me to stop, baby."

She shook her head as I buried my face against her. "No, just until you get hard again."

"That'll be in about thirty seconds, the way I feel about you."

"The sooner, the better." She gazed at me, her eyes fluttering as she rose to the cusp on my tongue. "I need you inside me."

I made her come twice, and she went over the edge screaming my name.

She lifted up, after she'd recovered from the second one, and gazed at me, eyes raking down my body. "Nearly there," she said, eying my hardening cock. "Maybe I can speed things along a little."

She shoved me to my back, roughly, and straddled me. Slid down my body. Bent over me.

Her mouth brought me to full erection in seconds. "Condom?" she whispered.

I reached up, opened a drawer over my head, yanked a box out. She took it from me, ripped it open, tore a condom off the string, snagged it open with her teeth. Rolled the condom onto me with both hands, and then lifted up.

"I've been waiting for this," she said. "I wanted to ride you like this the day we met. I just didn't know it."

I was going to say something, but all thoughts were blasted out of my head as she lifted up, guided me to her slit, and sat down on me. Took all of me, fast and hard, sinking down with a loud cry of ecstasy.

"Fuck, fuck *yes*," she moaned, head dropping forward as she braced her hands on my chest. "Fuck yes. You feel so good inside my pussy, Crow."

"The way you talk dirty makes me so fuckin' hot, Charlie."

She grinned, rolling her hips. "Yeah? You like it when I talk dirty?"

"You're so sweet, so innocent. Make you come a couple times, and you're a fuckin' dirty, nasty little wildcat. I love it so fuckin' much."

"I can't help it," she murmured. "You woke up something inside me, and it won't' go back in."

"Good," I said. "Let it out. Go as fuckin' wild as you can get. Show me how bad you want it, how much you like it."

She leaned forward, hands braced on my chest, and circled her hips, moving nothing but her hips in slow rolling sensuous maddening circles. "I love your cock, Crow. I want to ride all night, all day. I want you to bend me over this bed and fuck me till my ass hurts from the way you pound into me." She sank down, groaning. "I've come so many times, remembering how you fucked me over that sink."

"Fuckin' so good."

"Can we get a mirror so I can watch us?" She raked her claws down my chest. "I want to watch us fuck. I want to watch myself ride your cock. I want to watch you fuck me from behind."

She was moving faster, now, and I had no choice but to meet her there. Faster, harder. She braced one hand on my chest and used the other to finger her clit, helping herself get there faster, better.

Her tits shook, bounced with our movements, and I lifted up, latched onto one and suckled until she whimpered, and then she came, my cock deep inside her, my mouth on her tits, her fingers on her clit.

She came all over me, and I watched her come.

"Crow, god, ohmygod, Crow!" She cried, screaming as she rode me through her orgasm. "Fuck, I love you so fucking much, Crow!"

When she stopped coming, she slowed her hips. "You come yet?"

I shook my head. Lifted her off me. Rolled her to her knees. She fell forward, thrust her ass up, presenting herself to me. I pushed in, her fingers guiding me home. Drove deep.

"Talk to me, Crow. Talk to me while you fuck me."

God her mouth, so dirty.

My hips slapped against her ass, and she cried out. I groaned, knowing this would be fast.

"Can't fuckin' stand it, like this. Too fuckin' good, the way you feel." I set a rhythm, and she shoved back into me, begging for more, begging for faster, for harder. "I fuckin' love you, Charlie. You're everything I never knew I needed and wanted, baby. I want to make love to you every single fuckin' day of our lives till we're a hundred and twenty."

"Just once a day?" she teased. "Promise me at least twice a day."

"As much as you can handle, love."

"Everything you have, Crow. That's what I can handle. Just love me. Just fucking love me forever."

"Touch your clit, Charlie. Let me feel you come around my cock one more time."

She obeyed, and started shaking and losing her rhythm within seconds.

And that was all I needed. I felt it rise like a volcanic eruption, and I didn't try to stop it.

I pounded into her sweet sex, her ass shaking and jiggling as I drilled into her, like she'd begged me for.

I came, and she came with me. She called my name as she came, and she told me she loved me about a hundred times:

"I love you, Crow, Crow, Crow, I fucking—I fucking love you, Crow. I love you, Crow, oh god I'm coming so hard!"

I saw stars, felt faint. I came until I ached, and we collapsed together into a heap on the bed.

I cradled her in my arms.

She touched my cheek with her lips. "Is this our forever, Crow. Promise me it is. No matter what?"

"No matter what." I turned my face to hers, captured a long, slow, deep kiss. "Forever love, Charlie-girl."

"You going to make an honest woman out of me?"

I laughed. "That what you want?"

"I mean, every girl dreams of it."

"You realize, in terms of our time together, we've known each other, like, a week?"

"It's crazy, I know. Doesn't have to be soon." She

laughed. "I just wanted to see if it would scare you off."

"Nope." I tapped my chin. "Matter of fact..."

I sat up, dislodging her from my chest. She sat up, watching me. I rummaged in a drawer over the bed, my junk drawer.

Not junk, just random stuff. The box I pulled out certainly wasn't junk.

The box, a small wooden thing, made by River Dog, was smooth, made of walnut. No design, just the wood, the top lifting off. Within was a cushion of velvet. A small, old, delicate ring made of twisted gold.

"This was Mammy's. She and River Dog were never married, you know. Not in the white culture sense. They were just... them. This is the ring River Dog gave her when he asked her to be his forever." I showed it to her. "He made it. She wore it every day of her life. And when she passed, the day she knew she was going, she gave it to me. Didn't say nothin', but didn't have to."

"Crow..." she gasped. "I wasn't asking you to—"

"I ain't askin' you to marry me. Maybe someday, if we decide that's what we want. This is just me askin' you to be mine."

She took the ring from me, slid it onto her right hand ring finger. "I already was, Crow. But now I've got your ring on so everyone knows."

I fell to the bed, taking her with me, holding her on my chest. "Love you, Charlie-girl. I love that you don't hesitate to try the crazy shit. To wear my ring when we barely met each other."

"Time is irrelevant, Crow. I know you. You know me. My heart knows how I feel about you. My body knows it's meant for yours. My mind says this is a little crazy, a lot fast, but my brain is an idiot. My brain picked Glen because he was safe, and the good girl choice."

"I sure as shit ain't the good girl choice."

"But you're the right choice for me," she said. "Now. Feed me, and make love to me again. This time, on a blanket outside. I've always wanted to have sex outside." She giggled. "The blowjob doesn't count as having sex outside. But it was hot."

"Hot? Woman, you about killed me."

She grinned. "I think I just might be a fan of giving you blowjobs." She wiggled her eyebrows, silly, goofy, but hot as fuck. "This is good news for you."

"Keep talkin' about blowjobs, Charlie darlin', and you won't get food before we go again."

"Oooh, baby, threaten me with a good time, why don't you," she purred, reaching for me, finding me nearly ready again. "God, how fast can you be ready again? It's been what, ten minutes?"

I laughed. "Honey, it's *you*. You do things to me."

"Well, I like doing things to you." She pulled at me. Drew me closer. Hauled me down over her and slid me home. "I can wait to eat."

I groaned at the feel of her, bare. "I ain't wearing a condom."

"You'll just have to pull out and come all over me, then, won't you?"

I bent, laughing into her breasts. "You lost your damn mind, woman. You really want that?"

"I want everything, Crow. I want it dirty, and rough, and wild, and sweet, and messy."

I made her come two times. Three? I lost track, so did she. And when she knew I was close, she pushed me so I pulled out, and her sweet soft quick hands stroked me slowly until I made a godawful mess all over her belly and breasts, and she traced designs in the mess, smiling at me.

"You made a mess," she laughed.

"I'll clean it up." I fetched a paper towel from the kitchen, only to find her licking the finger she'd been dragging through the mess. "Damn, girl. What kinda tiger did I tie onto?"

She just laughed and let me clean her up. "I don't know, honestly. We're both finding out together." Her eyes became serious, then. "And I'm loving every minute of it."

"You sure do seem like a good girl on the surface,

Charlie Goode. But get you naked and horny, and you ain't so good after all, are you?"

"Only for you, Crow. You're the only one who ever has and ever will get the not-so-good version of me."

She kissed me, then, and we nearly didn't make it out of the bed for dinner.

Forever with her suddenly seemed like an awful nice prospect.

THE END

EPILOGUE

Lexie

THE BOX CAME ABOUT TWO MONTHS AFTER CROW LEFT for Alaska.

The tour was over, and Myles and I were playing house at his sprawling penthouse in Dallas.

It was a big wooden box, delivered by DHL. Postmarked Ketchikan, Alaska.

From River Dog Custom Guitars.

Myles used a claw hammer to open it. Inside was a hard-sided leather guitar case, with Myles's initials monogrammed into the leather. He opened the case, and sank to his knees, speechless.

Holding the guitar as if it might explode, he cradled it in his hands. I saw him literally in tears.

"Myles?" I crouched beside him. "What is it?"

He traced the whorls in the wood. "This."

"I don't understand."

"Crow. He finished it."

"Finished what?"

He touched the strings—nylon. "River Dog and Crow were making this guitar together when River Dog died. Crow never finished it."

"And that's it? The guitar they were making?"

He nodded, then moved to sit on his butt, cradling the guitar against his chest. He strummed the strings with a thumb, delicately—the sound it made was honey and light with a soaring purity.

"It's Spanish cedar. River Dog made a guitar and traded it to a tonewood exporter for a batch of this. It's not just any wood. It was handpicked for the best quality, the best visual appeal and sound." He strummed it again, and his fingers danced on the strings, picking a flamenco-type melody. "He said it was going to be the best guitar he ever made. He died before they could finish it, just the neck and strings were left. It's the last pure River Dog guitar there will ever be. All Crow had to do was attach the neck, bridge, strings, all that. The real work of it, River Dog and Crow did together, years and years ago."

I marveled at the pure sound of it. "It's incredible."

"Custom guitars are an art form. What River Dog

could do? It was more than art. It was…it was holy. Sacred." He shook his head, eyes closed, head turned to the side as he listened to a note quaver. "Hear that? The resonance? It sounds like it's…like it's resonating clear up to heaven and back to earth."

"He finished it, and gave it to you," I said. I stood up, glanced in the case, saw the note—gave it to Myles. "Here."

He read it out loud. "'Myles, brother. You firing me was the best thing ever happened to me.'" He cut off, laughing. "Poor bastard can't spell for shit, though. 'I'm reopening River Dog's shop, but it's going to be a real shop, here in Alaska. That there guitar is the first, and you know damn well which one it is. He wanted you to have it. He told me so himself, day he died.'" His voice shook, broke. "'I never told you he meant that guitar for you, because I was too scared of failing to try and finish it. Well, I did, and I think it turned out pretty all right. Make some beautiful music on it. Love you, brother. I'll miss the tour, but not the bus. That thing was a shithole.'"

I laughed, teary-eyed myself. "He's funny."

"Pretty all right," he echoed. "It's the most beautiful guitar ever made."

"What's the P.S.?" I asked.

"'P.S.: Lexie, your momma and sisters miss you. Charlie ain't told them shit, but they miss you something awful. Get your ass up here to see them, so they will quit bugging me to call Myles. He knows I don't talk on the phone.'" He laughed. "He tried calling in a pizza one time, ended up cursing out the pizza guy on the other end and hanging up. He hates phones."

"I'm not sure I'm ready to see them." I swallowed hard.

Myles set the guitar in the case. "You can't run from it forever, Lex."

"I know. But she'll just be so disappointed in me."

"She's your momma. You got lucky, babe. Your mom loves you. You told me as much." He clicked the latches closed. "We're going."

I shook my head. "I'm not ready."

"You'll never be ready." He cupped my cheek. "I got you, Lex. I'll be with you. We go up to Alaska, you get shit sorted with your family, and then we go on tour."

"Where do we go next?"

"Japan, Moscow, Germany." He grinned at me. "You and me can test our new songs together."

I shook my head. "You mean you can play them."

"Nope. *We* play them. You and me, together."

"You're asking for too much, Myles." I heard my voice shake.

"You're woman enough to face it, Lex. First your mom, and then the world."

Want the rest of the story?

GOODE TO BE BAD

May 8, 2020

Also by
Jasinda Wilder

Visit me at my website: **www.jasindawilder.com**
Email me: **jasindawilder@gmail.com**

If you enjoyed this book, you can help others enjoy it as well by recommending it to friends and family, or by mentioning it in reading and discussion groups and online forums. You can also review it on the site from which you purchased it. But, whether you recommend it to anyone else or not, thank you *so much* for taking the time to read my book! Your support means the world to me!

My other titles:

Preacher's Son:
Unbound
Unleashed
Unbroken

Delilah's Diary:
A Sexy Journey
La Vita Sexy
A Sexy Surrender

Big Girls Do It:
Boxed Set
Married
On Christmas
Pregnant

Rock Stars Do It:
Harder
Dirty
Forever

From the world of *Big Girls* and *Rock Stars*:
Big Love Abroad

Biker Billionaire:
Wild Ride

The Falling Series:
Falling Into You
Falling Into Us
Falling Under
Falling Away
Falling For Colton

The Ever Trilogy:
Forever & Always
After Forever
Saving Forever

The world of *Wounded:*
Wounded
Captured

The world of *Stripped:*
Stripped
Trashed

The world of *Alpha:*
Alpha
Beta
Omega
Harris: Alpha One Security Book 1
Thresh: Alpha One Security Book 2
Duke Alpha One Security Book 3
Puck: Alpha One Security Book 4
Lear: Alpha One Security Book 5
Anselm: Alpha One Security Book 6

The Houri Legends:
Jack and Djinn
Djinn and Tonic

The Madame X Series:
Madame X
Exposed
Exiled

The Black Room
(With Jade London):
Door One
Door Two
Door Three
Door Four
Door Five
Door Six
Door Seven
Door Eight

The One Series
The Long Way Home
Where the Heart Is
There's No Place Like Home

Badd Brothers:
Badd Motherf*cker
Badd Ass
Badd to the Bone
Good Girl Gone Badd
Badd Luck
Badd Mojo
Big Badd Wolf
Badd Boy
Badd Kitty
Badd Business
Badd Medicine
Badd Daddy

Dad Bod Contracting:
Hammered
Drilled
Nailed
Screwed

Fifty States of Love:
Pregnant in Pennsylvania
Cowboy in Colorado
Married in Michigan

Goode Girls
For a Goode Time Call...

Standalone titles:
Yours

Non-Fiction titles:
You Can Do It
You Can Do It: Strength
You Can Do It: Fasting

Jack Wilder Titles:
The Missionary

JJ Wilder Titles:
Ark

To be informed of new releases, special offers, and other Jasinda news, sign up for Jasinda's email newsletter.

Made in the USA
Monee, IL
30 January 2021

59246387R00239